AGNES HAHN

RICHARD SATTERLIE

PRESS®

Medallion Press, Inc.
Printed in USA

AGNES HAHN

RICHARD SATTERLIE

DEDICATION:

For Alison, Jake, Erin, and Tricia,
and to my brothers, Dave and Bob.

Published 2008 by Medallion Press, Inc.

The MEDALLION PRESS LOGO
is a registered trademark of Medallion Press, Inc.

Printed in the United States of America
Typeset in Adobe Garamond Pro

ISBN# 978-193383645-4

10 9 8 7 6 5 4 3 2 1
First Edition

ACKNOWLEDGEMENTS:

Thanks to Tricia and Alison for their critical reading of the story in its various drafts, and to Stacy M. for a critical read of the final version. Helen and Kerry of Medallion Press have been fantastic throughout the editing and production process. Finally I'd like to thank everyone at the Absolute Write Water Cooler for their help and encouragement, including Uncle Jim, Ray, Kevin, William, Teddy, Rob (both of you), and all of the other guys; Trish, Maryn, Kathy, Sass, Cath, Jay, Elaine, Kristie, and all of the other girls.

CHAPTER 1

AGNES HAHN IS A DONUT. IN A SCONE WORLD.

The entry under her photograph in the high school yearbook was funny when the ink from her classmates' signatures was still fresh. But as the pages yellowed, the lines lost their humor.

Agnes relaxed and her shoulders slumped with an exhalation. Even when Gert and Ella were still at home, something had always seemed to be missing, like there was a hole in her life. Not the kind of hole a mate or a best friend could fill, but one that was more visceral, more emotional. Yet something seemed tangible in the void. Something around its edges provided random reminders of her vacuity. It had always been subtle, like there was someone she should consult every time she had to make a decision—an inner voice that would provide an objective opinion.

Today, it was strong.

Agnes had been aware of the voice since the day she went to live with her great-aunts. In fact, she couldn't remember much else before that time. Nothing of her mother or her father. Only the voice. But even then it was capricious, stirring occasional feelings of uneasiness.

It wasn't there to argue when she decided to go back to work the day after Gert's funeral. She didn't have to convince it that it wasn't too soon, that the animals needed her—the plain ones, the damaged ones, the mean ones, the ones no one wanted to adopt. They all needed her. Not like at home where no one needed her anymore.

Agnes cinched her belt a hole tighter. The jeans hadn't shrunk as much as she'd thought they would. She was wrong again, keeping her string alive—always assuming shrinkage would produce the perfect fit.

She thrust her arm into the flannel shirt, pushed her other arm into place, and paused as the soft fabric surrounded her. Unbuttoned, the shirttails fell to the middle of each thigh. A medium when a small would do. Cotton head-to-toe, in-to-out. Even the bra. And they could be found without the wires. Cantilever brassieres projected the wrong impression—an exaggerated importance of body parts that somehow had attained a cult status.

Her hands threaded each button through its button-hole, upward, all the way to the lapels. Others seldom used the final button. Why put one there if it wasn't intended to be fastened? Like all things in her life, the top button had a purpose.

The weather report blared from the cheap speaker of the bedside clock radio, and Agnes flicked the switch to off as she hurried past. The station broadcast was from Santa Rosa, but the weather this far up the coast was considerably different. The best way to judge was to open the garage door and take a deep breath.

The Honda hummed along Reese Drive without complaint, living up to its rating in the *Consumer Guide*. Agnes settled into the cool fabric and let her mind run ahead. What was the challenge today? Two more strays brought in? Maybe three? One adoption if luck was working? The real challenge was to find something interesting to say to her co-workers, to stay in a conversation for more than one unscripted turn.

A murmur pulled Agnes's foot from the gas pedal. She swung her head left, then right. What was it? It sounded like a muffled moan. She slid her foot back to the accelerator. Her system of mental Post-it notes usually didn't kick in until after morning tea.

A left turn onto the coastal highway and she buzzed her window down all the way. The morning chill invaded the car in company with the smell of the ocean. The short jog to the animal shelter turnoff, south of Mendocino, had always invigorated her. She loved the Pacific Ocean, the beauty of the rugged shoreline, the power in the waves that scoured the beaches of all but the largest grains of sand. But lately, even this part of the drive had turned mundane, as if something had tamed the water, turning the brassy surf zone into the humdrum stretches of sand found in the southern part of the state. Baggy. Cotton. No wires.

The car looped into the parking lot like it had a homing device, past the packed column of employee cars, to the last space in the empty second row. It was her spot, by squatter's rights. She glanced at the other cars in her side mirror. Every morning her co-workers filled the narrow slips, jockeying for the one closest to the building, presumably in the hopes of saving a calorie. And their cars bore the scars of the thrift—their sides were chipped and wrinkled with door dings. It reminded her of the huge SUVs that would run three laps around the Wal-Mart parking lot, waiting to squeeze into tight spaces on the near side of the cart-return corrals.

She closed her window, flipped off the ignition, and pulled out the key.

It's time.

Agnes spun around, swinging her knees onto the seat. Who said that? No one was in back; no one else was in the car. All windows were up, doors locked. But she had heard a voice.

She turned in the seat and sat still for a moment, but the only sound was her heart, hammering deep in her chest. The dashboard clock turned over to eight, and the simultaneous flash of three changing numbers caught her eye. Three minutes. That's how far she'd set all of her timepieces ahead of the punch clock in the shelter.

She swiveled out of the car and looked around the parking lot. No one was near. It must have been her imagination. With a deep breath, she checked the top button that pulled her lapels tight to her neck. Another glance and she walked toward the shelter.

A police car waited near the doors, but that wasn't unusual. The police were her heroes. Around here, they pursued those who abused animals with the same fervor as those who abused other humans or drugs or property. They brought in the lost and the wounded. They cared.

She picked up her pace as she pushed the door open and slipped into the tile and glossy-paint reception room. Janie, the receptionist, didn't return her greeting.

Two of her heroes stood near the far side of the front counter. Officer Steven Wilson approached, followed by Officer Loreen Didier.

Agnes didn't smile a lot, but she always smiled for the police. "Good morning, Officer Wilson. Bring in another stray for us?"

Her smile wasn't returned. The officers positioned themselves on either side of her.

"Miss Hahn, please put your hands on the counter," Wilson said.

Agnes looked up. Janie's eyes were large, her lips tight.

"Miss Hahn?" Didier said.

Agnes squinted at Janie. "What's going on?"

"Put your hands on the counter. Now."

Each officer grabbed a wrist and forced Agnes's hands onto the high counter of the reception desk.

Agnes let out a muffled whine. "Why—?"

The cuffs clicked around her left wrist, pinching her skin. She wanted to rub the pressure away, but couldn't. Wilson bent her left arm around behind her back and forced her forward, into the counter.

Didier pulled on her right wrist, but Agnes resisted, looking the officer in the eyes. Just last week, Officer Didier had brought in a critically wounded beagle mix, peppered with buckshot. Agnes had cried with Didier when the vet gave the prognosis, and they had comforted each other when the euthanasia solution was administered.

"Relax, Miss Hahn," Didier said. "Don't make us use force."

Agnes blinked back tears. "I haven't done anything wrong." Her right hand met her left and another click sent a ring of pain around her right wrist.

Hands touched her, down her sides, around her

waist, down her thighs. She closed her eyes tight.

Fight.

Her eyes shot open. She looked left, right. Who said that? And why hadn't anyone responded?

Wilson reached into his pocket and pulled out a laminated card. He turned Agnes to face him. "You have the right to remain silent. Anything you say can and will be used against you in a court of law."

Fight what? What is happening?

Wilson's voice droned, like it was coming through a cheap speaker, strings of words without punctuation. "Do you understand each of these rights I have explained to you? Having these rights in mind, do you wish to talk to us now?"

Agnes looked at Janie again, then at the far doorway where her other co-workers crowded, staring.

"Why? I haven't done anything." Her throat constricted, threatening to choke her. She needed to calm down. Maybe it was a joke. Of course it was a joke. She didn't press the speed limit and she always stopped at yellow lights. What could she possibly be arrested for?

"Do you understand your rights, Miss Hahn?" Wilson grabbed her shoulders and gave her a slight shake. "Miss Hahn? Do you understand your rights?"

But jokes shouldn't be so painful. And no one was laughing.

"Miss Hahn? Do you—?"

"Yes. Yes, I understand."

"Good. Come on." He pulled on her left elbow, directing her toward the front door.

"But why? What did I do?"

Didier stepped alongside the two. She glanced at Janie, then at the far doorway. Her voice was low. "We'll explain at the station."

Agnes stopped and twisted her arm from Wilson's grip. "Tell me now. What did I do?"

"Not now." Wilson hooked his arm in hers and started her walking again.

Didier stepped ahead and pulled open the front door. *Fight.*

Agnes jolted again, then shook her arm free and turned to face Wilson. "No. I won't go until you tell me what I've done." Her voice was loud, shrill. "What are you arresting me for?"

Wilson shoved her through the open door and swung around to face her. He pushed his face close to hers, his lower teeth showing through his lips. "Murder," he said, his voice a low growl. "Three of them."

CHAPTER 2

WHAT DID THE TWERP WANT THIS TIME? A COMMAND to appear in Mulvaney's office never sat well with Jason Powers, particularly when it came like today's: "Get your ass in here right away."

Jason sank into the fake leather easy chair and mouthed a curse when the worn springs dropped his hips several inches below his knees. The armrests boxed him in to shoulder height so he pinched his elbows against his sides. The Mulvaney straightjacket.

Christian Mulvaney lit a cigarette from the last flickering glow of the previous one. He paced behind his desk, dwarfed by it.

In the six years Jason had worked at the *Santa Rosa Press Democrat*, he'd seldom seen his boss sit in the high-backed chair behind the oversized desk. Mulvaney paced when he talked. Paced when he read. Paced when he was on the telephone. Seven ashtrays were positioned around the office, and he used every one of them.

"I hate to say this, Powers, but your seniority is about to go in the toilet. You need to show me something right away or I'll have to send you back to the daily room."

Jason shifted his six-foot frame as much as the chair allowed. "You have a problem with my stories?"

"Your stories are fine. But for the last several months you've been slow with them."

"I'm slow because I'm thorough."

Mulvaney tapped a half-inch ash into an ashtray on a small table by the window. He lifted his leg and swung one hip up onto the edge of his desk. His next drag consumed nearly one-fourth of the remaining white paper of the cigarette.

Jason pulled his ankle up to cross his knee, but it wouldn't stay there. He returned the foot to the floor. Sitting, Mulvaney disrupted the equilibrium in the room. It felt like the earth's magnetic field was in the middle of a reversal.

"Let me put it this way, Powers. You're an excellent investigative reporter. Trouble is, you need to be a good investigative reporter." Mulvaney paused for another long drag. "Know what I mean?"

Jason shifted in the chair again. No sense answering. An explanation followed each of Mulvaney's stingers, whether or not comprehension was acknowledged.

"Look at it from my desk. Fewer and fewer people

are reading newspapers these days. I don't know what it is with the younger generation, but they don't want solid reporting or meaningful comment. They want flashy sound bites and attractive women reading from tele-prompters with those fake color contact lenses."

"And that's my fault?"

Mulvaney stayed on the desk. "Television and the Internet are the competition. They can get news out as it's happening. We're tied to evening deadlines and once-a-day distribution. We report yesterday's news, so we can't let it slip any later than that." He finished off his cigarette, lit another, and walked behind his desk.

Jason leaned forward and put his elbows on his knees. "The stuff I do isn't straight news. It doesn't have the same deadlines. And my writing is good."

Mulvaney pivoted, throwing ashes from the end of his cigarette. "Yeah, but even the best writing is useless if it's stale. You still have to be quick and good. Like you were before."

Before? Jason blew a full breath and inhaled quickly to keep the thick, smoky air from entering his lungs. "Before what? I've maintained regular submissions. The bigger stories take time. They need more attention."

Mulvaney stabbed his half-smoked cigarette into an ashtray and flopped into his chair. He rolled toward the desk and the casters squealed like they'd run over a family of mice.

Jason's eyes locked on to the source of the rising smoke-snake on the desk. Mulvaney never wasted a butt.

"Jason." Mulvaney took a deep breath and let it out with a suppressed cough. His voice was soft, missing the usual rasp.

Jason? That was a first.

"Someone needs to say this," Mulvaney said. "And I know what's left of your family won't do it."

The cigarette continued to smoke itself in the ash-tray. What was he up to? A show to motivate him?

"I know what's been going on. Everyone does."

Jason raised his elbows toward the armrests but gave up. "Going on with what?"

"Your productivity." Mulvaney pulled a cigarette from a half-crumpled pack, but he didn't light it. "Ever since your fiancée walked out on you."

Eugenia? "That has nothing—"

"Let me finish. I'm worried about you. You've always had a bright future in this business, but you're about to throw it away."

Jason folded his hands together on his lap. How long was Eugenia going to haunt him? "I'm turning in quality stories." His voice was near a whisper. "That hasn't changed."

"Jason, this newspaper is my life. This isn't a stepping-stone position for me. You may not realize it, but I'm proud when our reporters move up to a major market. I like to think it's because of what they've learned here. What they've learned from me. I have high hopes for you. But you're about to blow it."

Jason flicked his hands upward and let them slap back down on his thighs. "How?"

"That's what's been bothering me. Ever since . . . your problem . . . I don't know how to say this." Mulvaney twiddled the unlit cigarette between his fingers. "Most people would go into a funk, neglect their work. Not you. You've been working day and night. Harder than everyone else. But your productivity still has gone down. Think of what I said earlier. I think you're being too good. You don't need to triple- or quadruple-verify a source when a double check will do. You don't have to dig back into everyone's childhoods to explain their actions. Here's a good journalistic quote for you: Thoroughness isn't served by redundancy. You get it now?"

Jason gripped his thighs. Righteous bastard probably never had his heart ripped out with no hope of reattachment.

Mulvaney lit the cigarette and inhaled the tip red. He exhaled the smoke through his nose. "I'm trying to help you here. You have to get back on track. Do you know how much competition there is for positions at the *Chronicle*, or in LA, for the *Times*? You think I'm rough on you? They won't give you the benefit of an ass chewing."

"This is an ass chewing?"

Mulvaney stood and walked around the desk. "No. This is an ass nibbling. I'm not good at motivational speeches and rah-rah camaraderie." He took another drag. "Try this." Smoke punctuated each word. "You've got someone breathing on your heels. She's sharp as hell. Not bad to look at, either."

"Yolanda?"

"You could learn from her."

"I could pierce my belly button, too."

Mulvaney half-laughed, half-coughed out a cloud of smoke. "Good idea. I could attach a chain and give it a yank when you dally."

"I don't dally. I told you, I'm thorough. Maybe she could learn something from me."

Mulvaney massaged his temples. "Okay. Good cop, bad cop time." He finished off the cigarette and mashed it into an ashtray. He pulled another from the pack. "Don't go Pulitzer on me. You young hotshots think you know the news. Here's a flash for you. You ain't shit. You're just a grunt doing the fieldwork. Save your dreams for the nights and give me what I want when you're on the clock. But get that girl out of your mind. She's gone. It's over. Move on, damn it."

Fuck him. Eugenia was everything. Someone like her couldn't be stubbed out like a cigarette butt.

"I mean it. Forget her."

Jason scooted to the edge of the chair and saluted.

"Yes, sir. Is that all, boss?"

"No. You just don't get it. How long are you going to let her ruin your life? She did you dirt, what, four months ago? She's long gone and you're letting her do it to you over and over every day. I'm giving you one more chance to get back to where you were. And it's a good one." Mulvaney lifted a manila folder from his desk, but didn't open it. "You're on the Menstrual Murderer story. Female serial killers are as rare as honest politicians. But don't slip into redundancy. Don't try to psychoanalyze everyone and their cousins. I'm throwing you a softball here."

Jason inched farther forward. "That'd be great if anyone knew where she was, or who she was."

A smile pulled Mulvaney's lips tight against his cigarette. He shook the folder. "This is why I like my job. I got a tip. Something just broke on the case. Up in Mendocino. You need to get up there right away."

Jason covered his face with his hands. Not Mendocino. Anyplace but there. He raised his head. "They don't like me much in Mendocino."

"God damn it. I can give the job to Yolanda, if you want."

Jason shook his head. Mulvaney didn't have a clue, didn't remember. All this hadn't started with Eugenia. It had started in Mendocino. Two years ago. Eugenia had taken his heart, but Mendocino had taken his soul.

"Powers? Do you want the assignment or not?"

"Yeah. Yeah, I'll get on it."

"Okay, but if you don't curl my toes with this one, I'll yank you like a leashed Chihuahua. If I call you in and you stop to piss, you'll be working obituaries." He reached for the cigarette pack. "You got it?"

Jason pushed hard on the armrests and struggled, but stood. "Right in the tailpipe, boss."

"Good." Mulvaney tapped the filter end of a cigarette on the desk and turned to the window. "And remember what I said. I want the old Jason back."

Jason paused at the door and pushed a framed diploma crooked on the wall so a slash of pristine white paint showed against the surrounding yellow. It was a game he played every time he came into the office, and the diploma was always straight on his next visit. He opened, then slammed the door hard enough to keep the pollution in the office, but not hard enough to alert his co-workers down the hall. He dusted his clothes with his hands. His first impulse was to rid himself of Christian Mulvaney. To be the apple that fell far from that tree. But Mulvaney was a master at invoking the laws of Sir Isaac Newton. For good reason—he was right.

Jason pounded his fist against his thigh. Because of Eugenia he had thrown himself into his work, but now he realized it was just to stay busy. That's why he was so deliberate. What had Mulvaney called it? Redundant. It was all done to keep his mind off of her. Worked really well, huh?

This time he'd do it right. It was time to show Eugenia she couldn't hurt him any longer. No. To show himself, not her. He would survive Mulvaney and the *Press Democrat*. Survive Eugenia.

Jason relaxed his fist and his hand fell to his side. Surviving Mendocino was another story.

CHAPTER 3

Nightmares didn't hurt. But Agnes's wrists stung, even though the handcuffs had come off five minutes ago. Or was it ten? They were on again, off again through the booking. And the whole while, the pain persisted. Not a nightmare. Or was it?

The room was bare, painfully bright, and filled with apprehension. It triggered a brief flicker of a memory— of another room, about the same size. But it was dim, gloomy. And cluttered. Could opposites produce identical feelings of trepidation? At that, her mind turned away as if a heavy door had slammed the second room shut. All that remained was the glare of fluorescent lights, illuminating a stark table and three chairs, and a round clock on the wall that seemed to make a *tsk* sound every time the second hand jumped. And why only three chairs? A table had four sides. Four sides, four chairs.

She rubbed her left wrist. There was no need to cuff

her at the shelter. But they had. They knew her, knew of her, and yet they felt the need for restraints. And now, they were gone. Off to catch a real criminal, or to pick up an injured animal and deliver it to the shelter.

She was now in the hands of Detective Art Bransome. Why had she remembered his name? Probably because he had pronounced it like it was spelled in all capital letters. With an equal emphasis on each syllable—an accent mark for each. He had tilted his torso forward and then back with each sound, bending only slightly at the waist, like the inflatable, bobbing punching bag she had played with at a friend's house when she was young.

Detective Art Bransome. Didn't he realize she was innocent? That this was a ridiculous mistake? Had he brought her in to apologize?

She looked at the reels of the tape recorder, spinning slowly. He had pushed the button without a word to her. He spoke only to the machine. Something about the date and her name. The words were all lowercase, no accents.

Then he had started to pace. With each step, his large belly pushed his shirttail farther across his belt. She caught a good look at the belt before it disappeared. The dark brown leather faded at the margins, frayed with wear. Her frown gave way to a squint. His shirt-tails billowed from his waist, such a bright white they hurt her eyes.

Why was he waiting? Why wouldn't he say something?

At the far end of the room, Bransome pivoted on his heels. Agnes's eyes fixed on his black shoes. They were either patent leather or spit-shined to a military mirror finish.

"Ms. Hahn, would you like a lawyer present for this questioning?"

Yes.

Agnes's head jerked upward. He didn't hear it. But it said, "Yes."

"Ms. Hahn. Do you want a lawyer?"

Bransome seemed to fill the room. He used three people's allotment of oxygen, and he bragged about it—his heavy inhalations drew across his tongue with a slurping sound.

"Ms. Hahn?"

"No." It had said yes, but it didn't understand. She was innocent.

"Okay, then. Let's get started. Where were you last Saturday night?"

Silly question. Same as always—at home, watching television.

"Ms. Hahn, did you hear me? Don't make this any more difficult than it already is. Where were you last Saturday night?"

Agnes's eyes followed the wood grain on the table. The lines were two-dimensional. "At home."

"All night?"

"Yes."

"You weren't in Anchor Bay?"

Anchor Bay? On a weekend?

"Ms. Hahn?"

She kept her arms and legs tucked close, within the confines of the chair, like it was a floor-to-ceiling enclosure. "No."

"Can anyone else confirm you were at home?"

She looked at the table again. It wasn't real wood. The grain pattern repeated.

"Ms. Hahn?"

"No."

"Why should I believe you, then?"

Agnes looked up at Detective Bransome's massive chest. "I never travel at night. Especially on weekends." Her eyes returned to the table.

"Why not?"

"I don't like to drive at night. And people drink on weekends."

"So you were in Mendocino, at your house, all night Saturday night, but no one can verify it. Right?"

"Yes."

Bransome walked over and centered himself across the table from her. He leaned forward, his huge hands pushing into the fake wood grain. The table groaned. "And, last month, on the fourteenth. That was a Saturday night, too. Where were you that night?"

Agnes's eyes scanned halfway up his shirt before the glare drove them back down. "If it was a Saturday night, I was at home. I don't go out."

"You never go out on Saturday nights?"

"No."

"Any nights?"

"No. Unless there's something I can't avoid."

"So, you weren't in Bodega Bay on Saturday, July fourteenth?"

Bodega Bay? A month ago? Her mind flew through her mental calendar. "No."

"How about June fifteenth? That was a Friday. Were you in Cotati?"

A frown. "I don't think so."

"What do you mean you don't think so?"

"I give talks. To schools and libraries. About animal adoption and pet care."

"So you can't remember if you were in Cotati on Friday night, June thirteenth?"

No need to think back. "Not on a Friday night."

"How are you so sure?" Bransome leaned on the table again.

"I schedule the talks for the mornings so I can get back here in the afternoons. I don't drive at night."

Bransome resumed pacing. "Let's go back to Anchor Bay, last Saturday night. What if I told you a motel operator identified you coming out of a room at eleven o'clock, last Saturday night?"

"It was a mistake."

"She said she saw the pet shelter woman. She attended one of your presentations with her children. She gave a complete description. Do you want to change your story?"

Agnes gripped the table edge with both hands. "No."

"Maybe this will jog your memory." Bransome opened a manila file folder on the table and pushed an eight-by-ten glossy photograph across until it touched her hands. It was a man. Nude. Blood everywhere. His throat was cut and his penis was severed, sitting on his chest, covered with blood.

Agnes felt the room spin. She closed her eyes tight but the turning wouldn't let up. Her stomach lurched, then went into spasm. Vomit gushed from her mouth, splattering the photograph and half of the table.

"God damn it." Bransome jumped back, agile for a man so large. He found an unsoiled corner of the photo and lifted it, letting it drain on the table. "Shit." He dropped it back in the puddle.

Agnes's head pounded. She didn't want to look at the photograph, but she couldn't look away, either. Did they think she could do something like that? She closed her eyes tight.

The door slammed and Agnes flinched. She looked

around—Bransome was gone. Why was he asking about all of those places and dates? Sure, she traveled in Mendocino and Sonoma Counties, even Marin County, to give her talks. All carefully scripted and recited. But she was always back by midafternoon.

She glanced back at the photo. The straight, red line on the man's neck looked clean, like the incisions on the television surgery shows. Her fingers curled into fists and she twisted her feet together under the chair. She couldn't even kill a spider.

Agnes scanned a wide arc. The new room was nearly the same size as the previous one, and the table and chairs looked like clones. This one had a window, with bars, so it was flooded with natural light.

She relaxed her focus. Her mind floated beyond the window and wound around the cliffs that overlooked the rough Northern California shoreline. Normally, her mood was like the backwater of a protected bay, lapping at the shoreline, rising and falling with a tide of only inches. Today, she felt like huge breakers were pounding in her head, leaving only the coarsest of sand on the beach.

Her thoughts looped back in the opposite direction. The room was within a tiptoe peek of the fringes of the great stands of redwoods. But even within the silence of those fog-shrouded towers, she found no peace.

The tape recorder button snapped. Agnes jumped, her mind once again imprisoned with her body.

Bransome repeated the flat introduction and sat down this time, on the opposite side of the table. "Ms. Hahn, have you ever been arrested before?"

The words pulled together in slow motion.

Bransome leaned forward and spread his hands, palms up.

"Yes."

Bransome retreated to the chair back. "How many times?"

"Once." Her eyes followed his hands as he opened the manila file and turned a couple of pages.

"When?"

"Late eighties. I was nineteen, so it was 1989."

"You were a member of the Animal Action Committee?"

"No. It was called the Animal Protection Committee."

"That's not what it says here." His right index finger stabbed the page like he was trying to hurt it.

"The name changed later. I didn't know they were breaking into labs. I didn't know they hurt those people."

"But you were arrested."

"Yes, but the charges were dropped."

"Well, we brought up your fingerprints, along with the ones we took today, and compared them to a print we found at the Anchor Bay murder scene."

Agnes's eyes locked on Bransome's. "It didn't match. It couldn't."

"It wasn't a perfect print. We can only use the general shape and pattern."

"It didn't match."

"At that level it did."

Agnes held her stare. "You're making this up. I was at home."

"There's one way to tell for sure. Would you consent to a DNA test?"

No.

Agnes shifted her eyes to the left, then to the right, then back to Bransome. It would clear everything up. They'd see it was all a mistake.

"Ms. Hahn. Can we take a DNA sample from you?"

"I was at home."

"The test should answer that, shouldn't it?"

"Yes."

CHAPTER 4

THE SQUEAK OF NIKE SNEAKERS ON THE CLEAN FLOOR echoed in the corridor of the Mendocino Police Station. Jason froze. What was it about this place? The basketball court traction on the sheet linoleum, the smell of wintergreen disinfectant. They dredged up two-year-old memories that brought him to the tip of dread in an instant. He tiptoed to the door and ground his molars together. Would Bransome remember his squeaking shoes? He'd remember everything else. Bransome had come within inches of breaking some of his own laws two years ago. He'd said so, and Jason had believed him. But right now, Jason worried about the sounds. He wanted to get inside the room before Bransome heard him coming.

Jason took a deep breath and pushed the door open.

Bransome faced the door, his face crimson. "What the hell are you doing here?" He slammed a file folder shut on his desk. "You've got balls, coming back here. Why don't you stay down in Santa Rosa and leave us alone?"

Jason reached out his hand, then pulled it back when it didn't receive a glance. "Detective Bransome. It's been a while. I'm here on business. Heard you caught the Menstrual Murderer yesterday."

"Those details aren't public knowledge. You call her that in print and I'll have your ass. Only this time, I'll do it the back alley way."

Bransome's squint honed Jason's memory to a fine edge. Bransome hated reporters. What had he called them? Sensation-peddling headline hounds? That was it.

"Relax, Detective. That's just what I call her."

Bransome took a step closer, violating Jason's comfort zone, which was five feet with Bransome. "God. You're still taking a bath in that damn cologne."

Minotaure. It was Eugenia's favorite. She had bought it for him after their first night together. Said she couldn't resist him in it.

"If you're here to check on the DNA lab again, it's clean," Bransome said. "The old one went out of business because of you. Two friends lost their jobs."

Jason inched back. "I did what I had to do. The contamination was jeopardizing evidence. I did the right thing."

"The right thing?" Bransome's voice bounced around the walls like a racquetball. "Do you know—?"

"I've been following Ramirez since he was let go." Jason tried to match Bransome's resonance, but he didn't come close. "I did a story on him last year, and again this year. He's an upright citizen, married, stable. You know he was innocent."

Bransome balled his hands into fists. "Really. And the others?"

"I did what was right." This time, Jason barely heard his own voice.

"Keep saying that. Maybe you'll convince yourself. I can think of two families you'll never convince. I'll take you to meet them if you want to try."

The wintergreen scent burned Jason's nose as much as the words burned his ears—a pleasant smell in proper mixture, but irritating here in Mendocino. Everything in this place screamed of two years ago. He had to turn it all off.

"I'm here about the murders. That's all. They're big news in Santa Rosa and the whole Bay Area. They started in our backyard."

"You still with the *Press Democrat*?" A slight grin pushed on Bransome's cheeks. "I thought you'd be in San Francisco by now, with the *Chronicle*."

Powers straightened his back and pushed his voice to full volume. "Santa Rosa's home, unless there's an opening here at the *Beacon*. I'd like nothing better than to work for a small town rag, especially if I'd get to see you every day."

"So you expect me to cooperate with you—give you information. Is that right?"

"Right now I'm doing background work on Agnes Hahn. I'd like to interview her, though."

"People with balls the size of grapefruit shouldn't come within a leg's length of these shoes." Bransome lifted his foot and pulled up his pant leg.

"I presume she's allowed visitors. I'll make my request through formal channels if I have to."

Bransome huffed.

Powers took a deep breath and let it out quickly. "Do you know how rare a female serial killer is? And one whose killings are this gruesome? It goes beyond big news. This is sociologically important. This is book material. Don't you want your name immortalized as the man who caught this depraved woman?"

"I want my name immortalized as a man who did his job. And the best way I can do that is if you stay out of my way."

"Like I said, I'm doing some background work. I'll be happy to share anything I find if it will help your case. In return, I ask you to tolerate my rights. Deal?"

Blank stare.

"I'll take that as a yes."

Bransome lifted his shoe again.

Powers fished his hand into his back pocket and

pulled out a piece of yellow paper. "By the way, you should be congratulated. I was only going five over the limit, but you got me." He held the paper at arm's length, eye level.

A full smile puckered Bransome's cheeks. "You still driving that silver Volvo? I didn't think they'd remember. Who got you? Wilson?" He squinted at the form. "I'll have to give him a raise."

"So I can expect this every time I go out?"

"Only if you break the law."

"I was only going five over. Cars were whizzing past me."

"You were exceeding the speed limit. What does the word *limit* mean to you?"

Powers balled the paper in his hand and cocked his arm, but stopped and shoved it into his front pants pocket. "I understand Agnes Hahn is being interviewed by a psychiatrist. Is she taking the insanity angle?"

Bransome stomped to the door, yanked it open, and slammed it behind him.

CHAPTER 5

AGNES PAUSED BEFORE SITTING AT THE INTERROGATION room table. The woman in the opposite chair smiled as her jaw worked an invisible wad of gum so vigorously it bulged her temples with each chew.

"I'm Dr. April Leahy and I'd like to talk with you for a while. Do you mind if I call you Agnes?" The chewing stopped. "I'm glad they let you wear your own clothes."

Agnes slid onto the chair. A doctor? The last lady had told her she could make a phone call. Who was she supposed to call? Now, a lady doctor? She didn't look like a doctor.

Dr. Leahy was about her size, but looked smaller. Maybe because her skirt and jacket were tailored tight to her body. Disposable clothes, if they shrank. Throw-away society. But she was attractive. Maybe the kind of attractive that robbed an hour of sleep each morning. It'd be fun to see her without all the makeup, and without the revealing clothes. Agnes raised her shoulders.

"You can call me April if you'd like."

Agnes looked down at her own clothing, flannel and jeans, and shook her head.

"Why not?"

She seemed nice. Not threatening. "Gert and Ella taught me to show proper respect."

Dr. Leahy smiled and jotted a few notes on her green steno pad.

Agnes cringed—the pencil on paper sounded like the tip of a knife drawn across soft wood. "Can I go home?"

"I'm sorry, Agnes, but that's not for me to decide. If you answer some of my questions, talk with me, I'll do what I can to help you. Okay?"

She lies.

Agnes looked up at Dr. Leahy, then around the room.

"Is anything wrong?"

Agnes folded her hands in her lap and shook her head.

Dr. Leahy frowned and looked around the room. "You sure you're okay?"

Agnes nodded.

"Okay. Who are Gert and Ella?"

"My great-aunts."

"And you've lived with them? For how long?"

"Since I was about four."

Dr. Leahy scratched more notes. "Can you tell me about them?"

Gert would fix this. Agnes struggled to hold back tears. "Agnes?"

She cleared her throat. "Gert died six months ago. The day after we put Ella in the home. Ella has Alzheimer's. She doesn't recognize me." The tears released.

Dr. Leahy took a soft pack of Kleenex from her briefcase and pushed it across the table. "I'm so sorry. Do you want a few minutes?"

Agnes pulled a tissue from the pack and clenched it in her fist as if it were some vital force, like it would keep her from falling apart. "No."

Dr. Leahy tapped the pencil eraser to her lips. "You live in that beautiful Victorian house after the first bend of Reese Drive, right?"

"It's not so beautiful."

"Why not?"

Agnes kneaded the tissue in her hand. It was soft, unlike the stiff mattress and scratchy blanket they had given her. Was this all she was allowed from her life of two days ago?

"Agnes?"

"Gert said they ruined it when they built the strip mall down the street. Then they put the self-storage center right behind us. She planted junipers along the back fence, but you can still see the rows of storage units from the upstairs windows."

"What was Gert like?"

Agnes looked up and frowned. Where was the woman's gum? She hadn't spat it out. Swallowed it?

Dr. Leahy nodded. "It's okay, Agnes. I'm here to help you. I want to talk about your family. I want to help you understand what's happened. We can stop anytime."

Agnes's eyes returned to the table. "She was strict, but nice. When I was little, I used to sit on her lap . . ." Her eyes flicked to Dr. Leahy's face, then lowered. She looked kind. Concerned.

Dr. Leahy didn't move, like she'd been caught in a game of freeze tag. The wall clock *tsk-tsk*ed the seconds.

"You said she was strict. Did she punish you?"

Gert and Ella had been her life. The house, too. And the animal shelter. What would happen to the dogs at the shelter?

"Agnes? Did Gert punish you?"

"Sometimes, when I did something bad."

"How would she punish you? Did she hit you?"

Gert wouldn't do that. "She spanked me a couple of times when I was young, but mostly she'd lecture. Shake her finger in my face. Then she'd give me a hug and tell me I was a good girl who had just made a mistake."

Dr. Leahy scribbled a few more notes.

The sound grated on Agnes's ears. She gripped the edge of the table.

"And Gert never married?"

"No."

"Why not? Did she talk to you about it?"

Agnes fingered the grain of the table. "She was engaged once, but Ella said she caught her fiancé kissing another woman."

"Ella caught him?"

"No, Gert."

"What did Gert say about it?"

"Men can't be trusted."

"All men?"

"Just some men. She wanted me to find one of the good ones."

Dr. Leahy scribbled on the tablet. "Gert didn't have any other men in her life?"

"I think another man wanted to marry her, but she said no because Ella wouldn't have anyone to take care of her."

"Why would Gert do that?"

"They were twins. Not identical, but they were very close, like many twins."

"So, you think Gert did the right thing?"

"Family is the most important thing in life."

Dr. Leahy scribbled. "What do you remember about Ella?"

Agnes exhaled. "She was nice to me, too, but she didn't do much around the house. Just the cooking."

"Did she let you sit on her lap?"

Agnes smoothed the tissue on the table. "No. Because

of her artificial leg. She always kissed my forehead. When I was little, she let me put extra sugar on my cereal."

"How did Ella lose her leg?"

"A car accident."

"Were you with her?"

"No. It happened when she was young. She and Gert were out dancing. They both were drinking. Gert was driving home when the car went off the road and ran into a tree." Why was the doctor still smiling?

"How do you feel about that?"

"I don't drive at night, especially on weekends."

"Tell me more about Ella. Did she punish you?"

Agnes looked up and frowned. What was the big deal about punishment? "No. Sometimes she'd tell Gert to go easy on me."

"When Gert spanked you?"

"No. When she lectured. Gert would go on and on."

"Was Gert angry when she lectured you?"

"No. She always seemed concerned. Not angry."

Dr. Leahy paused to write a few more sentences. The constant grin on her face was nearly as irritating as the sound of the scribbling.

"You said Gert hoped you'd find one of the good men. Do you have a boyfriend?"

Agnes picked at the rubber liner on the edge of the table with her fingernail. "I had one in high school."

"Was it a romantic relationship?"

The corners of Agnes's mouth tugged into a smile. "We kissed a lot."

"Anything else?"

Agnes felt heat radiating from her face. She looked up at Dr. Leahy. Her expression was different. The smile was gone, but she still looked friendly, concerned. "He tried to touch my breasts one day."

"Did you want him to touch your breasts?"

"Gert said it wasn't proper. Only after marriage."

"Did Gert find out?"

"I told her."

"What did she do?"

Agnes shook her head. Gert always took care of things. "She told him to get away from me and never come back."

"How did that make you feel?"

"He wasn't one of the good ones. He was just after one thing."

"When you were kissing him. Do you remember how you felt?"

Safe, comfortable. Agnes shrugged.

You liked it.

Agnes looked around the room, then at Dr. Leahy. She hadn't heard it. Agnes crumpled the tissue in her hand.

"After you knew he wasn't one of the good ones, did you still want to kiss him?"

Why couldn't she hear it? It was clear.

"Agnes? Did you want to kiss him?"

"Of course not." Agnes looked up, not quite making eye contact.

"Why not?"

"I couldn't trust him. It's not right to be romantic with someone who can't be trusted."

"Did Gert tell you that?"

"No. That's how I felt."

"Did you get mad at him for trying to touch you?"

"I was disappointed. I thought he was one of the good ones."

"You didn't want to hurt him for touching you?"

Hurt him.

Agnes glanced up into Dr. Leahy's eyes and dropped her head, shaking it. "Hurting people doesn't solve anything. It would've made me just as bad as him."

Dr. Leahy smiled and wrote on her pad. She flipped the page and continued writing.

Now the pencil sounded like it was being drawn across sandpaper. And she held the pencil wrong—between her first and second fingers. Gert said that was the wrong way. Agnes pressed the tissue into a tight ball in her palm. Ask another question. Ask anything. Just stop writing.

Dr. Leahy stopped writing. "Sorry. Can I talk about the rest of your family?"

Yes. Yes.

Agnes flinched. "Yes."

"Do you know much about them?"

"Not a lot. I know Gert and Ella had another sister—my grandmother."

"You didn't meet her?"

"No. She lived in Illinois. Her name was Rachel Carrington."

"Lived? She's not alive?"

"Gert said she died before I was born."

A few more notes.

The pencil looked dull. Maybe it wouldn't make so much noise if she'd sharpen it. The lead barely extended from the wood.

"How many children did she have?"

"Who?"

Dr. Leahy pulled her hand from the page. "Your grandmother."

"Just one. My mother."

"Why didn't your mother raise you?"

Agnes put her hands on her cheeks, resting her elbows on the table. The balled tissue pressed against her skin, and she could still feel its softness. "She died right after I was born. Gert said it was a hemorrhage."

"How do you feel about that?"

"Sad. But Gert told me it wasn't my fault. Mother gave me the ultimate gift."

"How about your father?"

Agnes pulled her hands from her cheeks and shrugged

her shoulders. "Don't know about him. Just what Gert told me. He divorced Mother when she became pregnant with me. He didn't want kids. Mother came out here to live and changed her name back to Hahn so he couldn't find her if he changed his mind."

"How does that make you feel?"

"She was lucky to have family."

Dr. Leahy pursed her lips and then smiled. She wrote a few more notes. "I'd like to change topics again, if you don't mind. Is that okay?"

Silence.

"Agnes, what makes you angry?"

The pencil. It was like a scalpel now, dissecting her. Dissecting her past, her life. What was left of it.

"Agnes?"

"People who hurt animals."

"What do you want to do to them?"

"Tell them off. Call the police."

"Do you want to hurt them for hurting the animals?"

"No. I let the police handle it."

Dr. Leahy scribbled.

Grab the damn pencil.

Agnes's hand twitched.

"Were you angry when Gert died?"

"No. Sad."

"Do you know how she died?"

"The doctor said she had a stroke, but I think she

gave up when Ella stopped recognizing her. And then Ella went into the home."

"How did you feel when Ella went away?"

"I was sad then, too. But not as sad. The worse her memory got, the less she seemed to suffer. Her leg always hurt her. She felt pain in her leg, even though it wasn't there. The doctor called them phantom pains. Some nights I'd sit up late rubbing her back to make her feel better."

"The police found pain medication in your house. Did you give it to Ella?"

"Yes." Agnes smoothed the tissue on the table again. A small rip stretched the center. She had always needed Gert, but toward the end, Ella needed her. "I had to hold back, though. She always wanted more than the doctor said to give her." Her throat tightened.

"How did that make you feel?"

Agnes's eyes watered. "I cried, but not in front of her. I wanted to take the pain away, but I was afraid the extra medicine would do something bad to her."

Dr. Leahy uncrossed her legs. "Do you need a few minutes now?"

"Yes, please."

Dr. Leahy stood. "I'm going to get a cup of coffee. Do you want anything?" Her jaw dropped, then settled into rhythmic chewing movements.

"Some water, thank you."

After a few minutes of counting ceiling tiles, Agnes's

mind went blank.

Dr. Leahy walked in, twisting the top from a water bottle with a crackle. She handed the bottle to Agnes, sat down, and crossed her legs. Her jaw relaxed. "Agnes, what do you do at the animal shelter?"

"I coordinate adoptions. And help take care of the animals."

"Do you work with men?"

"Yes."

"Do you get along with them?"

"They're nice to me."

"You never had a problem with any of them?"

Agnes bobbed her head. "There was one man who used to tease me."

"How did you deal with it?"

Hurt him.

Agnes looked up at Dr. Leahy and paused before dropping her eyes to the table again. She really couldn't hear it. "I tried to stay away from him."

"Did you report him?"

"No!"

Dr. Leahy flinched at the increase in volume. She wrote a quick note. The blunt tip of the pencil squeaked across the paper.

Agnes folded her hands together, the tissue between them. "What good would that do?"

"What happened to him?"

"He was fired. He didn't do his job very well."

"Did you have anything to do with his firing?"

"No." Barely audible.

Dr. Leahy turned a page of her tablet and wrote a few more squeaky words.

"I'd like to ask a hypothetical question now. What are your views on the use of animals in medical research?"

"It's necessary. I just wish there was another way."

"Would you sacrifice all of the animals in the shelter for research if it could bring back Ella's memory?"

Agnes looked at Dr. Leahy's lap. The pencil was silent. So was the voice. But it was an easy question. "Yes, but only if it would help all of the people who suffer from Alzheimer's. I wouldn't do it if it was only for Ella. That'd be selfish."

The pencil squeaked.

"I have one more thing I want to ask, then I'll let you go. I know you're getting tired. Why do you dress like that?"

"Like what?"

"Your clothes don't fit very well. They're too big."

"They'll fit. Cotton shrinks."

How do you feel about that?

CHAPTER 6

JASON POWERS TIPTOED INTO THE OUTER OFFICE OF Dr. April Leahy, MD, Psychiatrist, trying to silence the squeak of his shoes on the hardwood planks. Since the office was on the second floor, he expected the floor to creak or groan with each footstep. But it was solid, a credit to early-twentieth-century craftsmanship. Unlikely to give up any of its secrets.

The building was close to downtown Santa Rosa— far from the myriad of generic medical suites that had sprung up like suburbs around each of the area hospitals, but within a heartache-and-a-half of Eugenia's former apartment. With downtown parking so tight, he had found a spot on this very street on more than one occasion and jogged the two blocks to be with her.

He inched over to a long, brown leather couch and sat. It had the look and feel of Ethan Allen. Abstract artwork bore original signatures, and three of the four pieces could easily have doubled as Rorschach inkblot tests.

He couldn't appreciate the comfortable feel of the couch. The space was too much like the living rooms of yuppie condos. They were the perfect birth control—no mop-and-bucket sex in there. To yuppies, foreplay probably consisted of spreading a paint drop cloth on the guest bed duvet. He massaged the soft leather and inhaled its musky scent. Strictly feet-on-the-floor furniture. Not like at Eugenia's—

A loud click shot through his daydream. At the far end of the room, a crystal doorknob turned. The door flew open and a thirtyish woman glided into the room. She wore creased slacks and a matching charcoal vest over a red, collared blouse. Her jaw hinged up and down without swallowing, and a muffled snap accompanied nearly every meeting of her molars.

Jason stood. "I have a two o'clock appointment with Dr. Leahy. My name is Jason Powers."

She frowned and popped her gum. "I'm Dr. Leahy."

"I'm sorry. You're just . . . I didn't think . . ." His face felt like it was on fire.

A slight smile curled her mouth. "I can only give you about ten minutes. A patient just called."

Natural light flooded the inner room, streaming through a south-facing bay window. A circle of three over-stuffed chairs complemented the arc of the room. A large desk dominated the side away from the windows. It must have been hell to bring the desk up that narrow staircase.

The woman motioned to the ring of chairs and followed Jason. She sat to his left.

Clever move on her part. When two cars reach an intersection at the same time, the one on the right goes first. He had the right-of-way.

"I want to discuss Agnes Hahn," he said.

He watched her eyes scan him, but they stayed soft, and her eyebrows maintained a welcoming arch.

She crossed her legs and jiggled her foot. "You're not police. What's your interest?"

Gut feeling—she already knew. "I'm with the *Press Democrat*. I've been researching Agnes and her family. I just wanted to know if she said anything about her past that might help explain her actions."

Dr. Leahy's eyes half-closed with her smile. "And I'm sure you know all about doctor-patient privilege. Right?"

"Yes. But I'm finding inconsistencies in what's been released and what I've uncovered. I think we could help each other out on this one. I don't have to know all the details. I'm interested in your general impression of her mental state, and in some specifics about her family."

"So you can misquote me?"

"This is all background. No quotes. If anything you say comes out, I'll state it as my conjecture. It won't be referenced."

"I can't see where any of this can help Agnes. That's

my main concern here."

"The background information I've turned up could help. But I'll need something in return to give it up." He cringed. He hadn't intended to sound so crass.

Dr. Leahy shifted and recrossed her legs. Her expression pushed him back in his chair. He expected anger, or at least resistance, but her look showed him something totally different. It blended with the smells of the Victorian and the sounds of downtown, and suddenly he was two blocks away, a bottle of Coors in his hand and Eugenia curled against his side. He shook his head as if the motion could clear the memory like an Etch-a-Sketch.

With Eugenia, he had felt the gravitational pull of instantaneous infatuation. What some people called love at first sight. But after what she did to him, he couldn't, or wouldn't give space to that kind of feeling ever again. He hadn't shut down all feelings toward females. Hope occasionally elbowed in—that somewhere he could find a woman who would turn Eugenia from yesterday's headline into a dusty archive.

Dr. Leahy glanced at her watch. Her jaw reactivated as she swung her leg over and put both feet on the floor. A forward lean showed a triangle of flesh from her open collar.

"Can you come back at six? There's an Italian restaurant around the corner. A small Mom and Pop place with checkered tablecloths. Great food, and the people are like family. I eat there more nights than not. Let's have dinner and see what comes up."

Jason stood. He knew the place. "Should I meet you here or there?"

She stood close enough for him to get a full nose of her subtle perfume. "There." She pointed. "It's right around the corner. You can't miss it." She glanced at her watch again.

"At six, then."

Her jaw stopped long enough to show a full-toothed smile.

CHAPTER 7

JASON PUSHED THROUGH THE DOOR OF THE POLICE STA-
tion and slowed his gait. Today, the hall to Bransome's
office wasn't long enough. He had a bomb to drop, but
he'd have to lower it gradually. The full impact of the
information wasn't apparent when he had talked to Dr.
Leahy. Now, Agnes Hahn might become a free woman,
even though the DNA evidence from the murder scenes
matched hers.

Dinner with Dr. Leahy had been pleasant. She was
casual, professional, and intrigued by his information.
There was no doubt she gained more from the conversation than he. But he didn't mind. For some reason, she
reminded him of his mother. Solid, stable. And she had
reminded him of the unwritten rule between him and
his brother. If you want something, ask Dad. If you
need something, go to Mom. In the end, the meeting
hadn't gone exactly as planned. He was the one who had

prattled on like a magpie.

But in his mind, two of her comments had exposed her soul like a plate glass window. She complained that all of the good men her age had already been taken. Then, something really curious. She had a small degree of empathy for single women who pursued romances with married men.

Jason slowed his foot-squeaking walk even more. He had to get back on track.

The legal impact of his new information was minor compared to its potential personal consequences. He was about to do something that would take him back two years with Detective Bransome. And he knew those sores were still open, still raw. His information didn't prove Agnes Hahn was innocent; it just opened the possibility that she was. Any lawyer with half a brain could use it to get her released.

But what if she was guilty? He'd be letting out another criminal. What if she murdered again? The haunting memories flooded back. Detective Bransome was wrong about him. He did agonize about his earlier actions. He had done what was right and it turned two felons back on the street. One innocent man and two felons. What was right had become a technicality in the eyes of most people. He'd nearly quit his job over it.

The reporter in him took charge. Now, like then, the truth was at stake. So was an opportunity. If Agnes was released, he could get close to her. Find out more about her. He wouldn't knock Mulvaney's socks off on this one; he'd knock him out of his underwear. And if he was able to get close enough to Agnes, find out enough about her, there could be a book in it. But he'd have to work fast. Mulvaney had a deadline for losing his undergarments.

A stomach cramp nearly doubled Jason over as the question came back to him. What if Agnes was the murderer? He froze at the detective's door.

Jason took a deep breath, opened the door, and walked into the detectives' workroom.

"What the hell are you doing here?" Bransome came at him, fast.

Jason thought about backing out of the room. About running like hell. He braced himself. "Sorry. Should I have knocked?"

"Get the hell out of here." Bransome grabbed his arm and steered him to the door.

Jason yanked his arm away. "I have some information about Agnes Hahn you might want to hear."

Bransome pushed him.

"It'll probably get her out of here."

Bransome stopped and swung Jason around by his arm.

"You never stop, do you? Do you have something against my police department? Or is it just me?"

Jason held his tongue. He wanted Bransome to cool

down, and the look on the detective's face scared him. "So what did the shrink say about Agnes?"

A slight grin spread across Bransome's cheeks. "She's got a problem with men."

That's not what I got from Dr. Leahy. If I interpret her comments correctly, Agnes's attitude toward men was a little skewed, but not enough to produce the type of fury in these attacks.

"Is she sane? Competent?" Again, Jason already knew the answer.

"Enough to stand trial." Bransome circled his ear with his right index finger.

Dr. Leahy had said she was fine. No indication of pathological anger or resentment. Jason gritted his teeth. It was time. But how would Bransome react? Jason thought back. Bransome was right-handed. He took a step back and locked his eyes on Bransome's right fist.

"What would you say if I told you Agnes Hahn wasn't born in Mendocino?"

"Big deal." Bransome grabbed Jason's arm again and pushed.

"She was born in Petaluma."

Bransome pushed harder.

Jason was at the doorway. He stiffened. Bransome's right hand was still in his visual field. "Okay. What if I told you she was the first of identical twins born to Denise Hahn in Petaluma, California?"

Bransome stopped his charge. His jaw relaxed.

"Both were live births. Agnes and Lilin Hahn. Both around five pounds. And I haven't found any evidence that Lilin Hahn has died. Actually, I haven't found a trace of her anywhere."

Bransome opened his mouth to speak, then closed it.

"I know what you're thinking. But the DNA would be identical. If you had a good fingerprint, that would do it, though. Identical twins have unique prints. Not in the general characteristics, but in the fine points—the whorls and turns. It's like the old nature versus nurture argument. Only both play a part in human development. Identical twins are the proof." He knew the answer to his next question, but he asked anyway. "Do you have any good prints?"

Bransome turned around and walked back to his desk, shaking his head. He spun around. "I suppose you've talked with the DA."

"Not yet. I wanted to talk to you first. As a courtesy."

Bransome rolled his eyes.

"And I'd like a favor."

"I knew that was coming. You're incredible."

"I'd like to meet with Ms. Hahn before she's released. I'd like to tell her about her sister."

"Get the fuck out of here." Bransome lunged at him.

Jason jumped back, into the doorway. That look was back on Bransome's face. The look of a man just this side of crazy. "Don't you want to see her reaction before her lawyer gets to her? I'm not an authority figure to her. I think I can get an honest reaction."

Bransome stopped. "And I'm sure your motives are pure as snow."

"You know my motives. Mine just line up with yours in this case. I told you I'd like to work with you, not against you on this one. I could have gone to the DA first."

Bransome rubbed his fingers over his eyes. "What if she doesn't want to talk to you?"

"Tell her I have information that may help with her case. Tell her I think she's innocent. Tell her anything you want."

Bransome shook his head. "Do your ethics ever fly higher than half-mast?"

Mulvaney's early lessons flooded back, and they made Jason's stomach ache. In his business, ethics were conditional. And this was one of those blurry times. It didn't sit well for a moment, but the uneasy feeling lasted only until Jason's adrenaline took over. And he was doing what was right. The end justified the means. The public had a right to know.

"I can hold my head high," he lied.

CHAPTER 8

THE NATURAL LIGHT IN THE ROOM WAS DIFFERENT THIS time. It seemed gray, muted, even though it was mid-afternoon. And this man was different. Agnes had never seen him before. He said he wasn't with the police, but he didn't say where he worked. Only that he wanted to help with her case.

He probably wasn't another psychiatrist. They'd let her wear her own clothes with Dr. Leahy. This time, they grabbed her from her cell and steered her into the conference room, still in her jail-issue jumpsuit.

Agnes made eye contact, briefly. Nice looking, athletic. His jeans fit well but not too tight. Her eyes stopped at the polo player insignia on his button-up shirt. The smooth texture of the shirt, with the creased sleeves, screamed dry cleaning, starch. A waste of money.

But his voice was slow, calm. She looked up again, and then down, but she stayed on his face long enough to catch his smile. Was he one of the good ones?

Not a good one.

Agnes looked down and scanned her orange jumpsuit, then tugged upward on the collar, cinching the lapels together. She wanted to look up at him again, but she didn't want to give him the wrong idea.

"Miss Hahn, I have some information that might get you out of here. But it might shock you."

"You can get me out? Really?"

Jason leaned across the table. "I think so. But you have to listen to what I say. It's about your family."

Agnes focused on the spinning wheels of the tape recorder. This was one of the pocket-sized models. What family? There wasn't any left.

"First, I found out you weren't born in Mendocino. You were born in Petaluma."

She kept her eyes on the recorder and shrugged.

"Your mother passed away right after your birth, but both you and your twin sister were fine, healthy babies."

"Twin sister?" She looked up and held his stare. Her head bobbed up and down. "I have a sister."

"You already knew that?"

Her eyes danced around the room. *That's what's been missing in my life.* "Yes."

"You didn't mention it before."

"It was just a feeling." *But now, she talks to me.*

"Have you had that feeling long?"

A wide smile. I have a sister. "As long as I can remember."

"Have you ever seen her? Talked with her?"

No.

"No."

"Did your aunts ever tell you that you had a sister?"

"No."

Jason drummed his fingers on the table. "Agnes, who is Edward Hahn?"

As far as she knew, she was the last of the Hahns, except for Ella, whose identity was lost in her ravaged neural circuits. She was the final progeny in a lineage of females narrowed by untimely deaths and marriage refusals. No, that wasn't right. She and her sister were the final ones.

"Agnes?"

"I don't know."

"You've never heard of him?"

"No."

"You told Dr. Leahy that your aunts' sister was your grandmother, and that she lived in Illinois. Right?"

"Yes."

"According to my research, your two aunts didn't have another sister. They had a brother, named Edward. He lived here in California. Around Petaluma. All I can find on him is that he fought in France in World War II. Got a Purple Heart. Then he vanished."

The bastard.

What? The voice wasn't making sense. Was it trying to trick her? Agnes shifted in her chair and picked the table grain with her fingers. "That's not what Gert told me."

"Edward Hahn had one child, a daughter, named Denise Hahn. Your mother."

Agnes slapped her hand on the table. "Gert wouldn't lie to me."

Jason pushed his chair back from the table and leaned forward, resting his elbows on his knees. "I'm sorry. I don't mean to upset you. I thought you'd like to know what I've found out about your family. Do you want me to go on?"

Yes. Yes.

Gert wouldn't lie. Neither would Ella. There was no way. Was there?

"Agnes? Do you want me to go on?"

She looked up. "I don't know." He had a kind face, his eyes filled with concern. His eyes. There was something in them. Was he one of the good ones? "I guess so."

"Edward Hahn was your grandfather, but I can't seem to locate him. There's no record of his death, so I presume he's still alive. If he is, he's not going by Edward Hahn anymore. I need to talk to him. As far as I can tell, he took custody of you and your sister after your mother died. Do you remember anything about that?"

Gert let me sit on her lap. Her lap was always a safe place. The only safe place. Agnes's eyes blurred.

"I know this is upsetting, but I need you to think back. Do you remember anything from before you went to live with your aunts? Why you ended up with them? Why your sister didn't?"

You know.

No. I don't remember. Tears tracked down her cheeks.

"Agnes?"

"No."

"Nothing?"

She shook her head.

"I'm sorry. This is really important. I can't find a trace of your sister or your grandfather. I need to find them. I think it's your sister who's doing all these terrible things."

Agnes waited, but the voice was silent. "Can I go home now?"

CHAPTER 9

JASON ROLLED UP THE WINDOWS OF THE VOLVO, punched a code for a stored number into his cell phone, and hit the speaker button before setting the phone on the passenger seat. A click followed the second ring—a world record.

"Hey, give me a second. Okay?" Tapping filled the silence.

Jason gripped the steering wheel, pretending it was his brother's throat. "Donnie? What's going on? You're not bent, are you?"

"Oh. It's you. What do you want, little brother? I'm kind of busy right now. And I'm expecting a call."

"I have a job for you. I need some information on—"

"Yes! I think I got it. Hold on." More tapping.

"Donnie? This is costing me."

Tapping.

"Donnie."

"Okay. Okay. What's so important?"

"I have a job. You want it?"

"What're you paying?"

"I'm already giving you two hundred a month. That comes with chores."

"Yeah, but I need more. You know. That doesn't even cover rent."

"What the hell are you on? You sound like you're half lit."

"Nothing, little brother. I swear. I'm just jazzed. I'm about to hack a hacker. Give him an eye-for-an-eye. Microsoft should give me a medal."

"Microsoft would probably give you a job. If you'd apply."

"You know I don't do the eight-to-five. Besides, they probably do urine tests."

"Why don't you turn the hacker over to the authorities?"

"They wouldn't do shit. Besides, he's just a soldier. He'd get probation. I've got a jail sentence I'm about to insert onto his hard drive. It'll tear his electronics a new one."

"So, how about the job?"

"Yeah. No problem. But I need you to get off the phone. Call back in about an hour and leave the information on the machine."

"You're not going to smoke any salad, are you?"

"Don't need to. I got a beep in to a young lady. She

should call any minute. Don't want to waste this natural high."

"Donnie, wear a rubber."

Dial tone.

CHAPTER 10

UNPLEASANT MEMORIES SURGED BACK WITH JASON'S first steps into the care home—bright; busy; the forced, homey feel of a Holiday Inn. Flowers everywhere reflected the unnatural colors of faded silk and plastic. He hated the sensations. A few years back, he had done a story on nursing home abuses, only to find that nineteen out of twenty were wholesome, healthy places with reasonable care and happy residents.

But he'd come away from the investigation with a strange feeling about the institutions. In the better homes, including this one, all of the residents moved as if their lives were carefully choreographed and monitored. Even at the busiest times, they slid through the hallways with calm efficiency. Like zombies.

He took a deep breath and entered the dining room. His timing was perfect. The cattle-like residents herded in for their evening meal, but once through the double-door entry, they changed. One after another called out greetings across the room in a ritual that bordered on spontaneous. Jason chuckled. Maybe their outbursts signaled relief when their mental head counts confirmed their ranks hadn't thinned in the last twenty-four hours.

Supper seemed to be the highlight of the day, and the clamor and gaiety reminded him of a junior high lunchroom, minus the airborne food. He pulled back a chair and nodded at the white-haired woman seated in a wheelchair. Ella Hahn returned his smile.

He hesitated, unsure why. He had expected erratic behavior or, at the least, a slight separation from reality. But the brightness in Ella's eyes seemed to draw energy from the room. He sat, momentarily mesmerized.

"Are you visiting today, dear?"

"I came to see you," he said.

"That's nice, dear. I'm going to have the chicken."

"The chicken sounds good." He pretended to read the menu. "Actually, I came to talk about Agnes."

"Oh, is she visiting, too?"

"No. She couldn't make it today."

"That's nice, dear. I think I'm going to have the chicken."

"You remember Agnes, your niece."

"Is she visiting today? It's a nice day for a visit."

"Ella, Agnes needs your help. Can you remember anything about her?"

"Who's that, dear?"

"Agnes. Your niece."

"Maybe she'd like the chicken. Is she visiting today?"

"No, she couldn't make it." Jason knew about Alzheimer's. Knew the symptoms and the prognosis. But this was his first conversation with an actual patient. Ella didn't even recognize a woman she had raised from a little girl. It was a good thing Agnes wasn't here.

"That's nice, dear."

Jason met the gaze of a gentleman across the table. He was decked in a gray pinstripe suit and bright red tie.

"You won't get much out of her, I'm afraid," the man said. "We call her Re-run. I think you see why." The gentleman reached his hand across the table. "Name's Earl. Been here for almost a year."

"Do you know much about Ella or her family?"

"No. She lives in the assisted-living wing. They let her eat supper with us. It really perks her up. My wife was the same way before she passed. I guess that's why I sit with Ella, to keep her company."

"Is she ever lucid?"

"I'm not the one to ask. You see that young lady over there in the purple tunic?" The man pointed with a crooked finger. "She's the one who looks after Ella during supper, and takes her back to her room."

Jason rested his elbows on the table to get a better view. The woman looked young, maybe late twenties.

Slim. She faced away, chatting and giggling with two of the dining room attendants.

From the back, she looked good, but more. A name came to mind. Eugenia. The woman had the same hair, the same figure. And her left hand was propped on her hip, inverted, the tip of her ring finger slipped into her back pocket. Just like Eugenia used to do.

He squinted, expecting to see a plain white-gold band and a three-quarter-carat teardrop diamond reflecting every bit of light in the room. But there was no ring.

He turned to the natty gentleman. "Do you know her name?"

"Who's that, dear?" Ella's voice was soothing, like the tranquilizing tones of a grandmother.

"The woman in the purple top over there. Do you know her name?"

"No. Is she visiting?"

Jason looked across the table and shrugged. He suppressed a chuckle, and covered his smile with his napkin. He pinched his own thigh as a punishment for the inappropriate response. "Yes. I think she came to see me. If you'll excuse me, I'll go talk to her."

"It was nice to see you, dear."

Jason patted Ella's forearm as he stood. He nodded at the gentleman, who returned an exaggerated wink.

"To be young," the gentleman said to the tablecloth.

Jason stopped short of the young lady's shoulder.

He felt the stir of past emotions, but his body refused to move. It wasn't Eugenia, but the draw was just as strong. He wanted to see the woman's face—needed to see it. But how would he react? Especially if she looked like her from the front. Conflicting feelings contributed to his paralysis. He wanted to know what happened to the ring. Not really. He already knew.

He stood back as if she radiated white heat. To him, she represented an incendiary mixture of anonymous mystery and passionate familiarity. And he'd only seen her back side.

Without moving closer, he reached out and tapped her shoulder with his finger. "Excuse me. I understand you take care of Ella Hahn."

She turned and grinned.

She wasn't Eugenia in a physical sense, but something in her smile, the way she tilted her head, reminded him of the good days. His smile was automatic.

"Who wants to know?" Her tone seemed more flirtatious than inquisitive.

He inched closer. "I work for the *Santa Rosa Press Democrat*. I'm covering the Agnes Hahn case."

Her eyebrows arched high. "I heard they caught her. I'd like to shake her hand. My old boyfriend did a number on me and I'd like to do to him what she's been doing."

A little closer. "The woman in jail is Ella's niece, and she may not be the murderer. I need to talk to you about Ella."

The woman scanned downward to his shoes, then back up to his face. She put her hand on his elbow. "I have to go get her now. I get off at ten. Meet me out front?" She brushed against him as she passed, slowly sliding her hand off of his arm.

He turned and watched her exaggerated hip-sway. "Your name?"

She glanced over her shoulder. "Ten o'clock. Out front."

Two evening hours were tough to kill in Mendocino, so Jason headed for his motel. He drove five miles under the speed limit, signaling for every lane change, veer, and twist. A yellow light meant stop here, and it gave him time to dial his cell phone—the number Mulvaney had given him.

"Officer Wilson here." The voice sounded distant. A cell phone?

"Hi. Jason Powers. Do you know if Agnes Hahn is going to be released anytime soon?"

"Detective Bransome is looking for you. Where are you?"

Jason rolled his eyes. "Thanks for the heads-up. I'll try to stay out of his way for the next couple of days. Is she going to be released?"

"Yeah. It's scheduled for the day after tomorrow, around one, I think."

"Why not tomorrow? You can't hold her that long, can you?"

"Bransome said the paperwork couldn't be processed until then."

Jason checked his speed. "And her lawyer bought that?"

"Why wouldn't he?"

"Never mind. You think she'll be released around one in the afternoon, or you know it will be at one?"

He heard papers shuffling. "It'll be at one."

"Good. I'd like to pick her up and drive her home. Do you think that'd be all right?"

Laughter. "You think Bransome would agree to that?"

"Can't you keep him busy with something around there? I'm working with you guys on this one, not against you."

More laughter. "Yeah. Right. The best I can do for you is pretend this conversation never happened. You're on your own with Bransome."

Jason mouthed a curse. "I really appreciate that. Don't tell him I'm coming. Okay?"

More laughter.

He folded the phone and threw it on the seat. His foot hit the accelerator hard, but he pulled it back, checking his mirrors. Bransome really knew how to hold a grudge. Maybe what had happened two years ago wasn't for the better, but it had been the right thing to do. Jason pounded the steering wheel with his fist. No matter how many times he repeated his justification, it didn't give him peace. Two years ago wasn't personal. But he knew Bransome wouldn't see it any other way.

Jason shook his head. To him, Bransome was an enigma. A previous background check had revealed that the detective hadn't served in Vietnam. He'd somehow managed a 2-S student deferment for six consecutive years of higher education, first at Santa Rosa Community College, then at Chico State, where he graduated with a degree in sociology.

Jason had found a picture of Bransome when he was in the debate club at Chico. It still bothered him. Bransome's hair was curly, kinky—the kind that yanked teeth from a comb in a single pass. In its current state the gray fringe that encircled his naked crown looked like steel wool. But that kind of hair was a source of envy in the late sixties when the Afro was in style. The bigger, the better. Yet, in the photograph, Bransome's full head of hair was trimmed short, nearly military, and his sideburns barely dipped below the bottoms of his ears. All other males in the photo had full beards or triangular muttonchop sideburns that teased the corners of their mouths. And Bransome was the only person, male or female, whose pant legs ran straight to the cuffs. The others had pants that ballooned below the knee into floppy bell-bottoms.

Jason grinned. Bransome had been a walking anachronism. A chuckle. Still was.

The August night carried a chill as tendrils of fog oozed around the corners and tops of the care home buildings, giving the yellow sodium vapor lights an eerie glow. It was ten minutes past ten and there was no sign of her. Jason leaned against his driver's-side door and pushed the lumi-glow button on his watch. He'd give her two more minutes. He crossed his arms against the cool mist.

A security guard appeared inside one of the side doors of the entryway and the loud click of a dead bolt echoed in the night. The main, automatic motion-sensor doors must have been locked sometime before ten. The guard pushed the door open, and the familiar purple tunic bounced through the door and onto the covered entryway.

The woman stopped and scanned the parking lot. She turned in Jason's direction, motioned for him to follow, and bounced away into the adjacent parking area. Jason stood next to his car and waited.

She slid a key into the door of a Saturn four-door

sedan, then turned in his direction and motioned to him again.

He nodded and climbed behind the wheel of the Volvo.

Jason felt the tickle of perspiration along his hairline. She drove nearly fifteen miles over the speed limit, zig-zagging through what little traffic was out at the hour. He squinted through the fog, trying his best to follow her darting taillights.

At a poorly marked intersection, she veered off the main road onto a street that seemed to disappear into the darkness and fog. Her red taillights barely defined the limits of the asphalt—streetlights and sidewalks didn't exist. His gut sent a loud signal. This might not be a good idea.

His foot twitched on the gas pedal and the slight lurch of the car seemed to second his indecision. A dim light appeared ahead. Her brake lights blared, then sputtered, and the red streaks shot to the right, toward a bank of overhead lights. A pair of long, two-story buildings appeared through the glowing fog, and her car slid to a stop between them. Before he could complete his turn into the lot, she was out of her car, heading to the building on the left.

His wheels barely stopped before she turned a key in the door of the second-in, ground-floor apartment. She paused and faced him, then disappeared into the building. Bright light flooded the open doorway.

Hesitation. Something seemed wrong. But the apartment was dark before she entered. At this hour, that meant she probably lived alone. His feet hit the parking lot before the next wave of caution hit. He shuffled toward the light as he tried to calm his internal objection. Ella. This was about Ella.

A tap on the door brought no response so he leaned in. "Hello?"

Movement to the left caught his attention, along with the sound of a refrigerator door closing. He stepped into the apartment in time to see her approach, a can of beer pushed in his direction with a stiff arm. He kicked the door closed and accepted the beer.

He preferred to drink from glass, not aluminum. A bottle was fine with him, but never a can. He scanned the apartment. The kitchen counter was littered with dirty glasses and dishes. A pile of rumpled clothing covered a chair and part of the couch in the living room. In his quick scan, he noticed three large stains on the beige carpet. Better to make an exception in this case.

She placed a hand-rolled cigarette in her mouth and thumbed a lighter. The scent of the first few puffs told him it wasn't tobacco. She took a deep draw and held her breath at the same time she took the joint from her mouth and held it out to him. "'Ere," she grunted.

He raised his hand in a stop motion and shook his head. "I want to talk to you about Ella Hahn."

The woman blew out the lungful of smoke and raised her beer can to her lips. Three noisy swallows and she pulled the can away, wiping her lips with the back of her hand. She took another long drag on the joint and stepped toward him, smiling.

She exhaled and motioned to the hall, but he didn't move.

"Do you know if Ella ever comes out of her trance? Does she ever make sense?"

"Information will cost you." She wriggled into his comfort space.

She reeked of weed. "I think you've been watching too many movies."

Her laugh echoed in the sparsely furnished apartment. "I have some of those. You can be the pizza man and I'll be the woman who doesn't have any money." She pulled him into her arms and leaned forward for a kiss.

He hesitated, then folded his arms around her, lightly. He leaned away from her mouth. "What about Ella?"

"Later." She put her hand on the back of his neck and pulled him into a kiss, her tongue thrusting into his mouth.

He terminated the kiss. His knees nearly buckled. The joking, the passion. Not only did she look like Eugenia, she acted like her, too. "Do you have a name?"

She giggled as she rotated out of his grip. She grabbed his hand and pulled him into the hallway, then into the bedroom. She took a long drag on the stubby joint and tossed it into an ashtray on a bedside table. In a quick motion, she pulled the purple tunic over her head. No bra.

His eyes locked on her breasts. But he needed to talk about Ella and then get out of there. He opened his mouth, but no words came out. All he saw was Eugenia.

She flopped on the bed. "What's the matter? You look like you've seen a ghost."

He never could say no to Eugenia.

She smiled. "Like I said, information will cost you."

"I don't think so. I don't even know your name."

She reached over to the table, pulled open a drawer, and removed a square condom packet. She waved it in front of her. "Hey, I'm clean. I have to go through all kinds of testing for my job."

"What about the weed?"

She giggled again. "There are ways around that."

He took a step back. "Good to know."

She stood and slipped her white pants below her hips. They slid to the floor revealing a pale pink thong. She waved the condom wrapper again. "If you want to talk about Ella, I'll talk. But I need something from you first. You won't regret it."

Her grin and her playful pout screamed Eugenia, and the woman's near nakedness fought against his hesitation. Maybe this was a way to begin easing Eugenia's memory. Maybe meaningless sex could erase the bond he had shared with her. But why wasn't he stepping forward? "Can't we just talk?"

"Yes. After." She slinked over to him and unbuttoned his shirt. She massaged his bare chest. "Nice," she exhaled.

His feet no longer shuffled backward.

She undid his belt, yanked open the buttons of his Levi's, and pulled the jeans off his hips.

He looked down at the bulge in his boxers, before her hand found it.

"Guess you're not ready to talk just yet."

He barely had time to roll on the condom before she pulled him into a coupling. Her animated movements created a challenge to stay in the union, and with each of his thrusts she gasped a loud, "Uh huh." He closed his eyes tight and Eugenia appeared.

As his tempo increased, her volume matched, and his thoughts jumped to the surrounding apartments. He pictured neighbors with ears pressed to the wallboard, laughing at the auditory performance.

"Uh huh . . . uh huh . . . uh huh . . ."

Despite the distraction, Eugenia returned, and he lost himself in one of his more memorable conclusions this side of his former fiancée. But as soon as he fell off of her, the vision disappeared, replaced by the woman without a name. Unsure of the proper etiquette in her universe, he reached out to pull her into a hug.

A quick roll and she was off the bed. In the dim light he watched her jog out of the bedroom, naked. The sound of the refrigerator door opening and closing signaled her return, another can of beer in hand. She flopped on the bed, outside of the covers, and jiggled her right leg in time to imaginary music.

"So what did you want to ask about Re-run?" A chortle punctuated the question.

Best to be blunt—to get to the point before her attention span expired. "Does she ever make any sense?"

A staccato, nervous laugh shook the bed. "That's funny."

"What's funny?"

"Make any sense. I'm not a good one to judge." This time, she belly laughed.

Jason watched her breasts bounce with her laughter, and had to force himself to stay on task. "Does she ever seem normal? Talk without repeating herself?"

"Oh yeah." She bobbed her head, further bouncing the bed. "I know what you mean. Sometimes. Right after supper. She seems different." The exaggerated head nods continued.

"What do you mean, different?"

"She wants to help. Clean up. She doesn't repeat herself. And she looks different."

"Looks different?"

The woman took a long guzzle of beer and crushed

the can in her hands. She threw it into the corner of the room. "You want another one?" She slid off the bed and hurried out of the room.

"No, thank you."

On her return, each hand held a can. She thrust one in his direction.

It went to the nightstand, unopened. "What did you mean when you said she looks different?"

A lunge onto the bed and her leg jiggling intensified. "Most of the time, she smiles. She's so nice. After supper. When she changes. She frowns."

"Frowns?"

"Yeah. She looks scared. Like she isn't sure where she is."

"Do you ever talk to her when she gets like that?"

"Once. I asked her if she knew where she was." She threw her head back and let the beer flow down her throat. A stream ran from the side of her mouth onto her shoulder. The back of her hand swabbed her mouth and partially muffled a cough.

Jason watched a dribble of beer run onto her breast, nearly to her nipple, baiting him. Eugenia would've appreciated a quick lick. He had to stay on track.

"What did she say?"

A drip fell to her hip. "When?"

"When you asked her if she knew where she was?"

"Oh yeah. She didn't answer. She looked mad.

Like she was going to cry. It kind of scared me. I don't talk to her anymore when she's like that."

"Does she get like that every night after supper?"

She rolled to him and arched her eyebrows. "I'm ready for another, and I don't mean a beer. I bet I can get you up for it."

"No. Does she get like that every night?"

The smile left her face. "Not every night, but most."

"How long does she stay that way?"

"Most of the time, only a minute or so. Sometimes ten minutes. No more than that." A loud laugh. "That's all I'm saying. Any more conversation comes with another payment." She reached and grabbed his crotch.

He pushed her hand away. "I'll settle for your name."

"Uh huh."

CHAPTER 11

JASON PUSHED ON THE GAS PEDAL, AND THE HONDA RE-
sponded with a slight thrust of acceleration. He let it
slide up, ten past the speed limit, and held it there. On
his better days, cleverness was a trait he checked off near
the top of his list of positive attributes. The last two days
were among his best.

To stay off Bransome's radar, he needed a different car. The budget for the job couldn't accommodate
a rental. Wrangling the keys to Agnes's Honda was a
major coup, even if he had it for this one trip. He looked
down—under twenty-two thousand on the odometer. A
faint hint of new car smell wafted from some untouched,
undisturbed corner of the upholstery. Not bad for a late-
nineties Japanese import.

He relaxed back into the seat and held down the button to the driver's side window. A jealous sky hid the sun
behind gray clouds that stretched between horizons like

a wall-to-wall carpet. The soothing smell of the ocean rushed in, like a breaker, and churned around him. With no risk of a revenge-based speeding ticket, the stiff breeze of illegality further puffed his chest with pride.

Yesterday, Jason had waited for Bransome to waddle off for lunch. Getting the visit with Agnes was easy, but convincing her to let him drive her home today, in her car, required all of the smooth talking in his extensive repertoire. His honorable intentions were confirmed when he insisted she tell the property clerk to take her house key off the chain. Only the car key was needed. What a smoke screen. No one asked how he planned to get the automatic garage door open. He smiled. The back door of Agnes's house had yielded easily to his lock-jimmying skills.

The dank, cool air, with the smell of a grandma's house, came back to him as if blown in through the open car window. He had found nothing remarkable in the house. Vintage furniture that would command a good price at an estate sale cluttered every room but one. Agnes's living space was ordered, plain, almost spartan, except for the decorative carved wood elaborations on all of the furniture appendages and picture frames.

Her clothing hung in a small walk-in, dominated by a row of flannel shirts as straight as a chorus line, the muted colors in spectral order. All garments were free of bloodstains, and none bore the telltale signs of recent, desperate scrubbings.

What had captured his attention was her bathroom medicine cabinet. With her solitary ways, her recent familial losses, and her timid nature, he expected to see at least one bottle of prescription, mind-targeting pills. All he had found was an empty circular card that once held a cycle of birth control pills.

A stiff gust of wind feathered his hair, bringing him back to the Honda. The speedometer read fifteen over, and he held it there for a few defiant seconds before letting it slide down by five. Birth control pills. She wasn't the type who needed contraception. Maybe they were for irregular cycles.

His mind flashed on the police reports he'd seen from the first two murders. In both, the killer was menstruating, and she used the victim's member after she severed it. Probably in the third as well. Otherwise Bransome wouldn't have reacted so strongly when Jason called her the Menstrual Murderer. In any event, there was plenty of DNA from the sites.

His foot pulled from the gas pedal. Female athletes used birth control pills to control the timing of their periods so they wouldn't be bothered during a competition. Murder dates paraded through his head—always on Friday or Saturday nights. Mental calculations came hard with the sudden infusion of adrenaline. The cycles couldn't all fall on weekends, could they? Random chance was a long shot.

His mind went back to the house. Letters had been strewn on the carpet under the belt-level mail slot in the front door. He had found nothing remarkable there either. A couple of utility bills, a *Sunset Gardening* magazine, and a card from the AAA auto club. No personal letters.

Jason looked at his watch and pressed on the gas pedal. Back up to fifteen over he risked detection, even in his camouflage vehicle, but he was behind schedule, nearly five minutes late.

A chest-level hedge protected the entry to the police station parking lot, so he couldn't change his mind once he'd made the turn. His foot jumped to the brake pedal, but he didn't slam it down. Bransome leaned against the rear fender of a police cruiser, arms crossed and resting on the top of his belly. He stared at the Honda.

Jason thought of swinging through the lot without slowing. With the diffuse glare from the cloud cover, maybe his features were obscured by a glint on the windshield. His finger hit the window button and the pane whined upward. Continuing on, he hoped to avoid detection by hiding in plain sight.

Bransome pushed away from the vehicle and withdrew the baton from his belt, as if he was pulling a sword from its scabbard. Stepping closer to the approaching Honda, he waved the stick at an empty parking space two down from the cruiser.

Jason exhaled his frustration, but obliged. He opened the door slowly, keeping his eyes on the baton.

Bransome blocked his entrance to the station, rhythmically slapping the rod into his cupped palm. Each impact produced a muted pop.

Jason closed the door and stood in place, but he kept his hand on the handle. If Bransome came at him, he would jump back in the car and lock the doors.

"I don't know what you're up to, but I'm pissed enough to use this. You better go straight to Ms. Hahn's house or I'll have you as a guest here."

"That's all I plan to do."

Bransome took a step back so Jason could pass. "We'll be watching twenty-four/seven, so if you're up to anything, we'll know. Ms. Hahn has instructions to stay in Mendocino. She leaves town, she's back in the clink."

Jason waited until he was three steps beyond Bransome, then stopped and turned around. "Have you talked with her aunt? Ella?"

"Why would I? If she has any useful information, it's locked up in that suitcase she calls a head."

Jason shook his. "I may be able to get through to her, but only briefly. I think she might be able to help. I'll let you know what I find out."

Bransome stepped forward and swung his baton into his palm with a single, loud pop. "I don't find ass-kissing an endearing trait, Powers. You find anything out, from anyone, you better get it here as fast as you can without getting a speeding ticket. If I find out you're withholding anything, I'll let this toothpick loose on your head."

Jason reached for the door, but stopped short. Officer Wilson exited and nearly plowed over him.

"Wait," Bransome said. "Have you talked with her lawyer?"

Jason glanced over his shoulder. "No. Why?"

"The pencil-dick is acting like he owns the place. I thought the two of you might be related." Bransome nodded to Wilson, who walked to an unmarked Ford that faced the parking lot exit. The officer swung into the driver's seat.

"I don't even know who he is," Jason said. "He must know what he's doing if you don't like him."

Bransome stomped over and poked his baton at Jason's throat, leaving it an inch short of the Adam's apple. "You play wiseass with me and I'll put you fifty IQ points behind Ella Hahn. I almost hope there's another murder. Anything happens from now on and I'll consider you an accomplice. You've got motive and opportunity. As far as I can tell, you'll do anything to get a book out of this. Even help Agnes carve up someone else."

This time, Jason knew Bransome wouldn't hesitate to use the stick. He needed to calm him down. "You still think she's guilty?"

"As sin. My guess is she's a real smart one. She's probably playing you. Playing that geek of a lawyer. Playing you all. But not me. I got a line on her. I can feel it. In fact, I'll bet a month's wage. You want to take it?"

Jason opened the door and hurried in, hoping it would shut Bransome outside. It did. He hurried down the hall to the booking room. Bransome was a seasoned veteran, the kind whose intuition didn't need corrective lenses.

Jason felt his shirt sticking to his back. How much did he really know about Agnes Hahn? Was he playing hunches, or was he doing all this to piss off Bransome? His hunches had served him well in the past. Or did he see dollar signs above all else? And what if Agnes decided to hone her razor on his crotch when they got to her house? He hadn't given that possibility a thought before now. He tried to put it out of his mind. Bottom line? Was he convinced enough to take Bransome's bet?

"No way," he said as he rested his elbows on the high counter.

Jason opened the police station door for Agnes, but she hesitated, shielding her eyes against the glare. He scanned the parking lot. Bransome was gone. The whir of a starter brought an engine to life, and Jason snapped his gaze to the white Ford. Officer Wilson stared back through the lightly tinted window. His hands gripped the steering wheel.

Jason ushered Agnes to her car, but paused by the hood. "Do you want to drive?"

Her focus stayed on the ground. "No."

He couldn't decipher her expression. Can one be truly blank? Indifferent, maybe.

A double push on the remote button, and the car doors clunked an invitation.

Agnes slipped into the Honda and settled into the seat like it was an old friend, but then she stiffened, staring ahead, hands on her lap. Her feet and knees clamped together, like she was uncomfortable, afraid.

As the Honda turned left out of the parking lot, Jason peeked in the rearview mirror. The Ford followed. He assumed Officer Wilson wouldn't bother giving tickets on this trip, but he pushed aside the temptation to test the theory. He signaled every lane change and turn, and kept the speedometer dead on the posted limit. Agnes remained silent so he forced a conversation.

"Are you glad to be out?"

Yes.

"Yes."

"Do you want to talk about Lilin?"

No.

"No."

"No, not now, or no, not ever?"

No answer.

He looked over at her.

"Not now," she said.

He smiled. "You'll tell me when?"

Silence.

Officer Wilson didn't follow the turn into Agnes's driveway. The Ford stopped directly across the street. Jason slowed and scanned the lot. Wilson's observation site gave an unobstructed view of the entire front of the house, as well as the garage and adjacent side yard.

As he pulled the Honda to the garage door, Agnes's hand shot toward him and he jerked back, bumping his head on the window. She thrust a pointed finger at the driver's side visor, jabbing at the black plastic remote switch. The garage door grunted, then slowly lifted.

Despite the tingling in his armpits and the heat radiating from his face, Jason forced himself to straighten, inched the car into the center of the double garage, and looked over his shoulder to judge the clearance of the rear of the car. His eyes strayed farther. Officer Wilson sat in his car, staring.

A thunderous roar sounded through the garage. Jason nearly came out of his skin, his heart thumping. The jarring sound gave way to a constant whir and he realized Agnes had pushed the remote button again. Moisture formed along his hairline.

He thought about throwing the Honda in reverse, flooring it to break the control beam and stop the descending door, but the dwindling light told him he was too late. He looked over at Agnes. She sat in her original posture, staring straight ahead.

He twisted the key and yanked it from the ignition as the light in the garage settled down to the glow of a forty-watt bulb. What if she was the killer?

Fumbling, he flicked the door handle and slid out of the car, slamming the door behind him.

Agnes remained frozen for what seemed an eternity, but was more like fifteen seconds. She slipped out of the car and walked to the front fender. He felt himself move to the rear, keeping the full width of the car between them.

She stopped, and a puzzled expression swept her face. "Do you want to come in?"

He looked around. There was no other choice. The side door of the garage opened into the house. The only other exit was the large garage door, which was now tightly closed. He could get to the remote on the visor before she could, but that would place him in a vulnerable position, inside the car. He shook his head. What was he thinking? She was as meek as they came and barely over a hundred pounds. The murders didn't involve guns—weapons of distance. Blades were close range. Intimate. He could handle her up close. Just like the victims?

"We can talk now," she said. "But only for a little while. I'm tired."

She keyed the door and walked in, leaving the door

open behind her.

He moved to the doorway and peered inside. He knew the layout. The small entryway led in two directions. The kitchen was to the back, living room to the front. Agnes walked to the front and he followed.

"Please sit down. Would you like some tea?"

He didn't want anything, particularly tea. But it might help get her to talk. "Would coffee be too much trouble?"

"I don't have coffee. Only tea."

"Tea would be fine."

She disappeared into the kitchen.

Jason pulled the drapes aside and caught a glimpse of the Ford across the street. Wilson had moved to the passenger side, and sat sideways in the seat, feet up. A pillow propped his head against the window. He guzzled from a green beverage can.

Jason turned and sank into a claw-footed chair. The clinking of china brought his mind back to the house. A low-pitched whistle ascended a musical scale and gained volume, then screamed to silence. The house was cold. He hadn't noticed that before. A warm drink would be welcome. Even tea.

Agnes entered, carrying a large tray with two cups and saucers, a board of cheese surrounded by a leaning stack of crackers, and a too-large knife. Jason stood. It looked like a steak knife, with a serrated edge.

The coroner's reports said the type of blade used in the murders was extremely sharp and smooth, like a scalpel. Or a straight razor. He shuddered. He had played with a straight razor once when he was a teen. The blade was paper-thin, but sharp enough to dive deep into flesh by just resting it on skin, from its own weight. His stomach churned like it had back then. It was the kind of churn he always got from a double Ferris wheel when the chair crested the zenith and nothing was between his feet and the distant pavement. His forehead tickled with sweat again.

Agnes placed the tray on a coffee table and sat in an opposite chair.

"I put sugar in for you. Two cubes."

To hide something else?

She tilted her head like a curious dog. "Was that all right? You look angry. People who don't drink tea usually like it sweetened."

Jason gazed at the ceiling and then back down. "I'm sorry. That's fine. I'm not used to being waited on." He looked in her eyes and she lowered them. She had fine features, a pretty face. With a little makeup, styled hair, and some feminine clothes, she would be pretty. And she didn't look a thing like Eugenia. Didn't act like her. In fact, she was as far from Eugenia as any woman he'd ever met. And it triggered an impossible sensation. Was he attracted to her?

She folded her hands in her lap. "What do you want to know about Lilin? I can't tell you much."

Her sudden bluntness startled him. He cut a slice of cheese and put the knife down with the handle facing his way.

"If you've never met her, how do you know she's out there?"

"I think she talks to me."

His eyes burned into her. Anthony Hopkins. *Psycho*. "Has she always talked to you?"

"No. Just recently. Before that, I had a feeling she was there. That's the best way I can explain it. Sounds crazy, doesn't it?"

Bats in the belfry. But her shy sincerity said otherwise. An urge swept over him. To pull her close. To comfort her. He shook the thought from his mind. Keep track of her hands. "No. Not to me." The reporter elbowed in. "When she talks, what does she say?"

"Not much. A word here and there, then nothing for a long time."

"Has she told you anything about the murders?"

Agnes shifted in her chair. "She doesn't tell me anything. Just words."

"Like what?"

She looked around the room and lowered her voice. "Like 'yes' and 'no.'"

He leaned forward a little. "She hasn't told you anything beyond that?"

"Just one thing."

Farther forward. "What's that?"

Agnes paused and bit her lower lip. "That you aren't one of the good ones." Her eyes met his for an instant and returned to the floor. She sipped her tea.

"Not one of the good ones? What does that mean?"

"Most men aren't good. Only some are."

A slight relaxation; he felt a bit of a flirt coming on. "How do you know I'm not one of the good ones?"

Agnes gripped her hands together. "I don't know that. Lilin said that."

"What do you think?" He smiled.

"I don't know yet." Her eyes flicked up then down. A faint smile revealed dimples.

So unlike Eugenia. "The tea is very good. Thank you for sweetening it."

"Ella isn't a tea drinker. I learned how to make it so she could drink it."

"Did she drink coffee?"

Agnes shook her head. "Gert said no coffee. If two wanted tea, the third should drink it, too. It was efficient that way."

Jason fingered his chin. Notes registered in his mental reporter's notebook, but they were incomplete. There was competition for Jason the reporter. From Jason the man. "Did everything have to be efficient with Gert?"

"It's the best way."

"Do you miss her?"

Agnes's eyes watered.

"Sorry. I shouldn't have asked that." The reporter took charge. "Can I talk about Ella, or is that too painful as well?"

"No."

"No, I can't talk about Ella, or no, it isn't too painful?"

"It's okay. I'm getting tired."

"I want to talk to her. Can you think of anything that might help me get through to her?"

Agnes's head bobbed and the corners of her mouth curved upward, her dimples deep. "Carnations."

"Flowers?"

"She loves carnations." A full smile. "She loves to smell them."

He downed the last sip of tea and shifted back in the chair. "I'll give that a try." He reached into his shirt pocket and pulled out a business card. "If you need anything, or if you just want to talk some more, give me a call. My cell phone number is here." He reached across the table.

She left the card on the tray without reading it.

The smile drained from her face. "Detective Bransome told me the people at the shelter don't want me to come back to work right now. Do you know anything about that?"

"No. Sorry." The man broke through. "People can be real jerks." The desire to pull her close returned. Her. Not Eugenia.

"Can I go to the bank? And the store? I need some things."

"You can go anywhere you want, as long as you don't leave Mendocino. You'll be followed." He pointed his thumb over his shoulder. "Do you have money?"

"Yes."

He assumed the house was paid for long ago. And she seemed like the type to bankroll most of her disposable income. And Gert and Ella. Were they the types who stuffed their mattresses with millions, twenty dollars at a time? He stood. "You'll call me if you need anything?"

They walked to the front door, and he stooped to pick up her mail. One more bill since yesterday, and two pieces of junk mail. "Thank you for the tea. I'll stop by tomorrow to see how you're doing." He thought he saw the dimples again.

"How will you get to where you're staying?"

"The motel is just a half mile down the road." He purposely pointed in the wrong direction. "I'll walk." He patted his stomach. "I need the exercise."

"Thank you for bringing me home." She closed the door on his smile.

Wilson was out of the Ford by the time Jason got to the road.

"What did you and the little lady talk about?" Wilson winked. "Or did you talk? The two of you got something going?"

"Thank you for not telling Bransome about the phone call. I really am on your side this time."

"Yeah, well, don't expect any more out of me. He found out. I really got my ass chewed. I'm lucky I gave you that ticket or I probably would've been busted down to janitor." He yanked the car door open. "Tell Mulvaney no more favors. Okay?"

"If I need one, I'll let you write another ticket first. How's that?"

Wilson laughed as he climbed back in the Ford.

Jason turned in the direction of his motel and started off at a fast pace. Out of the corner of his eye, he saw the curtains in Agnes's second-floor bedroom part. The afternoon carried a sudden chill.

CHAPTER 12

THE CARE HOME RECEPTIONIST PEERED OVER THE TOP of her half-frame glasses. "What's her name?"

"I don't know. She looks after Ella Hahn. Takes her to supper."

The receptionist scanned a list of names. "Ella Hahn. She's in the assisted-living wing. I don't know the aides over there. What does she look like?"

Jason had noticed at least three workers who fit Uh huh's general description, so that wouldn't help. And describing a nipple ring, and a tattoo of a skull smoking a joint on her right butt cheek would probably get him thrown out on his ear.

"Maybe if you could point me in the right direction, I could ask around."

The receptionist looked at the bouquet in his hand and frowned. "You have to be listed as a guest of a resident, or an employee. I can't let you go unless you give me a name.

For security reasons."

He knew the routine. But on his first trip, the receptionist hadn't made such an issue of it. Just a single question. Probably because he'd called ahead.

"I'm here to visit Ella Hahn, at supper. I wanted to talk with her aide first."

"I can put you down for Ella Hahn. What's your name?"

"Jason Powers."

"Do you have identification?"

He fumbled with his wallet.

"Normally, you have to make prior arrangements to have supper here. We can't have people dropping in."

"I don't have to eat. I want to talk with Ella at suppertime."

The receptionist peered over her glasses again. "I can put you down today. As Ella's guest. But you'll have to give advance notice in the future."

"Thank you. Where would I find Ella's room?"

"Second floor of the north wing." She scanned a ledger. "Room 238."

Jason used the stairs to the second floor and crossed a small outside bridge to the north wing. The difference was startling. In the main wing, the independent-living residents occupied one or two-bedroom apartments, and each door had a small shrine of decorations, some seasonally appropriate, some honoring grandchildren or great-grandchildren. In the north wing, the residents were more like patients, and the suites were more like private hospital rooms. The halls were nearly bare. Pictures were taped to an occasional door, but that was all. He felt like he had walked from a forest into a desert.

He spotted a young woman pushing a laundry cart. "I'm looking for a woman who works here. She looks after Ella Hahn in 238."

The woman turned as if startled. "The lounge is around that corner, on the left." She thrust out her finger like she was trying to hurt someone in the distance. "She's sitting on her butt, like always."

The woman was wrong. She wasn't sitting. Three aides stood talking next to a soda vending machine. He recognized the backside of the one facing away from him and walked up to her. "Uh huh?"

She spun around and threw her arms around his neck, crushing the bouquet of carnations between them. Her giggles were contagious, caught by the other two women.

"Come on." She grabbed his hand and pulled him from the lounge and into the hall. They turned right at a T-junction and hurried twenty yards down the austere hall, lined with naked, numbered doors. She jerked him to a stop, keyed an unmarked door, and pulled him inside.

A washing machine rumbled in the far corner of the large room, and the scent of fabric softener filled his nostrils. A huge pile of bedding and towels, all white, covered the floor in front of four machines, two washers and two dryers. To the left, three rows of floor-to-ceiling shelves filled the majority of the room, loaded with clean linens, paper products, and cleaning supplies.

The woman pulled Jason over to the pile of laundry and yanked his shirttail from his pants.

He grabbed her hands. "I just came to talk." He couldn't take his eyes off her face. The flip of her hair, the teasing arch of her eyebrows. They triggered a flashback of Eugenia, in an L-shaped Laundromat at two in the morning. How she had pulled him to the far corner of the empty room, against one of the floor-to-ceiling dryers. She lifted her skirt and dropped her panties in one quick motion. With another, she had freed him of his Levi's and had him inside her, moving to the tumbling rhythm and doubling the heat of the dryer.

The woman pulled her hands free, bringing Jason back to the care home laundry room. She grabbed the bouquet and hurled it to the floor, and tugged at the buttons of his shirt. He turned enough to break her grip.

Her shirt was off with a single pull and her pants followed a moment later. She laid down on the laundry pile, leaned back on an elbow, and parted her legs. Her smooth thong panty contrasted the rumpled bedclothes.

"This isn't what I came for."

"Yeah, right. What else do you need to know about Ella?" She sat up, legs crossed. "Whatever it is, you know it'll cost you."

"Never mind." He turned to the door.

She lunged and grabbed the waist of his Levi's, turning him back. The buttons of his fly gave a rip of staccato pops as they let loose.

He twisted, but her grip was firm.

She slipped her hand through the opening in his boxers. "Thought so." She laughed.

Damn Eugenia. Her image once again betrayed his intentions. Was this the only way he could have her?

The woman reached over to her discarded shirt and pulled a condom from the front pocket. She held the wrapper in her teeth, tore it open, and spat out the remnant.

Jason lowered himself and adjusted his position on the makeshift mattress. He didn't know what to say, and as usual, something stupid came out. "Do you always carry condoms at work?"

"I'm a real Girl Scout. Always prepared. And I knew you'd be coming around sooner or later."

Before he could say another word she sheathed and straddled him, quickly engulfing any remnant of dissent. Her vocalizations began immediately. "Uh huh. Uh huh. Uh huh."

The rhythmic utterances echoed throughout the room, overpowering the competing cadence of the washer. They threatened to awaken all but the hardest-of-hearing residents. He put his hand over her mouth to mute the grunts, but it did little to dampen her enthusiasm, or her volume.

"Mm hmm. Mm hmm. Mm hmm."

It was the sound Eugenia used to make in his ear when they made love.

The woman was good at her craft, and the spontaneity of the event triggered an early conclusion. Her oral crescendo vibrated the room and probably registered on the local Richter scale.

She pulled on her panties and slacks in a hurry and jumped to her feet. "You might want to get yourself together. This room gets used a lot."

He felt sluggish, like he was moving in slow motion, and the thought of being caught half-dressed did little to speed his movements. He fastened the last button on the Levi's and scanned the room for the carnations. The mangled bouquet was in the corner next to the washer. He retrieved it.

"Are those for me?"

"They're for Ella." He looked down. "Or, they were." He picked out the bent and torn flowers, tossing them to the floor. He gripped five of the original dozen in his fist. "She likes carnations."

"Nobody ever brings me flowers."

"Maybe if I knew your name, I would."

She planted a tongue-thrusting kiss on his mouth and pranced to the door, laughing. "Come on. Let's get out of here. We can talk in the lounge."

He followed her to the door. It opened to an audience; he jumped back a step. The two women from the lounge were joined by a third he'd never seen before, and they gave a rousing ovation. He slinked out, pulled by the hand of Uh huh. She gave a low curtsy and led him down the hall. Her laughter reverberated through the north wing.

The lounge was empty.

"What do you want to know about Ella that's so important you bring flowers to a woman you don't even roll with?" A pleasant blush filled her face. There wasn't a hint of hurt in her expression or her statement.

Anywhere. Anytime. Sex was a game. Just like with Eugenia. Although with her, it had also been a bond. They had done it in so many places, it had become part of their normal relationship. Relationship? He leaned back and focused on the woman. A relationship with this woman? He didn't even know her name. He shook his head. He needed information about Ella. But what did that make him? He shook the thought from his head.

"I want to get through to her," he said. "The real her. You said she was lucid sometimes after supper. Is there anything that helps bring her back? Any way to get her attention?"

The woman looked up at the ceiling. "When she gets like that, she always wants to help clean up. Maybe that's what brings her back. Cleaning up."

"Do you mention it to her, or does she just snap into it?"

"I don't do anything."

No surprise there. "When are you going to bring her down?"

She looked at her watch. "Oh, shit. I was supposed to start getting her ready five minutes ago." She didn't move.

He pulled a single flower from his fist and held it out to her.

A smile puckered her cheeks. She gave his crotch a quick squeeze and sauntered down the hall. At the doorway, she spun around, reached into her front pocket, and pulled out two attached, wrapped condoms. She swung them back and forth, winked, then disappeared into the hallway.

Jason looked down at the remaining four carnations and exhaled hard. Uh huh, it was.

Ella looked nice in her blue flowered dress, none the worse for Uh huh's tardiness. Uh huh wheeled her to the table and gave Jason a sloppy smile before slinking away to a far corner of the room.

"Ella, I'm Jason Powers. We talked the other day." He held out the bouquet of four carnations.

She cradled them in her arms and inhaled deeply.

"Are you visiting today, dear?"

Jason watched as Ella finished the last mouthful of her dessert. He pushed his dishes closer to hers and adjusted the position of the carnations on the table, trying to shake a little scent from them.

Ella reached for his stack of dishes and pulled them next to hers. Her expression seemed to change. It wasn't fear he saw, but more like sadness, in stark contrast to her normal jovial disposition. Her shoulders seemed to slump forward. And she aged before his eyes.

"Ella. Are you all right?"

"I'm fine, dear. It's time to clean up."

"I'm Jason Powers. I'm here to talk to you about Agnes."

"Is Agnes here? I'd like to see her."

"She couldn't make it tonight. But I need to talk to you about her. About her past."

"Is she in trouble?"

What made her say that? If Agnes was innocent, why would Ella's first thought be that she was in trouble? "Yes."

"What's wrong?" Her sad expression deepened.

He looked across at the dapper gentleman, who leaned forward into the conversation. Jason lowered his voice. "She found out she has a sister."

"Oh, dear." The creases surrounding Ella's eyes turned downward.

He waited for a few seconds. "I need to ask you about her sister, and about Edward Hahn."

Ella's entire face tensed, and her eyebrows pinched the bridge of her nose. "Eddie." She spat out the word and brought her fist down on the table. Her eyes flicked across the table, at the gentleman, then down to her lap.

Jason looked across at the gentleman and frowned. The man didn't raise his eyes from his plate.

"Please tell me anything you can about Lilin and Edward Hahn. It's important. For Agnes. Do you know where I can find them?"

Her expression slipped and her eyes glazed. Tears welled. "Family secrets." Her voice was soft, quiet. "Let them lie."

"What do you mean, family secrets?"

Tears rolled down Ella's cheeks, but her face dawned with a startling cheerfulness.

"Are you visiting today, dear? It's a nice day for a visit."

CHAPTER 13

ON AN EMOTIONAL LEVEL, NOTHING ABOUT A MURDER scene made sense to Bransome. And yet, he was expected to make sense of it. It grated, the way everyone tiptoed around, taking photos, acting as if the body were diseased, toxic. It was a person, someone's son, maybe someone's father or brother.

He turned from the motel room doorway and savored his last look at the Pacific before the sun extinguished into the liquid horizon. He'd probably see the light of tomorrow morning before he got home. A small bay to his left was partially hidden by a deep cliff, but he could hear the sound of the waves as they smashed into the rocky shoreline, sending salt spray skyward. The sound soothed him.

A man in a khaki uniform stepped forward, pulling Bransome's attention back to the room. The officer looked like he had graduated from the academy within the last week. He stopped and stood there, silent.

"Detective Art Bransome, from Mendocino." Bransome offered his hand.

"Officer Frank Tatum. I thought Ukiah handled the county stuff. How'd you end up down here on this one?"

Bransome tugged at his belt, but it slipped back down, under his belly. Cocky little rookie, probably his first assignment. He thought of a good way to cut him down to size, but that wouldn't make the job any easier. Besides, green or grizzled, the uniforms stood for a member of the fraternity, the good guys. "I get the major cases along the coast. Ukiah picks up all the inland stuff." Besides, this job would tear the rookie a new one soon enough.

"Lucky you," Tatum said. He swept his arm in a wide arc. "It's all yours. Mind if I watch? This might be number four. I've given it a quick look."

Bransome felt a twitch in his temple, followed by another in time with his heartbeat. "If you're right, she's moving up the coast. I hope she's not after anyone in Mendocino." He stepped close to the body. "Did you get the directive on what to look for?"

"They read it over the radio after I called this in. Nothing this big's ever happened around here before."

Bransome swung around. "A murder isn't an opportunity. It's not a blessing for a bored town." Or for a rookie officer, he thought.

Tatum stepped sideways. "Sorry, sir. That's not what I meant."

Bransome turned back to the body. The room was tidy, like it hadn't been occupied for more than a few minutes. Both lamps on either side of the bed were on, bathing the bed and the corpse in a bright wash of light. The bed was turned down on one side, but apparently not slept in, and the victim's pants were folded on an adjacent chair, his shirt draped around the chair back, and his shoes and socks lined up on the floor, like the chair was a sitting human caricature.

"Let's do a check-off to see if you're right," Bransome said. He leaned in over the bed. "Clean cut across the neck. Towels to prevent blood spray. What's that tell you, Tatum?"

Tatum's lips parted. "Um. I don't know what you mean, sir."

Bransome glanced over his shoulder, then back at the body. "If someone took the time to press towels against a slit throat, the victim was either on the way to death or somehow incapacitated." He glanced back again. "Right?"

"Yes, sir."

"Anything tell you which it might have been?"

"No signs of a struggle. The vic's clothing is folded on the chair." Tatum stepped around and pointed at the victim's chest. "And, two bruises, with small cuts in the middle." He pointed to the right side of the victim's midsection.

"Did you look at his shirt?"

"No, sir. Why?"

Bransome snapped a photo of the clothed chair and jotted a few words in his notebook. "Hand it to me."

Bransome pulled on a pair of latex gloves and clicked the nearside lamp to the high beam. He held the shirt up in front of it. "See on the right, where the bruises would be? No holes. What's that tell you?"

Tatum smiled and nodded his head. "It happened after he was naked."

Bransome grinned back. "Or, at least after he had his shirt off." He enjoyed working with young officers, as long as they didn't get too enthusiastic. As close as he was to retirement, his job included as much teaching as crime scene workups. And Tatum seemed like a nice kid. "Here. Hold it up to the light. Please." He clicked two more pictures.

"So far, so good," Bransome said. He took a step back, and Tatum followed suit. "What do you make of the penis?" He pointed to the severed organ, lying in the center of the victim's chest.

Tatum chuckled. "I don't know. It's not where it should be, I'll tell you that."

Bransome let him have his laugh. "Let's keep to the list. The cut is clean. Very little bleeding at the site. Tell you anything important?"

Tatum nodded. "The neck was cut first. He bled out, then . . . the other cut."

Bransome spun around and nearly knocked into Tatum. "Did anyone use the sink?"

"I don't think so. Why?"

"It's on the list."

Tatum shrugged and stepped around so he could see into the bathroom. "It's not wet, so no one used it recently. They didn't read me anything about the sink."

Bransome waved Tatum back over. He wanted to keep his voice down. "If it's like the others, the killer washed the organ before using it, so the blood on it won't be the victim's, it'll be hers."

"Her blood?" Tatum looked like he was going to throw up. "They didn't read that part, sir."

Bransome turned to face Tatum. "Are you okay?"

Tatum took a deep breath. "Yeah." He shook his head. "But one thing bothers me."

"Only one thing?" It was Bransome's turn to chuckle.

"Yes, sir. If the killer uses the . . . um . . . thing for pleasure, after she cuts it off . . . How? It'd be all floppy."

"Are you married, Tatum?"

"No, sir."

"Girlfriend?"

"Yes, sir. For a little over two months now."

Bransome held back an all-out laugh. "I'm going to do you a favor here. Ask your girlfriend to explain that part to you. You can't give her any of the other information on the list, that's for police eyes only. But I give you permission to reveal this one thing to her. Okay?"

"Yes, sir."

Tatum's vacant stare told Bransome to get back to the evidence. A loud rap on the open door startled him.

"Hey, Art. Is the party in here?"

Bransome's partner, Quint Saroyan, filled the doorway.

Saroyan stepped into the room, and Bransome saw Officer Tatum move back a step. It was fun to watch people's reactions to Saroyan when the quarters were tight. He was a shade over six-foot-five, with a bespectacled face that screamed pocket protectors and a belt-holstered cell phone. Below the neck, he could pass for a World Wrestling Federation bad boy. He was the rankler of midthirties men everywhere. Rather than a spreading waistline, he still sported a twenty-nine-inch waist that ballooned to thighs that challenged the fabric of even the baggiest of pant legs, and a V-shaped torso that defeated the back pleats of every button-up shirt.

"Looks like everything's under control," Saroyan said. "Shall I start dusting?" He glanced at Tatum. "Who's the uniform?"

"Officer Tatum. Local."

Saroyan offered a massive hand and Tatum shook it and let go like it was hot.

"I'm Quint. Second-in-command from Mendocino.

Good to meet you."

Tatum nodded. "I guess I'll be going." He side-stepped around the bed.

"Don't forget the question you have for your girlfriend."

Tatum's response, "I won't," came from beyond the doorway.

"What was that about?" Saroyan said.

"Just a little rookie education. Public service." He focused the camera and snapped a shot. "Looks like we have another one here."

CHAPTER 14

Jason peered through the peephole in the door. Why was she running away? And why had she rung the doorbell? She hated doorbells. Always someone you don't know, she had explained to him. Either bad news or, worse, a salesman.

She jumped into a BMW two-seater, the top down. The echo of the slammed door stabbed right through him.

The car spun its wheels and lurched. Who was driving? A man? In slow motion, the driver's arm reached out and surrounded her shoulders. His laugh pounded the door with another aural impact.

Jason yanked the apartment door open, but his acuity didn't change. It was cloudy around the edges, like he was still looking through the peephole.

A patch of bright white caught his attention. An envelope covered the WEL of the welcome mat. He picked it up and ripped it open.

The single page glared at him, so bright he had to squint. No salutation, just four bold sentences. And no signature. But the writing was familiar. The wide loops of each *L*, the small circles dotting each *i*.

He heard the slam of the car door again, and its echoes nearly jarred the note from his hands. He looked up but the car wasn't there.

As he read the words they echoed in his mind. "I can't do this anymore . . . do this anymore . . . do this anymore. You haven't been there for me . . . been there for me . . . been there for me. I've met someone else . . . someone else . . . someone else. Tell everyone it's off." The last sentence didn't echo.

The slam of the car door reverberated again, and Jason's full body twitch opened his eyes to a dark room. Where was he? His apartment in Santa Rosa or the weekly rate dive in Mendocino? The banging rattled the door, once, twice, three more times. A few sniffs told him he was in the motel.

More banging.

"Powers. Open up."

Bransome? What was he doing here? Jason glanced at his alarm clock. The red numerals glared a five and two threes.

"Open up or I'll break it down."

Jason swiveled out of bed and stumbled to the door, clad only in his boxers. He opened the door to the limit of the chain and peered out at Bransome and another man.

"Open it." Bransome took a step back.

The command floated in Jason's semi-awake mind. "Hold on. I'm not dressed."

A loud smack popped the chain anchor from the door frame, and the edge of the door slammed into Jason's forehead, knocking him backward onto the bed. He lay dazed as a warm trickle coursed down his temple and into his ear. A searing pain spun circles through his head.

Bransome was on top of him, lifting his shoulder, turning him over on the bed. He felt the click of the handcuffs before he heard it. Then the second click. He was yanked to his feet and spun around.

"I told you if anything happened, I'd be on you."

Blood leaked into Jason's eye. He tried to blink through it. "What are you talking about?"

"Nice act. She's only been out four days. Don't try to convince me you don't know."

Dizziness drained his head and settled in his knees. He went down, crumpled facedown on the worn carpet.

"I think he's hurt."

The voice came from near the door, behind Bransome.

"Get up." A hand pulled on his elbow.

Jason struggled to his feet. His legs wobbled. He felt like he was going to throw up. Bransome pushed him back on the bed, in a sitting position. "Get a towel."

Jason thought he saw a crew cut. Bransome's partner?

Bransome grabbed Jason's shoulders and shook them. "You're coming down to the station for some questions."

Jason squinted at the detective. The station? "What's going on?"

Two hands grabbed his upper arms and pulled him forward. The hot, sour breath was close, panting. He blinked, and squinted through the blood. Bransome's face was inches from his.

"I've been waiting two years for this day, Powers." His fingers dug into Jason's arms.

The answer was rehearsed so often, it was automatic. "Did what was right. Ramirez was innocent."

Bransome moved back and Jason shook his head to clear the view. Then he saw it. A huge fist cocked in the air. It crashed against his chest sending him backward on the bed. The next breath wasn't there. Or the next one. He strained to pull air into his lungs, but his chest muscles fought against one another. The room went dark.

Expanding light brought the familiar features into focus, again inches from his face. He heard his name. It echoed.

His chest ached, but air once again flowed in with each breath. He heard another voice, from behind Bransome, but he couldn't make out the words.

Then everything came back into perfect focus, including the pain. His chest dueled his forehead.

Bransome shook him.

The sneer on Bransome's face cleared his head. Where was the fist? Bransome's voice hit him just as hard.

"Ramirez was innocent."

Jason could feel Bransome's hands squeezing the blood from his arms.

"What about the other two? Did you do fucking stories on them?"

Jason felt a violent shake.

"Art. Calm down," the voice from behind Bransome again.

Another shake.

"Let me give you an update, asshole. Mullins moved down south, to Irvine. Three college girls were raped down there in a period of six months, all with his DNA. Clean DNA this time. They finally caught him on the third one. He won't get off this time. And Warne. He did himself proud. Pulled another armed robbery, but this time he killed the clerk."

The fist knocked Jason back on the bed again, but this time he could breathe. The pain was off center, higher on his chest. He was yanked upward again.

"Art. Don't."

Bransome's face was close again, his voice a low growl.

"The clerk had a family. Wife and two small kids. This is for them, and for the college girls."

The fist raised in the air again, and Jason closed his eyes tight. Go ahead, he thought. I know it'll make you feel better. Maybe it will make me feel better, too.

Nothing happened.

Jason opened his eyes to a squint. Bransome was frozen, his arm raised, the fist poised. But he looked different. Jason blinked to a better focus. Bransome's fist fell to his side. Anger no longer stained his face.

Bransome spun around and walked to the far side of the room. He flopped into the 1960s-style chair and leaned forward so his arms and forehead rested on his knees. "Get him dressed."

A huge man obliterated his view, and he felt hands pulling on his arms, releasing one of the cuffs, pulling a shirt over his head. He tried to focus on the man, but all he could make out were glasses and a crew cut. After a few minutes, the man snapped the handcuff closed and stepped back into the background.

Jason watched Bransome pull himself from the chair.

"We'd like you to come with us to the station for questioning. Your cooperation is strictly voluntary."

Jason yanked his wrists, pulling the cuffs taut. Voluntary, my ass. "And if I decline?"

Bransome leaned close to his face. He spoke slowly, letting each word hover for an instant. "Your cooperation would be greatly appreciated. If not . . ." He looked over at his partner and drew his face closer. His breath was hot against Jason's cheek, his voice low. "You may want to cooperate."

A drop of blood fell from Jason's forehead onto the bed. He looked at the red spot, then up at Bransome. "Okay. You win."

"You'll come voluntarily?"

"Yes."

"Of your own free will?"

He looked at the spot again. "That's what voluntary means."

Bransome clapped his hands together. "Good." He reached around and removed one cuff. "We appreciate your willingness to help."

Jason stood, wobbling. "What am I supposed to have done? I've been driving the speed limit."

Bransome unhooked the other cuff. "Don't play dumb."

The partner stepped forward, and Jason recognized him. Saroyan was his name. He put a hand towel in Jason's newly freed hand. "Put pressure on it."

Jason pressed the towel against his forehead. "I'm not playing anything. What did I do?"

"You don't know about it?" Bransome's voice hurt his ears.

"Know about what?"

Saroyan picked up Jason's shoes and tossed them to the foot of the bed. "There was another murder."

Jason looked around. Bransome was flanked by Detective Saroyan and a female officer he hadn't seen before. He touched the table in front of him. There had to be a master blueprint for police station interrogation rooms. He'd seen several, and they were all alike. "Where's Agnes?"

Bransome paced behind the sterile table. "She's at home. It's Wilson's shift again."

"You brought me in and left her at home? Who's the suspect here?"

"She has an asshole lawyer. You don't."

Jason touched the gash on his head. It still oozed a little fluid. "That could change." He paused. "Did Agnes leave her house? You had it staked out, right?"

"Didier had the night shift." Bransome turned to face the officer.

Officer Didier cleared her throat. "She's as regular as clockwork. Downstairs lights go out and the porch light comes on at 6:30. The light in her bedroom goes on, and then the blue glow of the television. Light and TV go off at 9:30 sharp. Nothing but the porch light until seven the next morning. You could set your clock by her schedule."

"How about last night?"

Bransome stepped forward and glared at Jason. "How about if we ask the questions?"

Didier looked at Bransome and then at Jason. "Same thing last night as all the others."

Jason rubbed his eyes. "Where was the murder?"

"You don't know?"

He looked down, shook his head, and exhaled. "I haven't seen Agnes since I dropped her off. I just got back in town yesterday, around suppertime."

Bransome stared, as if he were running a telepathic lie detector.

Jason blew out a breath. "Where was it?"

"In Point Arena."

Jason put his hands to his mouth. "They're getting closer." He slapped his hands on the table, startling everyone but Bransome. "Do you want to know if she went anywhere?"

"I thought you didn't know anything about this."

"I don't. When I drove her home, I wrote down the odometer reading." He pulled his wallet from his back pocket and lifted a scrap of paper from the money compartment. "When I pulled in the garage, it was at twenty-one thousand, four fifty-three. I don't know about the tenths."

Bransome turned to Saroyan. "You want to pay Miss Hahn a visit?"

Saroyan started for the door, but stopped. "What should I tell her?"

"The truth. Tell her there was another murder. Tell her we need to see her car. Don't accuse her of anything. Let's get our ducks in a row before her lawyer hears about it."

Jason chuckled.

Bransome looked at Jason, then back to Saroyan. "Go." He swung his head back to Jason. "What's your problem?"

"I thought you said the lawyer was an asshole. Seems like you're afraid of him."

"Fuck you." Bransome stomped to the door and let it slam shut behind him.

Jason looked at Officer Didier. "Sorry about the language. Must be a pleasure to work with him."

"He's not usually like this. The DA is really riding him on this one. I guess Agnes's lawyer is playing hardball."

"What should I do now?"

"You better stay put. He didn't say you could leave."

"What about you?"

"I better stay put, too."

Jason shook his head.

It took a half hour before Officer Didier settled in the chair opposite Jason. In different clothes, she could be decent looking. Why did a police uniform always defeminize female officers? Maybe the Kevlar vests.

Twenty more minutes of quiet and Jason threw his hands in the air. He pushed his chair back, lifting the front two legs from the floor. "You know anything about this one? Was it the same as the others?"

The question didn't bring Officer Didier from her trance.

"Come on. You people roused me from a deep sleep, cuffed me, and brought me here for something I didn't do. Now you say I should stay in this room and wait all day while you chase down leads you should've already had. I think I've been harassed enough here. The least you could do is talk to me. Give me some answers."

Officer Didier moved her arm from the table, but she didn't look up. "I don't know about it. I didn't go to the crime scene."

"Did you hear anything about it?"

"Yeah." She turned her head toward the door, then back to Jason.

He smiled. "What did you hear? Was it done the same way?"

"I shouldn't say any more."

Jason pointed to his forehead. "This is going to leave a nasty scar. And I bet I have two fist-shaped bruises on my chest. I'm thinking about filing a complaint. You want to be included?"

Didier took a deep breath and exhaled through pursed lips. "I don't know much."

"Was it done the same way?"

"That's what they're saying."

Jason leaned forward. "Who are they?"

"Detectives Bransome and Saroyan."

"Did they get any new information from this one? Any prints?"

"I know they got DNA. I heard Bransome order the analysis. Then he was yelling at someone else on the phone. He wanted them to keep dusting the place. That's what he kept saying. Keep dusting the place. So I doubt they found anything useful."

"Did you nod off anytime during the night?"

Didier straightened in her chair. "I do my job and I do it well."

"I didn't mean to suggest otherwise. Is there any way Agnes could have slipped out?"

"I'd have seen her."

"Did you take any breaks?"

"Not without relief."

"What about the back of the house?"

"Where would she go? The storage center has a six-foot fence with razor wire on top. If she'd gone out either side, I'd have seen her."

Jason rubbed his temples. "Do you know why I'm being hassled?"

"You'll have to ask Bransome that one."

"Probably because he can."

"He's the most thorough detective I've ever seen. He must have a good reason."

Jason rolled his eyes, then cringed. The laceration in his forehead complained with a burning bolt of pain.

The reporter worked through it. "You said the DA was on his back about this case. Shit runs downhill and I'm at the bottom of the slope. Right?"

"I bet there's more to it than that. He's probably checking to make sure you were where you said you were."

"So, I'm a suspect now?"

"I said he's very thorough."

"Pardon me if I'm not so impressed."

Officer Didier shrugged and settled back into her trance.

The door burst open, and a shock wave preceded Bransome into the room, jolting Jason from near sleep.

Jason's head shot up. He could feel the indentation between his eyes from resting on his arms. He blinked, trying to focus. Every nerve in his body came alive, as if somebody had taken a bat to his forehead.

Bransome folded his arms across his chest. "You can go now, but keep us informed of your whereabouts."

Jason tried to clear the cobwebs. "What did the odometer say?"

"Get out."

"I gave you the information. The least you could do is tell me how it was used."

Bransome blew a long, loud exhalation. "Twenty-one,

four sixty-nine."

Jason remained in his seat. "Agnes said she had to go to the bank and the store. It's what, thirty miles to Point Arena?"

Officer Didier stood. "More like thirty-five."

Bransome shot her a dirty look.

"That's still seventy miles round trip," Jason said. "Her lawyer know yet?"

Bransome mumbled something that sounded like an expletive. "You got back what you gave. Now take off. I have a lot of work to do."

Still sitting. "Don't you want to know what Ella Hahn had to say? She was lucid for a few minutes the other day."

"Will it help the case?"

Jason shrugged.

Bransome walked over and leaned on the table. "Well? What did she say?"

"She said, 'Family secrets. Let them lie.'"

"What's that supposed to mean?"

"It means there's something here that goes beyond Agnes Hahn."

"And I suppose you're going to keep poking your nose in the case until you find out what it is?"

Jason looked at his watch. "I have three hours of reasons why I shouldn't."

Bransome straightened and slapped his hands together. "Good. Then we can find you at your apartment in Santa Rosa if we need you?"

Jason forced a fake chuckle. "And I have a half million readers as reasons why I should."

CHAPTER 15

"WHAT THE HELL HAPPENED TO YOU?" EACH HOARSE word was punctuated with a puff of smoke from Mulvaney's mouth.

Jason feathered his brown hair over the butterfly bandage on his forehead. "I had an argument with a door. It's no big thing."

Mulvaney sauntered around the side of the desk. "How much longer are you going to be in Mendocino?"

Jason leaned against the closed door, trying to draw air from the hallway outside. "The story took an unexpected twist. It may take a while. But it'll be worth it. I guarantee it."

"I haven't seen anything about a twist. Have you sent in the latest?"

"It's unfolding. I've got to let it play a little while longer." He grimaced, and braced himself for the explosion.

Mulvaney sat on the edge of the desk. "I've got a problem here, Jason. The first story you sent was brilliant. And the hook at the end has the readers wanting more. It has me wanting more. That's the old Jason. But I didn't budget for a long-term stay. How do you think it's going to play out?"

"It looks like a multiple. That's about all I can say right now. This one isn't going to roll over in a one-shot story. This is the real thing."

Mulvaney stood and resumed pacing. His eyes stayed on the floor, as if Jason wasn't even there. He stopped and spun around. "I budgeted for just two more days on the expense account. I could squeeze out two more. Would that do it?"

"You've seen where it's headed, but it isn't coming easy. I'm dealing with an Alzheimer's patient, a story lead whose memory stops where I need to begin, and a detective who hates my guts." He brought his hand up to the bandage, but brought it back down when he saw Mulvaney staring.

"Four more on the expense account. That's all I can give you."

"I don't know if it'll play through by then." And the story needed to play through. A female serial killer who sexually mutilated men. A mysterious twin. And family secrets, whatever they might turn out to be.

"What about your other assignments? I haven't seen

anything on the county fair exposé yet."

"That one's in final edit." As soon as I finish the rough draft, he thought.

Mulvaney stubbed out a butt and pulled another cigarette from a fresh pack. "Is Mendocino worth going off account? Can you afford it yourself?"

Jason leaned away from the door. "Yeah. I'm staying in a cheap-ass motel, and I can do a couple of days there, a couple here."

"And what about the other stories? After four more days, I'll have to send an assignment load as if Mendocino is no longer active. Do you think you can handle the extra workload and still give me this kind of quality?" He picked up a section of the newspaper and waved it in the air.

A smile creased Jason's face. "I can handle it."

Mulvaney walked around behind the desk. "If you don't, I'll have to bring in Yolanda. You don't want her cleaning up any messes. She's a bright one."

"So you've told me."

Mulvaney chuckled. "Must be true, then." He took a long drag. "When can I expect the next story?"

"A day or two. Same for the county fair story."

Mulvaney plopped down in his chair. "It's that good, huh?"

"Looks that way."

"Do I have to say that it had better be?"

Clever. It was hard to parry Mulvaney's jabs. Jason flashed a syrup-sweet smile. Truth? He sure hoped it would be. This story really was make-or-break. It was a risk he wouldn't have taken before. Would he? And, why now? Because the potential was huge?

Mulvaney gave a backward flip of his hand and Jason walked into the hall.

Was there something else that drew him to Mendocino? To put up with Bransome, and the history? It all centered on Agnes Hahn.

CHAPTER 16

THE MOTEL PHONE WAS LOUD, OBNOXIOUS, AND THE rings were the old-fashioned kind, not the electronic noises made by modern phones. Was it Mulvaney? It'd be just like him to toss a zinger via long distance.

Jason reached across the bed, lifted the receiver, and took a deep breath before issuing a standard greeting. His voice came out more impatient than intended.

Composure. He rolled on his back and the coiled phone cord pulled the base from the nightstand. It crashed on the tattered carpet with a muted ring.

"Jason?"

The high-pitched voice sent him onto his elbow. "Agnes?"

Agnes opened the front door and tugged the flannel lapels tight against her neck. She turned away without saying a word.

Each time he got a brief glimpse of her face, it made him want more. Just once, he wanted to take a good long look. To look into her eyes. He felt he was pretty good at reading people's eyes, but Agnes seldom made direct eye contact. He didn't know why, but he wanted to see more of hers.

He followed her to the back of the house, into the kitchen. Wilson was on duty outside, so a call had already been placed to Detective Bransome.

Agnes stopped by the kitchen table and pointed. A single page letter, written in longhand, was spread open next to a personal-sized envelope. Jason leaned over to get a closer look at the envelope.

The postmark was from Point Arena, the day following the murder. He felt a slight resistance in his breathing. He turned to the letter, which was signed "Lilin." A red-brown smudge followed the signature. Probably blood.

He looked up at Agnes. She was pale, obviously frightened.

"Did you handle it much?"

"I just opened it and read it. I put it down right here and called you."

"Did you call the police?"

She shook her head. "No."

"Why not?"

"I wanted you to see it first."

Jason looked toward the street, as if he could see through the walls. "You know they're probably on their way right now?"

"I wanted you to see it."

He kept his gaze on Agnes. "Why me?"

"I want you to help me find Lilin. Before the police do. I want to talk to her. I think I can get her to stop doing these things."

He couldn't take his eyes off of her. She looked as helpless as a three-year-old in the dark.

Best to head this off with Bransome. He pulled his wallet from his pocket and fished for the detective's business card. The cell phone number would be best.

Bransome didn't disappoint, and Jason slapped the cell phone closed to terminate the conversation.

He turned to Agnes. "Bransome's going to ask why you called me first. I'd suggest you don't tell him what you just told me. Tell him you lost his number. Or something like that."

He looked back at the letter. There were only a few short sentences, each written in neat handwriting that tailed off into a scrawl at the end, like they were written with a purpose, but with a hurried hand. He concentrated on the message and gave Agnes a quick stare. A chill ascended his spine.

I WANT TO TALK TO YOU. IT'S BEEN SO LONG. I COULDN'T FIND YOU. THEN THEY KEPT ME AWAY. I'LL BE THERE SOON. I'M DOING THIS FOR US.

"Do you know what she means when she says, 'I'm doing this for us'?"

Agnes backed up a step. "No."

"Do you know who would want to keep you two apart?"

She brought her hands up to her mouth and shook her head. "No."

"Bransome's going to ask these same questions, but he won't be so nice about it. Do you want me to stay?"

She tugged on her lapels. "Yes. Please."

The doorbell rang in unison with the first of three loud knocks. Jason answered and Bransome pushed by him, followed by Officer Wilson.

"Where is it?"

"On the kitchen table." Jason pointed. He was left holding the door.

Bransome pulled back a chair and sat in front of the letter. He leaned in close as he examined the note from top to bottom, then he did the same with the envelope.

He turned and his eyes darted to Jason's hand, then to his face.

"Did you touch it?"

"No."

"Then your prints shouldn't be on it?"

"No."

He unbuttoned a shirt pocket and pulled out a pair of latex gloves. They snapped a tight fit around his thick wrists. He touched the letter by the corners, tilting it against the light, and turned it over and examined the blank side.

Wilson pushed two Ziploc baggies onto the table.

"I'll need a paper bag for the letter. Anything that has blood on it has to go in paper."

Wilson stared at Bransome. "I don't have one with me."

Bransome mumbled, his eyes still on the letter.

"I have one." Agnes disappeared into the adjacent pantry and reappeared with a brown lunch bag.

Bransome lifted the letter and slid it into the bag. He mumbled something that sounded like a thank-you, reached for the envelope, and turned it over. The top was slit.

"How did you open it?" He didn't look at Agnes, who was cowering against the counter.

"Letter opener." She pointed across the room.

Bransome examined the sealing flap. It was tightly tacked.

Jason took a step forward. "You may be able to get DNA from the glue, if she licked it. And from the blood on the letter."

"No shit, Sherlock. You worry about your involvement here. I'll worry about the forensics." He slipped the envelope into the plastic baggie. "It arrived today?"

Agnes nodded. "Yes."

"And you didn't do anything except read it and put it down?"

"No."

"Miss Hahn, will you please call us if anything else happens with this case? Mr. Powers doesn't represent the police. I want to get this to the lab right away, so I won't bother you with any more questions right now. I'll come back and talk about it after we do some tests."

Bransome snapped off the gloves and shoved them into his back pocket. He stood and faced Jason.

"If she calls you, you call us. If you come here, we'll know." He nodded at Officer Wilson.

"Are you saying I can't visit Agnes? She needs a friend right now."

Bransome turned to Agnes. "You really think he wants to be your friend? He wants to write a book about this case. He wants to make money off of you. That sound like a friend?"

Agnes took a step away from Jason and stared at the floor. Her hand went to her collar.

Bransome chuckled as he hurried out of the house, Wilson on his heels.

Jason looked at Agnes. She wouldn't look up. That prick, Bransome, got in a good shot. It was like Agnes pulled into a shell. Before, she had been coming around a little. He could feel it. She seemed more relaxed. She stood closer. And the brief glimpses into her eyes were getting longer, their draw irresistible. Now she might as well be curled into a fetal position.

He took a step toward her and resisted an urge to pull her into his arms. Honesty was probably the best way to go.

"I'm sorry about what he said."

"Is it true?"

"Agnes, I'm a reporter. I'm here to do a job. This case is very important, and the public has a right to know about it. But I can be a friend, too. I like you. And I want to help you."

Agnes stared at the floor.

"I am one of the good ones. Do you believe me?"

Agnes's face contorted into a frown and she swiveled her head left, then right.

"Agnes?"

"I don't know."

"Do you still want me to help you?"

She walked over to the table and looked up. A twinge of a smile tightened her lips. "Yes. Please."

CHAPTER 17

Agnes hurried down the hall from the kitchen and picked up the telephone receiver. The phone seldom rang. It had been two days since Detective Bransome had called requesting a meeting, and he had used her cell phone.

She twisted her finger through the coiled phone cord.

"Hello, Agnes."

Agnes fumbled the receiver, but caught it before it dropped. "Is it really you?" Breathing on the other end was rapid, almost panting.

"Yes."

"I want to meet you. See you."

Breathing.

"Where are you? Can we meet somewhere?"

More breathing. "No."

"The police are looking for you. I want to see you

before they find you."

"They won't."

"But I want to find you. A man is helping me. His name is Jason. He's a reporter. I think he's one of the good ones."

The breathing increased in frequency and volume. "No."

"Please. I want to see you. You can trust me."

The breathing slowed then stopped, cut off by a click and dial tone.

"Lilin . . . Lilin!"

Agnes eased the receiver back onto the cradle and stared at the phone. The voice sounded so close. But why didn't Lilin trust her? It must be Jason. She didn't trust Jason. He was getting in the way.

But how could she get together with Lilin without Jason's help? Lilin was still in hiding. She was close; the feeling came through clearly. But she was hiding— wanting to touch, but not wanting to be touched.

Agnes felt the chill of the empty house. Should she tell Jason about the call? What about the police?

She turned away from the phone and rounded the banister to the stairs. Maybe the police already knew about the call? Did they have the phone tapped? Even if they did, Lilin was too smart to get caught. That must be why the call was so short. She probably used a pay phone, or a cell phone. She wouldn't get caught. She couldn't get caught. Not yet. They had to meet.

Agnes circled the railing at the top of the stairs and slipped into her room. Her cell phone was on the nightstand, folded, but on. Should she call Jason? How else could she find Lilin before the police did? Lilin didn't want to be found, so it would be difficult. Hide-and-seek came to mind, twenty-some years too late.

Agnes paced the room, staring at the phone on each pass, hoping it would ring, willing it to ring. If Lilin's words could get through to her sometimes without a phone, maybe she could get through to Jason the same way.

She glanced at the clock. It was nearly ten. Jason wasn't going to call. He was probably in bed, asleep. No, he was a reporter. He'd stay up for the eleven o'clock news. He was awake. He must be awake.

She walked to the end table and picked up the cell phone. It was one of the few modern devices that appealed to her. It represented freedom, and freedom meant independence. And risk.

The hinged lid of the phone snapped open, illuminating the small screen. She knew the number; her mind was quick with numbers. Twice repeated, long remembered. That had been her trick in school, and it still served her well. But it was one thing to remember the numbers, another to punch them into the phone. Was he one of the good ones?

Don't do it.

She looked at the clock again. Nearly five past ten. He wouldn't like it if she called during the news. Maybe he wouldn't like it if she called at any time. But he said to call if she needed anything. He said anything.

She pushed the first three numbers and paused.

Don't do it.

He offered his help, and now she needed it. Was he serious or just being nice? Were his smiles sincere or was he using her for his own gain? Did it matter? She needed to find Lilin.

Agnes punched in the last four numbers and rested her finger on the talk button. If she called, she would be joining him in a pact. A pact that angled around the police. She wasn't out of trouble with them, and this would work against her in the long run. And Jason might not be one of the good ones. But his smile seemed sincere.

No!

She pushed the button.

Jason turned the dial on the hot plate. Instant coffee was nasty, but the goal was caffeine, not taste. The ring of the phone startled him. He froze.

One call had come in on that phone, from Agnes, but now it was late. She'd be in bed, asleep. Who else could it be? It wouldn't be his editor. Mulvaney disappeared around nine o'clock every night, without a trace. He couldn't be reached at work. He couldn't be reached at home. The word in the newsroom had him indulging in some undetermined excess that kept him busy until the wee hours.

Jason mopped his brow. He hadn't given the motel number to anyone else. He hadn't told anyone else where he was staying.

Another ring. Bransome would have the number, and more. He seemed to work day and night. No family? Maybe his kids were out of the house and his wife didn't mind. Divorced? It seemed to be a fate of too many law enforcement families.

Another ring. Maybe it really was Agnes. If she was still up, it must be important. He walked to the bed, sat down, and interrupted the next ring.

"Agnes. Why are you still up?"

"Lilin called."

"Holy shit." He looked the time. "If your lights are on, turn them off. And the TV, too. The police are watching, and they'll think something is wrong."

He heard shuffling and a click. More shuffling.

"Now, what did Lilin say?"

"That she doesn't want to meet me." Her voice sounded distant, sad.

"She probably knows the police are watching."

"Can they tap cell phones?"

Jason tugged on the phone cord. She didn't call on his cell. "Yes, but you don't have to worry about that."

"Why not? I don't want them to find her."

"Let's meet tomorrow. I'll explain it then. There's a Denny's about two miles up the coastal highway. On the right. Do you know the one?"

"Yes."

"Meet me there at noon, and don't worry. I'll already be there. I'll go about a half hour early and park a couple of blocks away. The police will probably stay outside in the car. I'll see you tomorrow."

CHAPTER 18

JASON BYPASSED THE WAIT-TO-BE-SEATED SIGN AND scooted into a booth centered on the back wall of the restaurant, prompting a dirty look from the midthirties hostess in the frilly dress. The place was about two-thirds full, populated by two sets of mortal enemies in a temporary state of détente. Apparently, locals didn't patronize this Denny's, so instead of a wide variety of human types, the patronage was dominated by the two very different groups. And they seemed to coexist in a fragile equilibrium.

At the tables, the working-class-retired hovered over breakfast plates, all bearing a common denominator—bacon. It was probably too messy to cook on the propane mini-stoves of their campers and thirdhand recreational vehicles.

Younger tourists occupied the window booths, club sandwiches and ham-and-swiss on rye waiting their turn behind the soup du jour. The boothed diners' eyes moved back and forth between the tables and the BMWs and Lexuses in the parking lot. Jason assumed they wistfully fantasized about working their autos' suspensions into a lather on the twisting, scenic Highway 1 unimpeded by their enemies' rolling roadblocks.

He imagined the meal ending in a *Le Mans* start, a sprint, or fast walk in some cases, beginning the race to the highway, and the jockeying for position for the long stretches between passing opportunities.

He silently rooted for the old folks. The BMW and Lexus drivers exuded a common air of entitlement; an option on most cars, but part of the standard feature package for these two. On a freeway, there was no governor on the young. But on Highway 1, the missiles and the behemoths were on a level field, and it satisfied his sense of righteous indignation.

He appreciated the drama. It passed the time. Meeting in a public place was important to him, although he wasn't sure why. Maybe it was the description of the carnage at the crime scenes, and the distant, hazy possibility that Agnes was involved. He wondered if the victims' throats were slit before the other carving. More hope than wonder. Could someone hate men that much to do it the other way around? Could Agnes?

The rush of rationalization was forceful. All of the murders took place in motels, all with outside-facing doors. And all of the men were large. One was six-foot-three and around two-twenty. These men had to be lured to the rooms. And what was the best way to do that? A way Agnes couldn't accomplish without both physical and emotional makeovers, particularly since the promise of the lure would have to be paid partially in advance.

His defense went one step beyond the conjured absurdity. Even if she were able to attract the men to the room, how could she subdue them to allow the butchery? She wasn't a physical match for a ten-year-old. His argument spiraled into a familiar circular path. Maybe the killer had an accomplice. But Agnes hadn't left the house.

The feeling of someone standing over him brought him out of his daydream. It was Agnes. He stood while she slid into the booth, but he didn't sit down right away.

Something about her had changed. Her clothes were the same, except the flannel shirt was blue today. Her face looked different, and her caramel hair fell around it with a little more shape. Her eyes had the faint contrast of eyeliner, and her skin looked smooth, without the light freckles that normally peppered her nose. A light dusting of makeup? She looked good.

But it was more than that. He'd only seen hints of a smile before, but today, her cheeks dimpled with a tooth-showing grin. And her eyes weren't glued to the floor. She still didn't look into his eyes, other than briefly, but their eye contact already seemed longer and more frequent.

"Have you eaten?" she said.

"I had a piece of pie. That's all I want."

"I already ordered on my way by the counter. It'll look better if Officer Wilson comes in. Besides, I'm hungry."

Jason sipped his coffee. His third cup.

Agnes seemed taller, more confident. She took a long sip of ice water.

"I've made a decision. I want you to help me find my sister. And I don't want the police in on it. I want to talk with her before they catch up to her. I think I can get her to stop what she's doing."

"What makes you think I can find her?"

"I don't know. I just do."

The waitress pushed a plate onto the table. Cheeseburger and fries. Jason looked around at the tables, then at the booths, and smiled. She wasn't in either camp. She was an original.

She held the burger in front of her mouth like she was teasing her lips. "Is it still safe to talk on cell phones? Last night you said it was."

"You asked if it was possible to tap a cell phone, and the answer is yes. But the police need a court order to do it."

"Do you think they'll try to get one?"

"They already tried, but your lawyer convinced the judge not to sign it. He's a sharp one. Maybe that's why

Bransome hates him so much. I worry about how long he can hold them off, though. Another murder and it could turn around."

"So we can use cell phones to talk?"

"For now, yes. But you called me on the motel phone both times. Why?"

Agnes smiled, and maintained eye contact.

"How did you find out where I was staying?"

Her smile widened.

He wanted to press for an answer, but an old couple caught his attention. They pushed up from their table and ambled to the front counter. He looked back at Agnes. Into her eyes. This time, he dropped his eyes.

Agnes's cheeks were puffed with a fresh bite of burger, so he moved on. "I think Ella is the key. I got through to her for a short time on my last visit. I think she knows something."

"Why do you say that?"

"It was what she said. Family secrets. Let them lie. Do you know what secrets she's talking about?"

Agnes's smile turned to a frown so fast Jason took too big a sip of the hot coffee. She turned her head to the right, then left. Her eyes settled on her plate.

He leaned down to try to draw her stare. "Do you?"

"No."

"She seemed to get mad when I mentioned Edward Hahn. Any idea why?"

"No. I don't know anything about him. Remember?"

"I have a strange feeling he figures into this."

Agnes took another bite, but pushed it into her cheek and mumbled around the lump. "Officer Wilson is coming in. What should we do?"

"Just keep his attention." Jason swiveled into the next booth, his back to Agnes, and pulled the collar of his Ralph Lauren shirt high on his neck. He slumped over the table.

Agnes pulled Jason's coffee cup across the table, within her circle of dishes, and wadded his paper napkin in her fist as Wilson slid into the booth across from her. Hopefully, the seat wasn't still warm.

Jason turned his head slightly so he could hear the conversation.

"How's the burger?" Officer Wilson said.

"Good."

"Are you going to be here long? I have to fill up with gas."

Jason heard Agnes chuckle.

"I have a ways to go," she said. "I won't leave until I see your car come back."

A deep laugh.

"Not exactly covert, am I?"

The waitress stomped over to Jason's table, a deep scowl on her face. He slid his finger to his lips in a shush sign and pulled his wallet from his Levi's. He withdrew a five-dollar bill and slid it across the table, his finger still to his lips. The waitress snatched the bill and stomped back to the greeting stand.

Jason picked up the conversation again.

"Mind if I grab a couple of those fries?" Wilson said. "They smell really good."

Jason didn't hear a response but the silence told him she'd offered the fries.

"I guess I'll go fill the car with gas."

"Take your time," Agnes said. "I'm not in a hurry these days."

Jason turned and watched Wilson exit the restaurant and walk to his car. He swung around into Agnes's booth. "Did he suspect anything?"

"He had a few fries. And he has to get gas."

"I can't believe he came in to tell you that." Jason snickered.

Agnes took a large bite.

He let her swallow most of it. "What did Bransome say about the letter when he came back to talk to you?"

"The DNA from the Point Arena murder matched the others, and it matched the DNA from the envelope glue. Lilin sent the letter. And it was blood on the letter—the victim's."

"Did he ask why you called me?"

Agnes's eyes met his. She grinned. "Yes."

He held the stare and smiled. "What did you say?"

She lowered her eyes. "I don't know."

"You don't know what you said?"

"No, silly. I told him I don't know."

He leaned down and tried to draw her eyes up again. "He accepted that?"

"Not very well. He had some more things to say about you."

"Like what?"

She shook her head and took another bite.

Jason edged forward in his seat. "Maybe I should leave while Wilson's getting gas."

Agnes raised her eyes again. "What do we do next?"

"I want to visit Ella again. See if I can get more information out of her."

"Can I come along? Every time I go, she doesn't recognize me. I really want to see her when she's more like her old self."

"Not this time. She was lucid for such a short time, I don't want it to go for hugs and kisses."

"But you'll take me sometime?"

"Yes." He pushed up from the seat. "Call me tomorrow. And use my cell phone this time."

"Maybe I will. Maybe I won't." Her smile made him want to sit down again.

Agnes made Officer Wilson wait in the restaurant parking lot for nearly twenty minutes before she headed out. She stopped at a Safeway and leisurely strolled three aisles, finally eking out a list of items she could use at home. The items weren't needed, but stopping at the store created the illusion that lunch was a side trip, not the primary mission. With efficiency of paramount concern, the selected items included nonperishable, eventual necessities.

Officer Wilson didn't try to hang back on the way home, so Agnes gave a backward wave as she pulled into the garage and pushed the button to lower the door. The light fell in the garage. She froze. Something wasn't right.

Back door.

She swiveled her head in both directions. No one else in the garage. She wanted to push the button again, to raise the door, but she knew Wilson would come running. Back door. What did that mean? "What do you mean?" she said, scanning the garage again.

No response. There never was a response to a direct question.

Back door?

She fumbled with the keys at the door to the house and dropped them. They hit the concrete with a loud jingle. It reminded her of something she saw on the Nature Channel the other night. Bats used a sophisticated type of radar to intercept flying insects. They emitted chirps of ultrasound, inaudible to human ears. But moths heard the ultrasound and responded with an evasive tactic worthy of fighter jet dogfights. They dove to the ground in a tight-turning swirl, hoping to land before the bat adjusted his flight. In the show, the narrator demonstrated the moth's response by jingling his keys, which, in addition to the audible sound, produced a burst of ultrasound pulses. Agnes was ready to dive to the ground at the slightest out-of-ordinary movement or sound.

The house was silent, cold. Filtered light illuminated the rooms through the drapes everywhere except the kitchen. With its southwestern exposure, the kitchen was always bright in the afternoon. No draperies to pull. The window curtains consisted of festooned ornamentals and decorative valances.

To the rear of the kitchen, a small anteroom was brightly lit by two narrow, high windows on the lateral walls that flanked the back door. A heavy, solid-panel door. No window. No peephole. She walked on her toes, more to stay tensed than for silence, ready to evade. She was a moth on high alert.

The dead bolt turned with a throaty clunk. She paused, listening for a sound, of movement, breathing, anything. She put her ear against the door. Nothing. Her hand found the doorknob, but she didn't twist. Not yet. She pulled back from the door and stood, silent. Listening. Listening for Lilin. If Lilin was close, maybe she could hear her. Maybe she would say something again. "Lilin?"

Silence.

Agnes turned the knob. She felt the door release in her hand, and she waited. Nothing happened. She opened it a crack, enough to let in a vertical light beam. Nothing. No movement, no sound. It was as if the back of the house was in a sound vacuum. An auditory black hole.

She opened the door wide enough to look out. The backyard was clear. Everything was in place. She stepped forward to look to either side and her foot hit something hard. She jumped back and closed the door to a crack. No movement. No sound. She eased the door open and looked down at a cardboard box. It was shoved to the side of the door, extending across the opening by only a few inches. There were no markings on the box, but it was sealed with clear packing tape.

She kicked the box, and it moved a couple of inches. Not too heavy. And the hollow sound suggested that whatever was inside included a lot of air. She stepped onto the porch, bent, and lifted the box. It wasn't heavy at all.

The box sat on the kitchen table where Lilin's letter had rested only a few days before. Agnes had the knife in her hand, but she stood, unable to cut the tape. It had to be from Lilin. Her mind flashed back to the glossy photo Detective Bransome pushed across the table to her in the interrogation room. If Lilin was capable of that, what might be in the box?

Agnes put down the knife and filled the water kettle. A cup of tea would break the tension.

Jason turned into the motel driveway and circled around the 1950s-style covered entry to the office. As soon as he made the left toward his room, he saw the police car. The round figure at the wheel turned slowly in his direction and the door swung wide.

Jason pulled in on the far side of the cruiser and quickly exited. He didn't want Bransome and his nightstick in his face.

Bransome waited at the front of the cruiser and motioned at the door of Jason's room. "We need to talk. I could take you to the office, but I'd prefer to do it here."

Jason didn't like the look on Bransome's face. "Can we talk out here?"

"No. Inside."

"Can you tell me what it's about?"

"Inside."

It wasn't a suggestion. It was a command.

"Could you leave your baton out here?"

Bransome pulled the nightstick from his belt, walked over to the car door, and threw the stick onto the seat. "Now, can we go inside?"

Jason looked at the detective's huge knuckles. Could they be left in the car as well? He left the motel door open behind him and pulled the cord that slid the dingy drapes open.

Bransome settled in the only chair in the room, and the aged Naugahyde crackled its displeasure.

Jason shuffled to the low chest of drawers. "You want some coffee? I only have instant."

"Sit down."

"Can I have some coffee?" He'd had enough at Denny's, but he wanted to stall. His mind plucked a quick snapshot from his past. Stalling never worked with his father. It never calmed the old man, never dulled the force of the paddle on his backside. But Jason remembered he never ceased trying the tactic. One never knew.

"Sit down!" Bransome's voice reverberated in the small room.

Jason settled on the side of the bed, more than an easy lunge away from Bransome.

"Do you know a Fiona Trapp?" Bransome said.

"Never heard of her."

"Come on, Powers. We know you've had contact with her here in Mendocino."

Jason fingered his chin. "I don't know what you're

talking about. I've never heard of a Fiona Trapp."

"So you didn't pay a visit to Ella Hahn last week?"

"Yes." Oh, shit. Uh huh.

"And you want to tell me you didn't visit this woman?" Bransome leaned forward and held a photo at arm's length.

Jason stood in a monkey hunch and grabbed the picture. "Yes. I know this woman. I didn't know her name."

"You didn't know her name?"

"No. She's an aide at the home. She's the person who brings Ella down to supper and delivers her back to her room. I talked to her, tried to get some information about Ella."

"You talked to her?"

"A couple of times."

"And you don't know anything about her?"

"No. I told you. I didn't even know her name."

"Really?"

"Yes, really. Why?"

"Do you know where she is now?"

"I know where she lives. In an apartment on the west side of town."

"We've been there. It's cleaned out."

My God, he thought. Could she be involved in the murders? It would take an accomplice to subdue even an average sized man. "What's she done?"

The ancient phone let out a loud ring, startling

Jason. He let it ring again.

Bransome motioned for the return of the picture. "You going to get that?"

Jason let it ring a third time and slid over so the cord wouldn't pull the base from the night table. He held the phone tight against his ear.

"Jason? It's Agnes."

"I'm sorry. I think you have the wrong number." He looked up at Bransome, who stared. Jason turned his gaze to the carpet.

"It's me. Agnes."

"No. No one here by that name." Come on. Get a clue. I can't talk right now.

"Why won't you talk to me?"

The hurt in her voice nearly floored him. He looked up at Bransome again. "This is a motel room. Maybe he was a previous guest. Good-bye." He hung up but kept his hand on the phone. He'd had to hang up on her. He had no choice. Would she trust him again?

Bransome's scowl burned through him.

"Wrong number." He hoped she wouldn't call on his cell phone. A quick change of topic was in order. "Why do you want that woman?" He pointed at the picture in Bransome's hand.

"Fiona Trapp isn't her real name. It's Francine Thomas. She has warrants for burglary, theft, and drugs."

"And?"

"And she did it again. She cleaned out some of the old ladies at the care home and disappeared."

A hollow feeling distended Jason's stomach. For two reasons. He'd spent three months investigating abuses at care homes, and this happened right under his nose, or right under his naked body. He considered reopening the investigation, using this Fiona Trapp, or Francine Thomas, or whatever her name was, as a focal point. The second reason was more disturbing. He thought he had used her to get information about Ella. But was she using him as a smoke screen for her thefts? "Did she get anything from Ella?"

"Not much from her, but she got quite a bit from three others. Are you sure you don't know where she went?"

"Why would I know that?"

"Just a feeling."

"My interest is in Ella Hahn. Not this Francine Thomas." At least that's the way it was a few minutes ago.

"Are you going to be in town for a while?"

"I have a deadline for a story, but I can send it electronically if I can get a hookup." He swept his hand around the room. "This place isn't exactly wired."

"Come in to the station. You can send it from there. I want you where I can find you for the next couple of days."

"Because you have a feeling?"

Bransome stood. "Yes."

Jason remained sitting. "I guess I can handle this

luxury for a few days straight, but I'll have to go down to Santa Rosa before the week is out. You're welcome to join me if you want."

Bransome opened the door and turned to face the bed. "By the way, the care home has security cameras. Everywhere. If I were you, I would've doubled up on the rubbers." The door closed on his laughter.

Agnes stared at the box. She was ready to open it, but Jason's reply to her call confused her. Scared her. Now the knife was back at her side, her caution raised like hackles on the back of her neck. Why wouldn't he take her call? Was something wrong? Was he all right?

She walked around the table, staring at the box. No markings anywhere. It was new, not recycled. The knife still in her hand, she picked up the box and gave it a shake. A rustle and a dull thump. Curiosity was winning. She put the box down, slit the tape on the two top flaps, and pulled them to vertical. The knife fell to the table.

A dress was on top. A pretty, maroon dress. She pulled it out and held it against her body. It was new, the tags still attached, and it was the right size. She laid it across the back of a chair and pulled object after object from the box. A cute pair of shoes with low heels, a package of panty hose, a black lace brassiere with underwires.

All the right size. A small bag held various items of makeup, hairspray, and an assortment of brushes, for her face and for her hair. She almost missed the note taped to the bottom of the box.

She piled the garments back into the box and hurried up the stairs into her room, where she spread each item on the bed. Slipping out of her jeans and flannel, she pulled the dress up across her hips, onto her shoulders. Its fit was tight, showing soft curves the outside world hadn't seen. The hem fell at midthigh, and a moderate vee-cut plunged at the neck, enough to show cleavage with the right bra. The black bra. Her face burned. She liked the look, even though her stark, white bra couldn't hide beneath the dress. And she had the legs for it. But she couldn't ever wear it outside. Could she?

The note. She tore it from the box and nearly shredded the envelope flap. It was written in the same longhand as the previous letter, but it didn't have the rushed scrawl at the end of each sentence.

The reflection in the full-length mirror caught her attention. A twirl to the right, then left. The dress fit perfectly.

The new Agnes turned the note to catch the afternoon sun.

I'M HERE, AND I'M WATCHING.
DON'T GO TO THE POLICE. YOU'RE
STILL SEEING THAT REPORTER.

HE'S NOT ONE OF THE GOOD ONES.
WEAR THESE CLOTHES. YOU'LL
SEE. THIS SHOULD BE OVER
SOON. LILIN.

Agnes looked in the mirror again, then at her purse. The cell phone was inside. Should she call Jason again? Would he give the same answer?

She twirled to the left, her eyes on the mirror. A new sensation swamped her thoughts. She liked the way she looked. But she was showing parts of her body that no one had ever seen. And yet, she liked the dress. And she wanted one other person to see it.

"Thank you, Lilin."

CHAPTER 19

JASON SAT OPPOSITE THE RECEPTION DESK AND RUBBED his temples. How many of the care home staff had seen the surveillance video? Things like that were usually passed around, like the pirated videos of Pamela and Tommy Lee, and that Hilton chick. He'd seen them on the Internet. Jesus, the Internet. He rubbed his temples again.

The receptionist gave him a double-take stare. It was the same woman who'd given him the third degree on his last visit. Had she seen the video? She was probably in her late fifties. What would she think of something like that? It wasn't too late to turn around, but he needed to talk to Ella again. And he needed to work fast. Mulvaney was getting restless. He'd begrudgingly allowed a little more time, as long as it didn't drag on too much longer. Jason sighed. He'd fight that battle again before he was finished.

"I'm here to see Ella Hahn."

"You're not planning to do any laundry tonight, are you?"

He watched her expression. Dissected it. A hint of a smile? A glare of disapproval? She'd make a great poker player.

"I called in yesterday. For supper."

"They're going to catch her, you know."

"Catch who?"

"Your aide friend."

"I don't know anything about her."

The blank stare again.

"Detective Bransome said we should let you talk with Ella. Otherwise, I'd have security throw you out. This is a respectable place. No thanks to you."

Had she heard about it, or seen it? "My intentions are honorable." Where did that assholic line come from? "I'm here representing Ella's great-niece, Agnes."

"She was here yesterday, to see Ella."

Why didn't he know about that? What had Agnes found out? "What time did she visit?"

"That's not your business."

"Was it for supper? You can tell me that."

Her eyes dropped to the ledger and returned to a silent stare.

Jason shifted his weight in the chair. A lie should do it, as long as it was a quick-thinking one. "I told Agnes if she came during a meal, I'd pick up the tab."

"No meal."

She probably didn't get through to Ella. "Can I go in?"

"You'll be watched. And you should know the directors aren't happy with all of this attention. If anything else happens, Ella will have to find another place to live."

He straightened in his chair. "Were the directors planning to notify Agnes about this? I presume there's a termination clause in the contract that gives reasonable notice." This was one area of abuse he'd found in some of the less scrupulous homes during his investigation. If a tenant became too much trouble, the relatives were pressured to remove the tenant.

The stare. "Enjoy your meal."

Jason had to hurry to get a seat next to Ella at her usual table. Earl, the well-dressed gentleman, sat across the table again and provided conversation to fill the uncomfortable gaps between Ella's repetitious meanderings.

Something was different in Ella's eyes this time. Like most of the residents, she appeared happy, or at least content. But the others had a dullness in their eyes, like something had been taken from them. Today, Ella's eyes twinkled more than usual. That was the best way to describe it. Maybe Agnes's visit registered deep within

Ella's brain, filling a void of loneliness.

Ella returned Jason's stare with a sweet smile and turned back to her plate. She didn't pick up the dozen carnations he'd placed above her place setting. If Agnes managed to touch her emotionally, it showed only in her eyes. Ella's grasp of the present hadn't received the same boost.

He turned to the gentleman across the table and shrugged. So far, he had heard about the old-timer's service in the army during World War II. How he had campaigned in France, then Germany. He heard about how the flood of servicemen returning from the war created a frustrating competition for good jobs. How several of Earl's friends had struggled for years.

Jason's mind drifted. Something didn't sit right with this Earl character. He seemed out of place here, like he was too together, too capable. The reporter kicked in. This was a good place to gain access to widows and their bank accounts. It was also a great place to hide. Hide from what, though?

The next breath wouldn't come. Jason jerked forward in his chair and gasped. The old man's stare seemed to go through him. Earl's connection to Ella—it was convenient. Was he Eddie? Eddie wouldn't be so brash to stay in such close contact with Ella, would he? On the other hand, it would be a great place to lie low. He thought of asking about a Purple Heart, but rejected the notion. If Eddie was ballsy enough to hole up in the care home, he'd lie about the medal.

Jason shook his head, trying to clear it of the thought. It worked, but his new track wasn't much better. He felt an overwhelming sadness. The dining room brimmed with life experience, with wisdom. But it leaked away right in front of him. Age contributed to one stream of loss, an inevitable one. But an additional breach produced an equal seep. He couldn't identify it with certainty, but he had a feeling it centered on a narrowing of the residents' lives, produced by their regimented existences. All of their basic needs were met. All according to set schedules. Spontaneity and individuality hid from sight, perhaps dusted off occasionally behind closed doors. Wisdom was maintained through use, and usefulness. Maybe they no longer felt useful.

A sudden urge captivated him. Their stories needed to be told. The reporter in him began sketching possibilities, but stopped dead. That job should fall to their families. He surveyed the room. But where were the family members? Not one head bore the vibrant hair color of youth. That was the story that should be told.

"Pass me your dishes, dear. Are these lovely flowers for me? I love carnations."

Jason turned in his chair. "Ella, I'm Jason Powers. We met earlier." No expression of recognition registered. "I'm here to help Agnes with a problem."

"Agnes has a problem? Does she need money? I

have a little saved up."

"No, she doesn't need money. It has to do with your family." That had an effect. Ella's look of concern turned cold.

"Why isn't she here? I want to see her."

"She can't come right now."

"Why not? I want to talk to her if she's in trouble."

He feared losing to her defiance. "She's in trouble. She needs your help."

"What can I do? I'm an old woman."

"Agnes found out about Edward Hahn." He glanced across the table. The old man didn't flinch. "She needs to know more about him. She needs to find him." A gamble.

"No." Ella slammed the dishes together.

"Why not?"

"It's family business."

"But Agnes needs to know. She's in trouble with the police. The only way to help her is to find Edward."

"Why isn't she here?" Ella shoved the dishes to the center of the table.

"She can't come until we clear this up. Can you tell me about Edward?" He hated to manipulate her like this, but it had to be done.

Ella's inhalation seemed to last forever. "Eddie is Agnes's grandfather."

"His daughter was Denise Hahn? Agnes's mother?"

"Yes."

"What about Agnes's father? Did Denise marry?"

"No!" The response jerked heads at nearby tables.

The reporter spoke. Pursue that line. "Agnes doesn't know anything about her father. Do you know who he is? Does Edward?"

Tears filled Ella's eyes. "I want to see Agnes."

"She can't come until we find out about Edward, about her past. Maybe her father can help."

"No. He can't."

"You know him?"

Ella frowned, then lowered her gaze to her lap. Tears released. "There's no other way?"

Jason leaned close to her. A twinge of conscience objected, but he forged ahead. "I'm sorry. No."

"It's Eddie." She buried her face in her hands and sobbed.

"What's Eddie? He's Agnes's father? I thought you said he was her grandfather? Oh . . . shit." He felt dizzy, nauseous.

Ella's shoulders heaved with her sobs. He reached over and put his hand on her arm, but she pulled away. He leaned closer. "Ella, I have to know. Did Eddie do anything to Agnes and Lilin? Is that why you took Agnes? And why Lilin didn't come, too?"

Ella looked up abruptly, sending Jason back in his chair. A wide smile contradicted her tear-glistened cheeks.

"It's nice to see you, dear. Are these flowers for me? They're beautiful." She hugged the bouquet to her chest and inhaled deeply.

CHAPTER 20

Jason held the cell phone away from his ear, waiting for the obnoxious voice mail announcement. The unexpected, live voice paralyzed his tongue. He coughed it to life.

"Glory be," he said in a singsongy voice. "I got through. Maybe I should buy a lottery ticket. Hold on." He pushed the speaker button and put the phone down on the passenger seat.

"Who is this?"

Jason cleared his throat, and his mind. "It's me, big brother. How you doing?"

"Shitty. The landlord said I better give him some money or he'll throw me out."

"Again?"

"I don't need you to get on me right now, okay? I'm really close to getting into a Chinese weapons manufacturer's computer. At least I think that's what they do.

Can you read Chinese?"

Jason shielded his eyes and mouthed a curse. "One of these times you're going to get caught. You know that, don't you?"

"I'm going to throw in some pop-up jokes. Something about Russians. They should get a laugh out of it. If they can read English." Coughing. "They won't be able to trace it back to me."

"That's what you said last year."

"I have a better security program now. Besides, I'm setting up the back door. I'll do the installation from a library computer."

Jason lowered his hand and rolled his eyes. "I can't keep cleaning up your messes. My savings account is nearly empty. And I'm not dipping into my pension fund."

"Are you forgetting who took care of that indecent exposure charge for you?"

"It wasn't indecent exposure. It was a ticket for urinating in public."

"You could have been branded a sex offender."

"Bullshit. Anyway, that was a long time ago."

"You're welcome, little brother."

Jason shook his head. "Let's not argue. I have some more work for you."

"Since you're an ungrateful son of a bitch, my fee just doubled. I have a reputation to uphold. Working for known sex offenders is risky." Chuckle.

"I'm not paying double. You'll get the usual amount. Take it or leave it."

"I'm about to get thrown onto the street. And you're being stingy? Nice guy."

"Well, this time use the money for your rent or for food."

"I do need some salad."

"Marijuana isn't food, jerk-off."

"You meat eaters are all alike. Just jealous because we vegetarians are so mellow."

Jason laughed. "Vegetarian? Your apartment has cheeseburger wrapper carpeting."

"Must be my evil twin."

"Well, I need the twin who doesn't smoke the salad. Are you high right now?"

"I don't have any money. Remember?"

"Good. I want information on an elderly gentleman from a care home here in Mendocino. His name is Earl Trent. I'll e-mail as much as I know to get you started."

Long inhaling sound. "What do you want on him?"

"God damn it, Donnie."

"Relax." He chuckled. "Just kidding."

Jason rubbed his temples with his thumb and fingers. "The usual."

"The usual general information or the usual in-depth stuff?"

"General. Start with voter registration here in Mendocino County. Go to a broker if you have to."

"A broker?" Donnie's voice turned to a bellow. "Screw you. You're asking me to do kindergarten stuff. I don't need a fucking broker."

"Then why can't you get anything on Eddie Hahn?"

"I told you. I'm working on that one. He's had some help. Some professional help. And he probably did it in the Jurassic—before computers." Donnie's voice returned to calm. "Do you know how hard it is to get something from back then?"

"Well, keep trying. Can you still get into the Social Security System?"

Donnie chuckled. "For the right price, and enough time, I can get into anything."

"I know you're good. If you'd use your computer talents the right way, you'd make a great living. Probably outearn me."

"I could do that selling salad part-time."

"Thanks. Don't rub it in." Jason checked his appearance in the rearview mirror. "I do what I do because I like it. Not for the money."

"And because a sex offender can't get a real job."

Jason thought of a good comeback, but it bordered on a sore subject—jobs. He took the safe road. "Oh yeah. On this guy, pay particular attention to aliases, previous addresses, things like that."

"Can you give me an advance?"

"No." Jason pounded his palm on the steering

wheel. "Shit, Donnie."

"Why? Don't you trust me?"

"I don't want you binging. I need results right away, not in a few days when your head clears."

An exaggerated exhalation. "I'll use the money on rent and food. I promise."

"Good idea. You don't want all that high-tech equipment tossed out in the alley again. And, Donnie. Do this one quickly and I'll throw in a bonus."

"I'll make you proud. I love you, man."

"Me, too, big brother. Take care of yourself. And use my cell phone. I'm not at home."

CHAPTER 21

THE HAMMERING ON THE DOOR RIVALED THE POUND-
ing in Jason's head. He squinted at the clock—7:10 a.m.
Just what he needed. Only Bransome knocked like a
Sumo wrestler with a bad case of the runs. The door-
jamb was pieced together after the last invasion, and it
groaned with each smack of Bransome's fist.

"Hold on. Don't break it down again."

The knocking stopped.

Jason struggled with his pants. Bending over
increased the throbbing in his head and scattered flickering stars in his peripheral vision. He limped to the
door and released the chain, then stepped back before
turning the lock.

The door didn't burst open. He turned the knob
and pulled. The flash of morning light flooded the
room and submerged his senses. Squinting turned the
sight of Bransome standing outside the door, hands on

his hips, into a surreal image.

"Room service." Bransome's laugh echoed throughout the room, or at least through Jason's part of it.

Jason leaned around the edge of the door and peered through the narrow opening. "Real funny. Do you have a home, or do you live at the police station?"

The laugher started up again, tinny this time. "You want to do this here or at my home?"

Jason pulled back the door and hunched to the bed. He flopped on the nearest corner.

Bransome slammed the door and hovered over the chair. "What, no coffee?"

Jason grunted to his feet and shuffled to the hot plate. He turned the knob and leaned on the counter. "What is it this time? I didn't do anything with Ella Hahn. She's not my type. I like them a little more spry." He straightened. "Is Ella all right?"

Bransome fell into the chair and the Naugahyde emitted a prolonged hiss. "There was another murder. In Fort Bragg."

"Jesus. That's just up the road. They are getting closer." Jason rubbed his sandpaper chin. "Did you check Agnes's odometer?"

"Just came from there. Twenty-one, four eighty-three."

Jason ran his fingers through his hair, as if that would clear the cerebral cobwebs. "I don't remember what it was before."

"Just fourteen new miles."

"How far is it to Fort Bragg?"

"Ten miles, one way."

"So Agnes is off the hook?"

"Yeah, but how about you? Where were you last night?"

Jason pointed at the door. "The bar down the street."

"When?"

"From around ten until midnight."

"You got proof? Can the bartender vouch?"

He lifted his wallet from the counter and fished in the bill compartment. "I charged out at"—he brought the receipt close to his eyes and squinted—"eleven past midnight." The receipt shook in his hand when he extended his arm.

Bransome took the paper. "So that's why you look so nasty." He pushed the receipt back to Jason.

"What was the time of death?"

"Don't know for sure yet, but the coroner guessed around eleven. I'll get back to you once it's established." Bransome stood as the water kettle tuned up for a good screech. Jason lunged for the hotplate knob.

"That's it? You're not going to ask me where I was before and after the bar?"

"No. I'll talk to the bartender. See if you were there the whole time." He stepped to the door.

"What about the coffee?"

"You drink both cups. You look like hell."

Bransome opened the door and stomped out. The door slammed and the shock wave reverberated through the room.

Jason grabbed his temples. "Bastard."

The pounding barely subsided when the motel phone rang, starting another cardiovascular drum solo.

"Come on, Agnes," he said and reached for the phone. "It's early."

"Hello?"

Silence

"Hello? . . . Is anyone there?"

He pressed the receiver to his ear. No dial tone, no breathing, just dead air. He hung up.

"What's she up to? Unless Bransome's messing with me."

The card with Agnes's cell phone number protruded from his wallet. He pulled it and unfolded his cell phone.

"Agnes? It's me. Did you call me on the motel phone?"

"No." Her answer sounded like a question.

"Are you sure? Someone called but didn't say anything."

"Did you see Ella? How was she?"

"Did you hear what I said? Someone called me but didn't say anything."

"I heard you. But I want to know about how the meeting with Ella went. Was she okay?"

"She was fine. She made sense for a little while."

"What did she say? Did she ask about me?"

If she only knew. "Not over the phone. Do you know about Fort Bragg?"

"Yes. I really need to find Lilin, Jason."

He wasn't so sure he wanted to now. "Where do you want to meet?"

"Can you come for supper? To my house?"

"When?"

"Tomorrow."

What's wrong with today? he thought. This is important. "You don't have to go to any trouble. Just fix something you already have there."

"It's no trouble. But I want to make something special."

What would be special to someone like her? Rude to ask. "I'll check with Bransome to make sure it's okay. I don't want him getting weird on me again. What time?"

"Six."

"I'll call back if there's a problem."

Jason fell back on the bed and immediately regretted it. The original plan for today was to run down to Santa Rosa to turn in some copy. He could have done it via e-mail, but he wanted to check on his brother. But he knew Bransome would come unglued if he returned and the place was empty. That meant a boring day would compound his hangover. He pulled his legs up on the bed. A good snooze would pass the time. A thin wisp of steam corkscrewed from the cup of coffee on the counter, heading for nowhere in particular.

Jason clicked the lid of the laptop closed and congratulated himself. Got up somewhere around one. Got a hot dog and a Thirst Buster at the 7-Eleven. Finished off most of an old assignment, one that hadn't recaptured his enthusiasm for weeks. It turned out to be a good day after all.

The afternoon shadows passed his window and the light took on an amber hue. That probably meant another nice sunset. Weariness crept up his back. What now—supper or sleep? A decision for the idle, the homeless, and the lonely. He fell back on the bed.

Leftover pizza and five bottles of beer crammed the knee-high refrigerator under the counter. He walked over to the TV and flicked it on. No remote control in this place. The newscaster spewed excitement as she read the latest breaking news, then broke for a set of commercials.

Jason stacked the two anorexic pillows and leaned against the headboard. The Fort Bragg murder was yesterday's lead. He'd have to wait to see if there were any new developments.

The phone jarred him from relaxation. He let it ring

two more times before he reached for it.

"Hello."

Silence.

He pressed the receiver tight to his ear. "Hello?"

A muffled scraping came through, as if someone was covering the mouthpiece.

"Who's there?"

The scraping stopped. Silence.

"This isn't funny. Tell your parents they want you—"

Giggling.

"Who is this, damn it?"

Dial tone.

CHAPTER 22

Jason jerked upright in bed. The inability to fall into a deep sleep had come and gone over the last several years of this life. On most nights, the slightest sound could bring his head off the pillow, particularly when he was away from his apartment.

A metallic jolt and a rough, sliding sound broke through Jason's confusion. His mind cleared almost instantly. Someone was trying to push open the window. The lock was nonfunctional, but a wooden dowel placed in the window slide did its job.

The sodium vapor lamp across the parking lot cast the culprit's shadow on the unlined drapes. Jason's flinch drew the covers into a ball around his knees as he pulled them tight to his chest. His heart galloped.

Was it a he, or a she? The shadow wore a baseball hat, pulled low. But the silhouette was short. Maybe. The angle of the lamp would shorten anyone who stood more than a few inches from the window.

The window frame jammed into the dowel again. He swiveled his feet to the floor. The screen had to be removed, or cut, to get to the window.

The shadow moved across the window, toward the door, and Jason launched himself out of the bed. He couldn't get his breath. He scanned the room for something solid to fend off the attacker, but the only thing he could find was his laptop. The hard drive contained the better part of the last three years of his life. He hesitated, wondering if he could actually bring it down on the shadow's head. His digital life for his organic life.

Holding the computer over his head, he slid behind the hinge side of the door. He tried to subdue his breathing, but gave up. The doorknob turned, slowly. It caught on the lock. It turned again, this time harder, but once again the lock held. A third twist was accompanied by a muffled bump against the door, which groaned its resistance.

Jason slid the computer under his arm. As the knob turned a fourth time, he slammed his fist into the door as hard as he could. The thump echoed through the room and rattled the door on its hinges.

He watched the shadow hurry across the window, hunched over in a shuffling run. He stepped to the drapes and pulled the corner out a few inches, but he could see only a short length of sidewalk. The room fell silent.

Should he call the police? It probably wasn't the best idea. The attempted intrusion would raise more questions. There was so much he hadn't told Detective Bransome about Agnes and Ella. And Eddie. In fact, Bransome didn't even know about Eddie, and Jason didn't feel like telling what he knew just yet. Besides, what could Bransome do about an attempted break-in? It might be unrelated to the Hahn case. The shadow could have been a crackhead looking to bankroll his habit. This wasn't the Hilton.

Sleep was impossible, so he opened the laptop and pushed the power button. It was one of the faster models, but it still took a few minutes to boot through the operating system and security programs. He reached over and unplugged the phone from the wall jack. He wasn't in the mood for any more crank calls.

The cell phone seemed safe. Or was it? He grabbed it and put his finger on the *off* button. The screen caught his attention. A voice message? He hadn't heard the ring—some obnoxious classical tune that grated on him. Perfect at grabbing his attention.

His finger hovered. He didn't recognize the number. He looked over at the window, the dowel. Someone was toying with him. Was this part of it?

The cell phone was his one secure means of communication. Was secure, or was still secure? His mind oscillated. Erase it. See what it says. Don't give in. It might be important. The button beeped under his finger. He hit the speaker button.

"Hey, little brother. I got something on your man. The Trent dude. He changed his name two years ago. Get this. Legally. I haven't been able to get the details, though. Don't know the original name. I can't get into the system. They must've closed the back door on me. I'm amped about finding another doorway, but I'm having a little problem with a virus at the moment. Imagine that. Bit by my own pet. Anyway, I'll keep plugging as soon as I clean out my hard drive. Oh yeah. His social security number starts with 557, so he's a California boy, at least originally. I'll get back to you in a couple of days. Whoever sent this bug is a clever bastard. I hate clever people. Before I go, can I have another fifty? Don't worry. I'm clean. Later, little brother."

CHAPTER 23

JASON PAUSED ON AGNES'S FRONT PORCH. WHERE HAD the day gone? The light of day had given him courage to sleep, and he almost missed all three meals, including this one. A stomach growl complained about his lapse.

He reached to push the doorbell and a loud click came from behind the door. It sounded like a cocking gun. He crouched, ready to hit the deck.

Another click.

He took a step to the side, out of a direct line with the doorway, still in a crouch.

The latch shuddered. One last click and it opened.

A dead bolt, not a gun. Great name for a lock. Jason straightened and stepped into the doorway, wishing he could kick himself for being such an idiot.

The slow, wide swing of the door revealed a beautiful woman in a fitted dress. A vision.

It was Agnes. He blinked to see if it was some kind

of hallucination. Agnes? His eyes widened. His reversed sleep cycle and recent stressful experience would allow it.

It didn't look like Agnes. It did, but it didn't. The neckline of her dress plunged to show cleavage, which was pushed upward and inward for emphasis. His eyes stopped at her chest.

Agnes crossed her arms, effectively blocking the show. She looked at the ground, but a small smile parted her lips.

He saw hints of eyeliner before her hair swept forward, partially covering both of her eyes. Same Agnes, but in a different package. For the first time, her gender elbowed past her role in the investigation.

"Wow. You look nice. All the flannels in the wash?"

She didn't laugh with him, but her smile remained. She stepped back from the door.

He followed her through the living room into the dining room, and noticed her hands didn't drop until she had her back to him. Her gait wasn't exactly fluid, but it wasn't mechanical either. His eyes locked onto her butt. The dress clung to her hips, showing a shapely derriere. He didn't know how he'd missed it before.

Agnes turned quickly to face him, her hands back over her cleavage. "Please, sit down." She left the room before he could comply.

His mind hit Mach 2. Was it really Agnes? Or was

it Lilin? He pictured Agnes, bound and gagged in one of the upstairs bedrooms. Was he Lilin's next victim? His mind danced in zigzags. Who had been calling him, and who tried to get into his room last night? Twins almost always had subtle differences in their appearances, sometimes more than subtle. She looked like Agnes, and definitely acted like Agnes. But she was wearing perfume, a bold, come-here rather than stay-away scent. If it was Lilin, would he be able to tell?

Jason sat on the edge of the seat and scanned the room. The nearest escape was the front door, unless he wanted to dive out a window. He shook his head. She was so small. But he would keep the table between them anyway.

Agnes crept back into the room carrying an envelope, pinched at the corner with her thumb and forefinger. Her other arm crossed her chest, her fingertips resting lightly on the top of her shoulder. She walked to the end of the table and slid the letter on the polished wood.

Jason stood and inched back a step.

"This came in yesterday's mail. It was mailed from here, in Mendocino." The envelope hadn't been opened.

He stepped forward to examine the envelope. The address was handwritten in a sloppy hand with a distinct shake. "Looks like a man wrote it."

Agnes shrugged.

"You should open it."

She disappeared again, but came back in a less than

a minute, a silver knife-like letter opener gripped in her free hand.

He flexed his knees, prepared to lunge.

Agnes stepped toward him.

Lower. Ready.

She pivoted and grabbed the envelope from the table. With three quick wrist flicks, she threaded the opener under the envelope flap and slit the envelope from side to side. Shaking hands pulled out the single sheet of paper and spread it on the table. The letter opener dropped beside it. Her arm crossed her chest again.

Jason leaned on the table, trying to regain his breath, then pushed the opener out of reach. The few lines of the letter were hard to read. Agnes leaned close, keeping her arm in position.

STOP WHAT YOU ARE DOING. STAY AWAY FROM ELLA. LEAVE FAMILY ALONE. STOP SEEING THAT MAN. OR ELSE YOU'LL BE NEXT.

Jason straightened up and looked at Agnes. Her eyes were on the letter, and her palms were flat on the table. He looked past the clear view of her cleavage to her face. Her expression showed more than fear. But what was the additional component? Understanding? Resignation?

Agnes's inhalation wavered. "Who's doing this?"

Good question. Eddie was a good bet, but it could be Lilin, too. "I don't know."

"Why would they want to hurt me?"

"They?"

A faint grin turned the corners of Agnes's mouth, but her eyebrows canted downward in a scowl. She stomped out of the room.

Jason glanced back at the letter, and his head spun. The look on her face—it scared him, but he didn't know why. He looked up. What was she doing in the kitchen? The closest window had a slide lock on top of the lower sash. And the path to the front door was clear.

The lights flickered overhead. He felt his heart rate hit red line. He turned, ready to bolt.

The door from the kitchen creaked. Instead of a weapon, Agnes held a pair of Ziploc baggies. She extended her arm. "Here. We should bag these for the police."

"What's with the lights?" His voice cracked.

"Oh, that. The wiring in this place is really old. They do that every time the refrigerator cycles on."

He looked up at the chandelier and blew out a breath. "You should get that fixed."

"They'd have to rewire the whole place."

He took the baggies and held one open while she pinched the letter at the extreme corner and slid it into the bag. No breast protection this time. They did the same with the envelope.

"Should we call the detective?" she said.

Jason didn't feel like answering Bransome's questions in front of her. "I'll drop them by the police station on my way back to the motel." He reached for the baggies.

"What about supper? I worked hard on it."

Eating fell somewhere between a dentist appointment and an IRS audit at the moment, but in the time it took Agnes to fetch the baggies, her demeanor had sagged. She obviously had spent a lot of time on her appearance, and the smells that wafted from the kitchen rivaled those coming from her body in terms of raw, visceral draw. The mention of food leapfrogged that aroma past her perfume in his sensory hierarchy.

Her lower lip quivered.

He couldn't hurt her right now. "Can I help?"

"No. Sit down. I have a cart." Calm returned to her face. "I've already dished it up."

She disappeared into the kitchen and reappeared a moment later, pushing a squeaky-wheeled serving cart. She slid a heaping plate in front of him and placed another, half-full, at her place setting.

The smells from his plate not only registered, they stimulated a twinge of hunger, but only a twinge. He watched her spoon gravy over the sliced beef roast and the mashed potatoes nestled in a half-potato skin. "The gravy smells great."

"It has bacon in it. It was one of Gert's favorites."

"Agnes, you said, 'why would they want to hurt me.' Who did you mean by 'they'?"

She took a large mouthful of meat and shrugged her

shoulders.

"Do you know anyone besides Lilin who's involved in this?"

"No."

"Then why did you say, 'they'?"

"I don't know. I guess because the handwriting on this letter is so different. That's not Lilin's writing." She barely paused. "Aren't you going to eat?"

The meat offered little resistance to his knife, and as soon as the gravy hit his tongue he cut another piece. "Are you sure you don't know anything about your family that you haven't mentioned to me?"

"I only know what Gert told me."

"You don't know anything about Eddie Hahn?"

"No. I'd never heard of him before you mentioned him."

"Why do you think Gert and Ella didn't tell you about him?"

"I don't know."

"He's their brother, and your grandfather." He paused, and decided to go no further. "Why wouldn't they say something?"

"I don't know."

"It doesn't make sense. Does it?"

"Nothing makes sense to me, and now it's all happening here." Her eyes stared, like they were defocusing.

Jason had seen the look before, on his brother's face,

when the two of them had to ask for their baseball back from the reclusive neighbor, Mr. Sillar, and 'fess up to breaking his window.

"What do you mean?" he said.

"The murders are getting close. Mendocino's next." She looked up at him. "Is she going to kill me? Is that what she wants? I'm her sister." Tears filled her eyes, but they didn't release.

"The police are always right outside. I don't think she'd try anything with them there."

"Yeah? They didn't see her drop off the package."

Jason jerked forward. "What package?"

"These clothes. And makeup." Agnes folded her arms across her chest. "Lilin bought them and left them in a box on the back porch."

Lilin? "How do you know it was Lilin?"

"There was a note."

"Why didn't you call me?"

She shrugged her shoulders.

"What did you do with the note? And the box?"

"I threw them away."

"Why?" It didn't make sense. It wasn't like her. "They were evidence."

"They didn't have anything to do with the murders."

"Everything has to do with the murders now. What did the note say?"

"Nothing. Just, here are some clothes. I guess she

doesn't like the way I dress."

He glanced around at the windows, then back at Agnes. "She's seen you?" *And she's been here?*

Agnes pushed back her chair and placed her dish on the cart. "You didn't finish it."

"You gave me enough for two men. Besides, I'm a little worried here. I'm worried about you." *Worried about me.*

She paused, and he thought he saw the hint of a smile.

She reached for his plate, making no attempt to shield her cleavage. "I still want to find her. I need to talk to her."

"But what if she really is after you?" *And me.*

"That's why I need to talk to her."

Agnes wheeled the cart back into the kitchen, and Jason pulled the baggie containing the letter in front of him. Whoever wrote it had a pretty bad case of the shakes. The way the pen left a small blob of ink when applied to the paper, and when removed at the ends of words, suggested a herky-jerky lack of coordination. He'd seen this kind of writing before—in his grandfather's letters.

Agnes returned holding a tray with two cups of tea. "I'm sorry. I didn't have time to make dessert."

"You did enough with the supper. It was fantastic. Thank you. I haven't had a meal like that in a long time." *Ever since his fiancée had stomped out of his* life, into the arms of that deadbeat who called himself a writer. Jason wished he had a dollar for every resident of Sausalito who claimed to be halfway through the next best-selling novel.

He regarded the cup of tea on the tray and his mind wandered back. What if she really was Lilin? She wouldn't know about the sugar. He scanned the path to the front door again and slid his chair back a few inches. He thought about the phone calls and the person who tried to break into his room.

Agnes pushed the cup and saucer across the table. "Are you all right?"

"I'm just freaked out about the letter."

"Me, too."

He studied her expression, but he couldn't read it. Was it the makeup? He tried to steady his hand, but the cup chattered against the saucer when he raised it. It brought her eyes up to his. He slid forward a little so his back was away from the chair, ready to spring if he had to. The cup touched his lips and he turned slightly toward the front door. A small stream of hot liquid crossed his lips. It was sweet. He leaned back in the chair and exhaled.

"You look like you saw a ghost."

"I'm sorry. I didn't sleep last night." His face felt hot. From the tea? "I was up late working on a story."

"Maybe you should get the letter over to the police station, and then get some rest."

"Will you be all right?"

"If Lilin comes here, if she gets past the police, I'll get what I've wanted. I'll get to talk to her."

"But what if she wants to hurt you?"

"She didn't write that letter."

He finished the tea and pulled the other baggie to him. "I guess I'd better go. As long as I know you'll be all right."

"I'll be fine. I can take care of myself."

Strange. Her smile and soft eyes assured him.

She walked him to the front door and held it open, leaning into it. Her free arm crossed her chest, blocking the view.

"Thank you for a lovely supper." He swept his right hand down in front of her. "And you look beautiful."

She straightened and let go of the door. "Do you like the clothes?"

"Lilin has good taste, but she obviously doesn't know you. I say keep the look, but go with something a little less revealing." He drew a V with his forefingers from his neck to his chest. "I don't think you're very comfortable with the neckline, although it's very chic."

She dropped her arms to her sides and smiled, showing teeth.

He reached for her left hand and pulled it upward to his mouth. A soft kiss and it was released. "Thank you again. If you need anything, call me. And don't worry about the time. Remember, someone will be in the car across the street."

She maintained the smile.

At the street, he turned back. She still stood in the open doorway, staring at him. He gave a wave and walked to the cruiser. Officer Didier didn't lower the window, so Jason rapped on it with his knuckles. It opened a crack.

"You may want to radio in to Detective Bransome. I'm heading over to the police station. Agnes got another letter. I have it right here." He held up the two baggies.

Officer Didier was on the radio by the time Jason got to his Volvo.

Detective Bransome was waiting behind the door of the police station when Jason turned up the walkway. He didn't look happy.

Bransome yanked the door open. "Why didn't Agnes call us as soon as she got this letter?"

"I don't know. I think you scare her."

Bransome rolled his eyes. "Where is it? Did you touch it?"

Jason held the baggies at arm's length. "Agnes is the only one who touched it, and she didn't open it until I got there."

"Why didn't she call me, damn it?"

"You'll have to ask her about that. I can't answer for her."

"Come on." Bransome stomped down the hall and into the detective's workroom. He pushed his glasses up on his forehead and examined the letter as he walked.

When he reached his desk, he placed the baggies on a large blotter. "Looks like someone else wrote this. Any idea who it might be?"

Jason stopped a lunge-and-a-half away from the desk. He took a deep breath. Time to get it out. "Maybe Eddie Hahn."

"Who the hell's Eddie Hahn?"

Jason took a step backward. "He's Agnes's grandfather."

"And why don't I know about this?" Bransome's face glowed red.

Jason's fingers found the healing wound on his forehead. "I found out about him from Ella. It seems she and Gert kept a secret from Agnes—about the family. They don't have any relatives in Illinois."

"Why didn't you tell me this before?"

"Like I said, I just found out about it myself."

Bransome paced in Jason's direction, slowly. "So what's this Eddie Hahn's story, and why did Agnes's aunts hide him from her?"

Jason took another step back and bumped into a

desk. He leaned against it and gripped its edge. He thought about revealing Eddie's other role, but stopped. He didn't want Bransome bothering Ella until he could get more out of her. She'd clam up if Bransome came in with his attitude.

"I don't know yet. I've been able to get a little out of Ella each time I go, but nothing else about Eddie Hahn yet. I'm still earning her trust. I'm heading back to see her tonight."

"They still let you in that place?"

"I thought you told them to let me visit." Touché.

Bransome's face reddened again. "And I'll leave it that way as long as you tell me everything Ella says. The one time I talked to the old coot, I couldn't get anything out of her except broken record pleasantries. You don't think she's involved in this, you know, that she's faking it at the home?" Bransome smiled. "You're a ripe one for being played."

"Those places are depressing. People go in but they never come back out, except in coffins. Why would she put herself through all that as a deception?" He thought about the old man across the table and one possible answer materialized. To keep an eye on someone. To keep that someone from talking. Or to hide out. Or both.

The detective rubbed his head. "Nothing surprises me anymore, and my gut's telling me something fishy is going on here."

Jason walked a few steps closer to Bransome and tried to redirect his focus. "I want to talk about Agnes. Can you give her more protection? She's really scared about this letter."

"We already have someone outside her place, day and night. That's all we can do. We're stretched pretty thin."

"There's nothing else?"

Bransome lifted his head and grinned. "After the Fort Bragg murder, the phone tap finally went through." A squint and he nodded. "We've been monitoring her calls."

"Her cell phone or her home phone?"

"Her cell. According to PacBell records, her home phone was disconnected right after her great-aunt died."

Jason tried to think of everything he had said to Agnes in their last phone conversation. Was it before the murder or after? He couldn't think straight. Time to change the subject. "Just for the record, were there any prints at the Fort Bragg scene?"

Bransome took a step closer. "You think you're entitled to that kind of information?"

"Come on. I'm working on Ella for you. I told you about Eddie."

Bransome's eyes shifted downward, then back up. "No prints."

"DNA?"

"Not back yet, but I'll put odds on it." Bransome walked back to his desk, turned, and folded his arms across his chest. "By the way, the time of death. It was eleven. You lucked out this time."

"So can I go down to Santa Rosa for a couple of days? I have to report in and file some stories." And try to Vaseline a little more time out of my editor to work on this story.

"Not yet."

"You can have someone follow me."

"No. Not yet."

"Come on. I'm asking. I really need to go."

Bransome lifted a manila file from his desk. "No."

Jason exhaled. "Why not?"

"We came across your old friend, Francine Thomas."

"Who?" Jason's mind flip-flopped. Uh huh. "Oh. Her. Where? Another care home?"

"No. A motel. With her throat slit."

Jason pushed away from the desk and retreated a step. "It wasn't me."

"Relax, hero. She was with a man. His throat was slit, too. And his penis was severed. It was sitting on her chest."

"Where?"

"Benicia. Know where it is?"

"Yeah. East Bay. Big oil refineries." Jason stroked his chin. Was Uh huh involved in this? "Same MO as the other murders?"

"Very perceptive. I'm heading over to take a look at

the evidence tonight."

"You think it's related?"

Bransome picked up a thick packet of papers and put them on top of the file folder. "Too many connections to be coincidental. Works with Ella Hahn. Runs away with some of Ella's money. Same cause of death. Same mutilation."

"Could be a copycat."

"We have a long list of things to look for. Several haven't been made public. Some you don't know about. I'll know if it's the same killer within a few minutes of getting there."

"Is that why you want me to stay put?"

"Just covering the bases."

Jason paced. "You think she was involved in the murders?"

Bransome's face contorted into a frown, then softened. "That's a new one on me. You think she was keeping an eye on Ella or something? Working with the killer?"

Jason's mind raced. Maybe more than that. Uh huh could have been an accomplice in the killings.

"If it was the same killer, there was plenty of motive," Bransome said. "The victim stole from Ella. A revenge killing."

"But that would make it unique for our serial killer. Revenge isn't a motive in any of the other ones, is it?"

"Our serial killer?"

"Yeah. Ours."

"Doesn't look like it." Bransome chuckled. "Okay. For the record. Where were you?"

Jason froze. Oh, shit. Did Bransome see cause? He knew about the fling with Uh huh. And she was with another man. A jealousy killing. "I was with Agnes."

Bransome's chuckle boomed into a belly laugh. "Great alibi. One suspect vouching for another."

"Why's that so funny?"

"Never mind." He walked around Jason to the door. "By the way. Why do you think Agnes needs more protection?"

Jason thought about mentioning the box. "I don't know."

Bransome stepped close. "Something else you're not telling me?"

Jason held his gaze. "No."

CHAPTER 24

ELLA HAHN DIDN'T GREET JASON WHEN HE SAT DOWN at the supper table. She stared at her plate, ignoring the carnations when he placed them next to her salad fork. Jason looked across the table at Earl and shrugged.

"She's been like this for two days now." Earl spoke like Ella wasn't there. "It's not like her. I hope she's feeling all right."

Jason studied Earl's face. Why would the old man change his name? And settle in an old folks' home like this? He lived in the independent wing, with a full apartment, but he was together enough mentally and physically to have a place on the outside. Jason turned his head.

"Ella? It's Jason Powers. I talked with you before about your niece, Agnes."

Her eyes remained on her plate.

Jason thumbed the printout of the entrée selections.

"The meat loaf sounds good. Can you recommend it?"

Ella dipped her shoulder and turned away slightly in her wheelchair.

He shook his head and looked across at Earl. "What do you suggest?"

The old man shrugged and slumped over his plate.

Tension ruled the table throughout supper. No one stayed on a topic long enough to pass the time quickly, so Jason was glad when the last of the meat loaf was gone from everyone's plates.

The desserts finished, Ella reached for Jason's plate, but froze. She looked frightened, like she'd seen a snake.

"Ella? It's me. Jason Powers. Do you remember me?"

She sat still, silent.

"I'm here to talk about Agnes. Remember? She needs your help."

Ella pulled her hands together on her lap and wrung them slowly.

"You do want to help Agnes, don't you?"

"I'm not supposed to talk to anyone," she said, her voice a hoarse whisper.

"Who told you that? The people here?"

"Please go away."

"I don't understand. Who doesn't want you to talk to me?"

"Please." This time her voice echoed through the room, startling everyone to silence. Heads craned in her direction. "Go away. Leave me alone."

Two aides appeared from the kitchen and fast-walked in their direction. Jason stood and pushed in his chair.

He looked across the table. Earl sat straight, eyes down, hands folded on his lap. The strained look on his face gave Jason a chill.

"I'm sorry, Ella," Jason said. "I was trying to help."

Ella stared at her hands.

A young man in employee whites stepped close to Jason and spoke in a low voice. "You're going to have to leave now. She's been upset for two days. We might have to stop bringing her down for supper."

"Do you know why?"

"I wish I did. She seems miserable."

Jason flicked a business card from his wallet and handed it to the new aide, a young man in his twenties. "Give me a call if you find out what's bothering her."

Halfway across the parking lot, Jason froze. The look on Earl's face when Ella went off had chilled him, and the thought of it repeated the response. What was this Earl's story? He changed his name about two years ago. He'd been in the home for a year. California native. He always sat at the table with Ella. Was he involved in this mess? Jason paused. A familiar thought surfaced. Was he Eddie?

"Can't wait for Donnie to come through on this one," Jason said to the pavement. Despite Bransome's objection, he had to go to Santa Rosa tomorrow. Maybe he should stop in on the way and visit Earl's apartment. Talk to him in private. Press him on his past.

CHAPTER 25

THE BENCH ACROSS THE LAWN FROM THE DINING ROOM windows was perfectly aligned to watch the lunch crowd. The table was in clear view. Earl faced in his direction, just over Ella's right shoulder. Jason knew the layout of the home. There was only one way to turn out of the dining room—to the right. A short hall with a lounge on one side and a reading room on the other opened to a small atrium that had mailboxes on one wall and the elevators on the other. The hall continued into the distance with apartments on either side. The third wall of the atrium had a locked glass door that opened to the lawn. He'd wait until Earl exited the dining room, then go to the glass door and try to attract the old man's attention.

Ella was wheeled away before Earl stood and stretched his arms upward. He was one of the last residents to leave the dining room. He paused to say something to the waitress, nodded to her, and ambled into the hall.

Jason hurried to the glass door. No one stopped him, or seemed to give him a second thought. He waited, but Earl didn't show. He didn't want to move, but dallying at the door was an attention grabber.

A severely hunched woman limped nearby and turned the dial on a mailbox. She tilted her head and gave a stained-toothed grin. Jason nodded and turned, looking at the lawn.

He was about to abandon his plan when the familiar suit rounded the corner, two books wedged between upper arm and ribs. Earl walked to the bank of mailboxes.

Jason tapped.

Earl turned a stiff neck. A look of initial confusion gave way to a vague smile. He pushed the door open and stood back. "Hello there, young man. Ella's probably in her room by now. You know where she lives?"

"I came by to talk to you."

Earl frowned. "About?"

"Ella. Can I ask a few questions? In private."

Earl pivoted. "I'm around the corner here. I got lucky. First floor, facing the lawn." His gait was quick and Jason jogged to catch up.

Earl's apartment was bright and clean. Sparse artwork decorated the white walls. But something wasn't right. Jason scanned the front room once, twice, a third time. What was it? Something was missing.

"Have a seat. Can I get you something? Coffee?"

Jason shook his head and fell into the soft-fabric couch. Photographs. That was it. There weren't any photographs. In all of the care homes he'd seen, photographs were a decorating staple. As far as he could tell, they represented family ties as strongly as if the subjects were in the next room. And they were always the first topic of conversation.

Earl settled in a thick-armed chair facing the couch. "What can I do for you? Is it Ella's niece again?"

"I've watched how you are with Ella. I wanted to thank you. Her niece thanks you, too. I told her about you."

"It's nothing. Everyone needs a friend. And consistency. Especially as we get older. I can be both to her."

"Did you know Ella before?"

"Before what?"

"Before you moved in here?"

"No. I just happened to sit at her table one day when her head cleared. We had a brief talk."

"What did she talk about?"

"Just pleasantries. She wanted to clean up the table."

"She didn't say anything about her family?"

"Not that I recall."

"Has she ever said anything about her family?"

"No. I know she has a niece, but I think that came from you."

Jason took a deep breath. "Do you mind if I ask a few questions about you?"

Earl seemed to melt into the chair. "Are you with the police?"

Jason watched Earl's eyes flick down to the carpet. "No. I think I told you before. I'm a reporter for the *Santa Rosa Press Democrat.*"

"What do you want with me?" The words were soft.

"I'm involved in the investigation of Ella's niece. I'm being thorough. Checking everything out. The detective wanted to question you, but I told him we'd talked a few times. I said I'd do it."

"Did the detective tell you what he wanted?"

Jason was on a ledge, but he inched out farther. It was time to turn the conversation, and mention of the police seemed to change Earl's demeanor. "He gave me a rundown."

Earl brought both of his hands up over his face and pulled them downward, leaving his fingertips on his jaw. "I knew it would catch up to me."

"Catch up?"

Earl folded his hands in his lap and fixed his stare between his feet. "My wife. Her mind went, just like Ella's. Started almost five years ago. Her memory went fast. Then she lost control of . . . you know . . . her body functions. She didn't recognize me, so she became belligerent when I tried to tend to her. Then she started hallucinating. Thought I was trying to attack her. This was the woman who shared my bed for over forty years."

Jason lost his edge, but the reporter peeked through. "Why didn't you put her in a care home?"

Earl spoke without emotion. His face was a blank screen. "She wouldn't have had the care I gave her."

A good story, or a good liar? A brash question might tell. "Were you relieved when she finally passed?"

Earl remained frozen. "For me? No. For her? Yes. She was the one in prison, not me. She was still the woman I loved. She didn't have the pleasure of remembering our relationship. She was alone and afraid."

"So why change your name?"

Earl's eyes flicked up to meet Jason's, then down. His voice wavered. "We had a pact. From before she got sick."

"What kind of pact?"

Earl stiffened in the chair. "I don't want to talk about it."

"I'm sorry." Jason slumped in the chair. Earl seemed sincere. "I don't mean to pry. Sometimes it helps to talk about things like this. And I'm a good listener. You've been good for Ella. Maybe I can return the favor."

"I won't talk about it."

"Sorry." Or maybe a good actor. "Are you in some kind of trouble?"

Earl slumped. "I don't know." His face seemed to drain of color.

He looked scared, close to a breakdown. Jason wanted

to comfort the old man. Maybe Earl needed reassurance. "You legally changed your name. That leaves a clear paper trail. If the authorities wanted you, they wouldn't have any trouble finding you."

"It wasn't the police I was worried about."

Jason paused. He had to think this through. "Do you have children?"

"No. We couldn't."

"Are you worried about family?"

Earl jumped to his feet. He thrust a crooked finger in Jason's direction. "I don't know why you're pushing me on this. Maybe it was me I was trying to get away from. A big piece of my life ended when she no longer recognized me. Then . . ." His eyes welled. He lowered his finger. "If you're thinking of doing a story on me, I don't give my permission."

"No. It's not that. I thought you had some connection to Ella Hahn—"

"I do. Every time she comes out of it, I want her to know she isn't alone here." He turned toward the window, and the green lawn beyond it.

Jason stood. "I'm sorry. I have what I need. You don't need to worry. Nothing will come of our conversation."

Earl didn't turn from the window.

Jason paused at the door. "Thank you for caring about Ella."

CHAPTER 26

THE DRIVE TO SANTA ROSA TOOK FOREVER, OR SEEMED to. Jason wondered why Ella had refused to talk to him. If something had happened to her, the memory must have survived her mental vacancy through most of the day. He didn't know much about Alzheimer's, but he assumed the event would have to be pretty bad to make a lasting impression. Unless she remembered more than she let on. At least Earl didn't seem to be involved. Although he could be a good liar. "Benefit of the doubt."

Jason picked up his cell phone and punched in the code for a stored number. He waited. It clicked into voice mail, as expected.

"It's me. I don't need the workup on Earl Trent anymore. I got what I needed. It might sound strange, but I don't want to know his real name. You can send me one piece of information, though. Is there anything outstanding from the police? And don't worry, I'll send full payment, plus a bonus. Thanks, big brother."

He threw the phone onto the passenger seat and swerved from the highway onto an off ramp. He swung over the overpass and drove about a mile before he flipped a U-turn and headed back. It was his third and last maneuver of this type before his turnoff in Santa Rosa. Ever since Agnes told him about the box, he'd paid as much attention to his rearview mirror as his windshield. Tonight, either he was clean, or his pursuer was really good. He banked on the former.

Glad to be home, he slammed the front door behind him and threw the dead bolt, then walked through to the sliding glass door and pulled it open. The patio faced the tee boxes on the seventh hole of a public golf course, but they were partially shielded by a stand of eucalyptus trees. The trees shredded the view, but they repelled nearly all of the wayward tee shots.

He liked the location, despite the limited view. He was on the end of his building, and the building was at the end of the development. Privacy squared. Besides, his parking space was right next to the side wall of his apartment. Easy in, easy out.

He liked the nights here the best. No golfers, and no upstairs neighbor, who worked nights at an aluminum plant that stamped cans for beer and soft drinks. He even liked it when it rained and the eucalyptus trees smelled like cat pee.

He leaned on the stucco half wall that separated his patio from the long, sparse grass of the golf course fringe. No rain recently. The air smelled fresh. It smelled of productivity. He'd bring his laptop out for a final tune-up of one of his stories.

A rustling sound shook a bush to his right, ten yards into the darkness. He cocked his head in that direction. A shadow moved behind one of the tree trunks.

"Who's there?"

Silence.

He turned to go back inside.

"Don't go in." The soft voice stopped him.

"Who's there?"

"Please. Don't go in. I want to talk to you."

He scanned the area, but there was no substance to the voice.

"Who are you? Identify yourself or I'll go in."

"No. Please. I just want to talk."

He turned and stepped to the sliding glass door.

"I'm Lilin."

He froze. "Did you follow me here?"

A dark figure stepped from behind a tree trunk and slowly walked toward the stucco wall. As she stepped into the muted light from his patio, his heart raced. From fear? From excitement?

The woman resembled Agnes, but only superficially. Her walk was more of a confident strut, even though she walked on a soft surface. She wore skintight shorts that barely covered two or three inches of her thighs. Her shirt, if one wanted to call it that, was tied just above her navel, and fell open two buttons up to reveal an ample cleavage that protruded with a natural, braless sway.

He tore his eyes from her chest as she came into the light. Her face was Agnes's, but with a different countenance, and not from the makeup, which was heavy but well done. Her eyelids were heavy, sensuous, like Marilyn Monroe's. And her hair was styled with a zigzag part that coursed halfway to her crown and disappeared into a slightly bouffant shell that fell to her jawline.

He stood, paralyzed in the glow of her advancing appeal.

She put her hands on the patio wall. "Help a girl over?" She held her arms out like a toddler wanting to be carried.

He hesitated. Which was dominant, the reporter or the man? It didn't matter. He moved to the half wall and placed his hands under her arms, then lifted. Her perfume teased his senses. It wasn't the same as Agnes's. It was more floral, ethereal.

Her midcalf, heeled boots clattered on the stucco. Her hands wrapped around his neck as she slithered against him.

His body reacted uncontrollably to her curves. He caught a prolonged view of her breast. She did nothing to hide it from him.

Intoxicating.

He shook loose and stepped back. Focus. He had so many questions. Which one to ask first? Cold shower. Think cold shower.

She straightened, thrusting her breasts forward. She tilted her chin and raised a brow. Hands on hips, she looked him up and down.

He stood with his mouth open like a spellbound teenager, cold shower forgotten.

"Now you've seen the titties of twins." Her voice broke the silence, much more bold than the calls from behind the tree. "A male fantasy unfolds, right?"

The topic caught him off guard, and he didn't know if he should duck for cover from her complaint, or laugh at her joke. Her tone had been playful, and her partially closed eyes didn't have the slant of anger, but something in those eyes told him to beware. They glowed with the full dilation of intent.

"I'm sorry." He stammered into his response. "What did you say?"

"I want to know your intentions with my sister."

"I've been trying to help her find you."

"Now we know your approach. What are your intentions with her?"

Her words were confrontational, but her tone and expression were teasing. She moved toward him, swaying her hips wide with each step.

"I like Agnes, but I don't have a personal agenda."

"Bullshit. I've seen the way you look at her."

Seen? He felt like he was teetering on the edge of a cliff, balancing on one foot. Her delivery was softer, sultry, and her exaggerated movements enhanced the sway of her breasts. Was she angry or flirting? Or both?

"I'd like to find a way to get the two of you together."

Lilin laughed. "A threesome. I should have known."

He balanced on the edge of the abyss, and she pulled and pushed at the same time. She looked like she enjoyed her game.

"No. Not that. Agnes wants to meet you. You're her sister. She wants to be with you."

"I'll meet her when I'm ready, and I won't need you to set it up."

He flexed his legs, ready to jump. "Then why are you here?"

"To judge your intentions with my sister."

"I told you what they were."

"I don't believe you. If you want to score twins, you'd better start with me. Now. I don't know where I'll be tomorrow, or the next day. Besides, it's going to take some serious work to get into Agnes's pants."

"I told you that's not what I'm after."

"You don't find us attractive?"

"I didn't say that."

"And you didn't diddle that woman from Aunt Ella's home after knowing her for what, a few minutes?"

She saw that? "It's different with Agnes."

"Pull the other one. You men think a woman is nothing but a playground. A teeter-totter, curly slide, and merry-go-round all rolled into one."

Her effervescence was fading, so he took another step back.

"I'll stop seeing her if that's what you want."

She tilted her head as a frown wrinkled her forehead. "You know that's not what I want. She seems happy when you're around. She's never had a man, and she's not likely to have many more chances." She paced parallel to the half wall. "I want you to do her, and then stop seeing her." A throaty laugh filled the patio. "I'm sure you can pull it off. It seems to be your style."

"I can't do that. That's not why I'm helping her."

"Sure you can." She pulled her shirt aside to expose her right breast and supported it with her left hand, giving it a slight shake. "She has everything you see right here, but it's low mileage. Not like me."

"I wouldn't do that to her."

"Yes, you would. The innocent ones always induce the best fantasies. I could do you ten different ways and your mind would still be on her."

Jason inched backward.

Lilin seemed to notice his movement. "So, I guess

this means you're not interested in having some fun with me tonight. Pity. I could've curled your toes like they've never been curled before."

"What about Agnes?"

"Don't try to tell me you have those kinds of feelings for her. I've been watching you. You're not one of the good ones." She reached down to her right boot.

The expression reverberated in his mind—not one of the good ones. He took a full step back as her right arm raised toward him.

He dodged left as a zing rang in his ears. A shooting pain ran up his right arm and down his right side. Then all of the muscles on that side of his body contracted into painful knots. He fell to the cement.

A Taser. She shot him with a Taser. He knew because he'd done a story on them. He'd even seen a demonstration in which an officer volunteered to be shot with one. But unlike the officer, he wasn't totally incapacitated, and his mind was still sharp.

He leaned up and swept his left arm across his chest. A lead was attached through his shirt. He yanked out the barbed probe, grimacing at the sting. He scraped his right arm. Nothing. It must have grazed him, delivering only a portion of its jolt. Movement terminated his analysis.

Lilin came at him, towering over him. A bright starburst of reflected light flashed from her raised right hand. A low, guttural growl parted her red, painted lips.

He waited until she was a step closer and raised his left leg. He kicked. His heel caught her square in the chest, knocking her backward against the apartment wall. She collapsed, straining for her next breath.

His right arm hung at his side, useless, and his right leg was only partially there, tingling from hip to ankle. Lilin staggered but stood, so he launched himself at the half wall. The stucco rasped the skin along his left side as he fell on the other side of the wall. A snarl crowned the barrier. He heard the swipe of her hand pass close to his right ear.

He jumped to his feet and ran for the cover of the trees, eyes on the wall.

A groan pierced the darkness as she strained. He glanced over his shoulder and saw her shadow come over the wall.

His right leg worked well enough to maintain a decent pace, but he ran with a significant limp. He sent a silent prayer of thanks upward for his dedication to his morning visits to the gym.

Staggering between two trees, he stumbled around a third and headed out onto the grass. He grunted as he turned left onto the fairway, then held his breath as he cut right to circle behind the elevated tee boxes. The crescent moon was unobstructed by clouds, so his silhouette would be easy to see.

Her growling turned away. His deception worked,

but only for a moment. The knee-high tees were still about ten yards away. Her snarl shifted in his direction, bouncing off the slick grass. Had she spotted him?

He circled the first tee box and ran to the far edge of the course. A waist-high chain-link fence separated the golf course from a flood control canal that maintained a trickle of water, even in the dead of summer. He rattled the fence with his arm, and kicked it a couple of times, then darted away from the fence, back toward the other two raised tee boxes. Halfway, he fell to his knees, then flat on his stomach as Lilin approached the fence, silhouetted by a distant streetlight. She raised herself over the barrier and ran to the edge of the canal.

She looked right, then left, then right again. She darted to the left. Ten yards down the canal, a tall stand of white oleander filled the space between the fence and ditch. She ran to it and pushed her way into the bushes.

Jason returned to hands and knees until he was behind the last tee box. He paused on all fours, struggling to catch his breath. The razor just missed his neck a minute ago. His neck, then his crotch. His abdomen tightened like he was leaning off the roof of a skyscraper.

Out of view, he ran in a low crouch across the cart path to the sixth hole. It was a par three with three large sand traps guarding the green. The largest one had a tall grass overhang that was probably responsible for a good proportion of the curse words he had heard leaking from the course during playing hours. The hole bent around his apartment complex, so the trap was within fifteen yards of his parking lot.

He dove into the trap and crawled as far under the overhang as he could get. Wiggling into the sand, he used his good arm to scoop more sand around him. He put his head down, trying to blend into the contour of the slope.

The wait wasn't a long one. Within a few minutes, soft footsteps and heavy breathing echoed across the short, even grass of the green. He tried to calm his own breathing. It was shallow, fast. He switched to mouth breathing, hoping it wasn't noisy.

The footsteps crossed the green at a leisurely pace, right to the edge of his bunker. Then stopped. A loud grunt sounded from right above him. He flinched. God, don't let her notice. Please, God, don't let her hear.

The footsteps started again, circling the bunker in the direction of the parking lot—the direction of his head. Boots. He saw boots. Shorts. Shirt. Lilin. All of Lilin. She approached another short chain-link fence at the edge of the parking lot. She spun around.

The human body can't flatten like some animals, but Jason did his best to become two-dimensional. He pushed himself farther into the sand, and felt it move between his parted lips with each inhalation and exhalation. He pushed his tongue behind his front teeth to keep the grains from going any farther.

Lilin scanned the golf course one more time. Hands on her knees, she hunched forward. Two slow, shuffling steps forward. Three. She stared directly at the overhang.

A low growl resonated across the sand. Jason held his breath.

The growl rocketed in volume. Lilin exploded into a sprint, directly at the overhang.

Oh, shit. Jason's entire body tensed. He closed his eyes tight. Sand grains ground against his molars. Involuntarily, his eyes opened wide.

A bird flushed directly behind him. Its wings hammered the air. A sound nearly escaped his throat, but he held it in. The bird shot past his left ear and banked away into the darkness.

Lilin froze again, hunched over at the corner of the bunker.

The seconds seemed like minutes. He wanted to scrunch farther down into the sand, but he didn't want to risk the movement. Did she see him? Was she preparing for the kill?

A cackle ripped the air. "Almost got a birdie."

Jason closed his eyes again. The cackling continued, but changed direction. Away from him. He waited until it was a ways out and opened his eyes.

Lilin boosted herself up on the short chain-link fence with straight arms and lifted her right leg, gaining a foothold on the top of the fence. She froze once again and turned her head toward the bunker, and laughed again.

Jason's Volvo was two spaces from the fence. Lilin stalked its rear bumper. She raised her fist and slammed it down on the trunk cover and let out another laugh before circling to the driver's side of the next car. She opened the door and swung in.

Jason knew the type of car—a late sixties or early seventies Pontiac GTO. The muscle car of all muscle cars. An instant wet dream for most males over the age of thirty. The car matched Lilin's growls as its engine came to life.

Jason relaxed and spat out as much sand as he could. He'd be grinding grains between his teeth for hours, maybe days.

The GTO backed up and swung its rear end toward the bunker. An unexpected bonus greeted Jason. The plate was one of the really old black ones, with bright yellow letters and numbers, and the lightbulb that illuminated the license plate well was missing its covering, so it was particularly bright, despite being pixilated by the chain-link fence. Before the howl of four hundred cubic inches of power spun the wheels on the pavement, he was able to make out all three letters, and the first of the three numbers: ZFZ 5.

The road to the apartment complex looped around the tee boxes of the par three hole and formed a T-junction with a major street within a hundred yards. Jason watched and heard the GTO accelerate around the par three, rat-tatting across the raised, reflective street markers that outlined the golf cart crossing. He watched its brake lights flare as it approached the stop sign. It screeched into a right turn on the next street and headed into the night.

Jason hurried from the sand trap, doing his best to shake loose the sand that covered him head to toe. His right leg was back to near-normal, and his right arm was tingling. Thawing out, as he called it when he was young and one of his limbs "went to sleep."

He tapped his right pants pocket. No car keys.

He was in the apartment long enough to lock all of the doors and windows and scoop his keys from the credenza in the entryway. No way was he going to stay there tonight, or any night in the near future.

As he turned onto the freeway on ramp, his foot came off the gas pedal. The disorientation of nearly losing his genitals must have clouded his judgment. A police report. He should file a police report. Get the Santa Rosa police on the trail of the GTO. Call 911.

Hesitation.

His foot stomped the gas pedal to the floor, kicking the Volvo into turbo. It lurched. To hell with the police. He had to get out of Santa Rosa. Now. His personal sanctuary had been violated, and it was an easy mark for future attack. But where would he be safe? The motel in Mendocino? No way. A different motel? Someone always seemed to find him no matter where he went.

He merged onto the freeway and let the speedometer climb. Strange as it seemed, only one safe place came to mind. As close to Detective Bransome's side as he could get. It was time to find out if Bransome really did live in the Mendocino Police Station.

Jason didn't pay a lick of attention to the speed limit as he wound through the near-deserted streets of Mendocino. He sought the company of police. Turning into the police station parking lot, he hit the brakes a little harder than he intended. Detective Bransome's car was in the lot. He hurried into the building and directly into the detective's workroom.

"What the hell happened to you? You get some action on the beach?" Bransome didn't laugh.

Jason hadn't realized it, but he was still covered with a light dusting of sand—everywhere. He rubbed his head and sand rained from his hair and peppered the floor. The relief of finding Detective Bransome fought against the pent-up panic of his interaction with Lilin. He couldn't catch his breath. "Went to Santa Rosa . . . Lilin came by . . . shot me with a Taser . . . I got away."

Bransome stepped toward him, his face intense. "What did you say?"

"Got away."

"No, before that."

"She shot me with a Taser."

"Son of a bitch. You're one lucky bastard. It was Lilin."

Jason edged toward panic. On the drive up, he had gone back and forth about whether it really was Lilin, or Agnes in disguise, particularly with what she'd said about not being one of the good ones. But Bransome seemed convinced it was Lilin. "How do you know?"

"In murders like these, we always withhold some of the evidence from anyone not directly working the case. In this one, a common thread in all of the murders is the use of a Taser to subdue the victim. If Lilin is as small as Agnes, she'd have trouble slicing them up unless they were brought down first."

Jason felt sick to his stomach. "They're the same size." This was the first time he fully realized how close he had come to joining the list of victims of Miss Lilin Hahn, serial killer, mutilator of men. He gripped his groin with his right hand and pictured his severed penis resting on his chest, the flashbulbs of crime scene cameras documenting it for posterity. "At least they didn't feel it."

"Maybe, maybe not. How come you got away?"

Jason raised his shirt to show a raw wound surrounded by an already forming bruise on his chest. "One of the leads got me here. The other must have glanced off my arm. The arm was dead for a while, and the leg on that side was numb. Good thing I live on a golf course."

"Huh?"

"Never mind."

"Did you file a report?"

"No. I got the hell out of there."

Bransome walked behind his desk. "I'll want to get some information from you, but I have something else I have to take care of first. You'll want to know about it anyway, so you might as well hang around."

Jason stopped him on his way out of the room. "You said I'd want to know about it?"

"Oh yeah. I'm a little spacey right now. Ella Hahn is dead."

"What?"

"As far as we can tell, she was suffocated with her pillow. In her room."

Jason slumped against a desk. "Poor Ella." He bolted upright and pointed at his chest. "I have an alibi for this one."

"Sorry, I'm not worried about that. The security camera got good shots of the guy who did it. An old guy. Hey. You want to take a look? Maybe you've seen him. As soon as Saroyan gets back, I'll have him bring up the clips."

Jason's head spun. Everything was happening too fast. His thoughts spiraled to Agnes. "Does Agnes know about Ella? Is she all right?"

"I just radioed Didier. Told her to let Agnes know. I can call her back and check with her."

"Please."

Bransome pushed his way through the doorway.

Jason started after him. "Wait. I forgot to tell you something."

Bransome poked his head back in. "I'm kind of busy right now."

"I got a license plate."

Bransome jumped back in. "Holy crap. Why didn't you say so?"

"I'm like you. A little spacey right now. I nearly had my prick sliced off and my throat slit."

"Forgiven. Let's get on the computer and see what comes up. I'll let Saroyan handle the Ella Hahn case for now."

Jason widened his stance and folded his arms across his chest as Bransome approached. "Wait a minute. I've got a condition."

"A what?"

"A condition. Kind of a demand. I'd appreciate it—"

"You're not in a position to demand anything. Either you give me the plate number or you go in lockup."

Jason's exhalation puffed his cheeks. "That's what I'm talking about. I'm trying to help you with this case and all you do is hassle me. What happened two years ago was unfortunate, but the people in the lab were the ones who screwed up. Not me. Can't we get past that? I want to help get this murderer off the street."

Bransome's lips moved, but nothing came out. He stood still with a blank stare, like he was mulling a career decision. "You've been a help, but you can shove your demand. I prefer an agreement. Since it doesn't look like you're going to go away, I suggest we go about our jobs in a professional manner and let the past be just that. But don't overstep. I can't push that situation too far back. You have to be open with me, though. Let me know what you find out. Let me know what you're thinking. Even if it's speculation."

Jason grinned. "And I get full disclosure from your end? Not the things that are held back from the press and public, but everything else? And could I get an occasional hint about what you're thinking?"

Bransome fell back into the vacant stare.

Jason shuffled his feet and glanced at the clock.

"Let's work on one thing at a time. I'll back off the attitude. I'll think about the other stuff. That good enough for you?"

Jason smiled again. "That's the biggie. I agree."

"Good. Come on." Bransome hurried into a back

room that had a bank of four computers lined up on a windowless wall. He pulled up one of the small roller-footed chairs and nearly enveloped the entire seat. Two fingers punched keys faster than Jason could with ten, and a password screen flashed, like a strobe. Bransome reverted to single finger keystrokes, each deliberately selected, and the screen went blank, then came back to life with a statewide motor vehicle registry site.

"What was the license plate number?"

Jason pulled another chair over and sat. "It was one of the really old black plates, with yellow numbers."

Bransome pushed a few keys. "The number?"

"The letters were ZFZ."

Tap, tap, tap.

"I only have the first number. It was a five." He cringed, expecting a disgruntled response, but Bransome seemed satisfied.

"With the old plates, that should be enough."

The computer froze, all except for a small rectangular box at the bottom that gradually filled with an enlarging blue line. When full, the screen flickered to a new display.

"Good. There are only two left. Was it a Volkswagen or a GTO?"

Jason sat up straight. "A GTO. Late sixties or early seventies."

"Sixty-nine. God, I love those cars. Let's see who

the owner is."

Jason crowded in to the monitor.

"It's registered to an Edward Hanson. The address is a post office box in Inverness."

"Inverness? That's on Tomales Bay, right? Not easy access, kind of wild?"

"Pretty area, although the yuppies have discovered it. It won't stay wild for long."

Jason smiled. "Edward Hanson. I'll be damned. Edward Hanson. Eddie Hahn. You think it's an alias?"

"Could be. It would fit."

"But what would Lilin be doing driving Eddie's car?"

"Hold on. Something's coming up. Says here the car was stolen. Not long ago." Bransome stroked his chin and scanned the ceiling. He slammed his hand down on the table, jiggling the monitor. "It was stolen about the time the murders started. What do you make of that?"

"It's about the time Gert Hahn died."

Bransome swiveled to face Jason. "Either Lilin and Edward are working together, or against one another. I don't think this is all coincidental."

Bransome's cell phone rang.

"Okay . . . Okay . . . He's right here . . . I'll tell him . . . You stay with her until she's feeling better . . . Okay. Thanks."

"That was Didier. She told Agnes about Ella. Poor

girl is really broken up. She's asking for you. You going to go?"

"Not tonight." Lilin was probably watching Agnes's house, expecting him to show up. "You have a cot or something I can use? I'm starting to fade."

"The main holding room has several cots. That's where I'll be sleeping, if I ever get done with all this. I'll throw in a breakfast for both of us. Go through that door and make a right. It'll be on your left. I have to contact the Marin County sheriff to get them on the trail of our Edward Hanson/Eddie Hahn."

Jason didn't drift off right away. Agnes had asked for him, but it wasn't safe to go to her right now. Not safe at home, not safe at the motel, not safe at Agnes's house. He scanned the holding room. Safe in jail. He'd find another motel tomorrow and check out of the old one. Could he do it without Lilin knowing? Was she watching? Was Eddie?

CHAPTER 27

JASON RAN THE VIDEO THROUGH A SECOND TIME. The old man hunched as he shuffled along the corridor, his thick white hair neatly parted on one side. That was about all the tape revealed on the murderer's inbound trip. The screen blanked, and the suspect's exit came up—same hunched, limacine walk. Same perfectly ordered white hair. The man's clothing was rumpled, his shirt partially tucked into faded jeans. Not Earl.

Jason hit the *stop* button, then *rewind*. He replayed the second clip again, hit *stop* and *rewind*. It was barely noticeable, but it was there. The old man's right hand had a slight, regular shake. The letter flashed in Jason's mind. The slant of the alphabet. Written by a right-handed man with the shakes.

The tape automatically rewound and started at the beginning. Jason let it play again. Come on, old man, he thought. Tell me about yourself. Why did you kill your sister? Was it because she refused to acknowledge you to one of your twin granddaughters? No. Probably not enough. Because you didn't want anyone to know that the twins were your biological daughters? That you molested their mother, your daughter? But that was old news. Or was it? Agnes didn't know. Did Lilin?

The tape started again. It had to be something worse than that. Did Ella say too much, or was she about to say too much? Something that needed to be silenced. Old man, did you molest all of your daughters? Is that why Gert and Ella took Agnes, and why she doesn't remember anything about her years before that? And why didn't they take Lilin, too?

He stopped the tape before another cycle. Someone was coming down the hall.

"What do you think?" Bransome's voice filled the room. "Does he look like the type to suffocate his own sister?"

"Too hunched to see his face. Besides, I don't know the look of siblicide. But I did notice his right hand has the shakes. He's probably the one who wrote the letter to Agnes."

"I didn't catch that. Good job. I'll have Saroyan work it up for the evidence file. Anything else?"

"Did he sign in?"

"No."

Jason chuckled, remembering the difficulties he had

at the entrance to the home. "I bet he walked in and greeted the receptionist like he lived there. No need for a disguise."

"My thoughts, too. You want to take a ride?"

Jason spun around on the wheeled chair. "What's up?"

"I'm heading down to Inverness, to meet up with the Marin County people. They talked with some guy at the post office there. He steered them to a small house just outside of town. They're planning to invade the place this morning. They offered to wait until we showed up, and I accepted. You want in?"

Jason didn't answer right away. It was the first time he'd seen a hint of a rounded edge in Detective Bransome's demeanor. But a quote came to mind, source unknown: Keep your friends close, and your enemies closer. Bransome didn't do anything without an objective in mind. But an opportunity was an opportunity. "I'm in."

"Good. We have to go right now. You'll be my cameraman. Just snap everything I tell you to. And don't go off on your own. Let me be the lead."

The house was really just a cabin—two rooms and a bathroom. The living area had a full kitchen along one wall, and was sparsely decorated with a table and two chairs, a couch and coffee table, and a rabbit-eared television. A double bed and chest of drawers nearly filled the small bedroom. The bathroom had a toilet, sink, and shower stall, so cramped a man could sit on the commode and wash his face in the sink at the same time.

The view out the front windows was beautiful. Through a part in the trees and shrubs across the road, the narrow band of pure blue water that was Tomales Bay reflected glimmers from the late morning sun. The area was quiet, pristine, not yet choked with condominiums and BMWs.

Bransome threaded a beige, canvas satchel over his head, onto his shoulder, and under his left arm. The bag had six small, mesh pockets on the front, and at least two large pockets in the back. It appeared to be homemade.

Each chamber bulged with goodies. A pocket-sized spiral notebook, evidence cards, various types and sizes of bags, fingerprint dusting kit, forceps and tweezers, metal probes, tape measure, assorted other implements Jason didn't recognize, and who knows what in the large, rear pockets. A sense of kindred preparedness warmed Jason's core.

Bransome pulled a quad-ruled sketchpad from one of the rear compartments and began sketching the main room. He pushed the tape measure around and between the pieces of furniture, jotting figures onto the diagram.

"Don't just stand there. Take photos from all four

corners." He tossed a notepad to Jason. "Number all of the photos, even if the flash doesn't go off. Make a notation for each photo. Subject, direction, things like that. We'll do the other rooms next. When we finish that, I'll start taking evidence, and I'll give you a tag number for each photo. Match that number with your negative number sequence."

Bransome preferred film to the convenience of modern digital cameras. He'd explained it as a distrust for the latter's long-term storage potential. More like a lack of confidence. And with the editing power of programs like PhotoShop, a crooked cop could create evidence at the push of a mouse. That was the distrust part.

The camera was a ten-year-old Nikon. Heavy, but nearly indestructible, as suggested by the numerous scratches and dings covering the body. The lens was a macro, capable of everything from an "infinity shot" to a close-up in which a single fingerprint filled the entire frame. And there were no worries about holding the camera steady for the close photos. Bransome's pride was a telescoping unipod that stretched to nearly five feet, and collapsed to around twelve inches. The camera mount had a ball-and-socket joint that could be locked in any position with the twist of a knurled ring. He had explained he had it custom-made years ago, complete with a leather case that clipped on a belt, or on a satchel.

Two Marin County officers charged into the cabin

and opened cabinets and drawers.

Bransome grimaced. "Do you people mind ransacking the place after I finish doing some police work? You're contaminating the evidence."

The officers pulled back to the front porch and mumbled something inaudible.

Bransome was methodical, but he worked faster than the flash recharge time of the camera Jason wielded. "Hold on" was Jason's main means of communication. In return, Bransome used a restricted repetition of three exclamations to punctuate his work. So far "shit" was leading "nice" by at least a twenty-to-one margin, and there hadn't been a single "holy crap" since he bagged a matchbook right after walking in the door.

He dusted and lifted prints from every surface. Each time, he requested a photo, recited a number, jotted a notation in his notebook, then filled out an evidence card before attaching the lifting tape to the card.

"With all the dust, there may not be enough oils left for good prints, particularly if they're more than a week or two old," Bransome said. "At least we have heat and humidity working for us. Still, we'll have to take a lot of them, hoping for a few good ones. We may have to smoke some of them. I'll leave them for last. We'll take the paper and cardboard back with us and ninhydrin them at the station."

Bransome walked to the refrigerator and dusted the

door and handles. More photos, more notes. He opened the lower door. The only items were old bottles of ketchup, mayo, and apple juice, all half-full. The freezer was empty.

One of the Marin boys peeked in the front door and after a quick look around, spoke in a timid voice. "You mind if we take off for a while? We're in the way right now. Looks like it's going to take you some time. The place is secure."

Bransome didn't look up. "Come back in two hours. I'll be about done then."

Once the officers' SUV fired up, Bransome exhaled with a loud wheeze. "Donut withdrawal."

"Just what I was thinking." Jason snapped a picture on Bransome's nod. Their collaboration had settled into an efficient interaction that didn't require verbal orders. "The first murder occurred down around here. Did these jokers work it up?"

Bransome lifted another print and logged it in his notebook. He nodded for a photo. "Don't blame them. They're not the crime scene people. They probably don't get much of this sort of thing around here." He let out a muffled grunt. "You have to understand. The second thing we do after we pin on the badge is go out and piss on the boundaries of our jurisdiction. That creates problems when there's multicounty cooperation. When a leader is appointed for a multicounty task force, someone pops a champagne cork and someone else impales a voodoo doll."

Interesting dynamic. The officers were Bransome's brothers. Jason nearly chuckled. And not his. Bransome was free to chew them out, but he circled the wagons when an outsider shot an arrow.

Jason lowered the camera to the floor. "What's the first thing?"

"What first thing?"

"You said the second thing you do is piss on the boundaries of your jurisdiction. What's the first thing you do when you pin on the badge?"

Bransome dusted another smudge. "Donut. We eat a donut." No flinch in his expression.

The more he watched Bransome work, the more Jason was impressed. Details he wouldn't give a second thought commanded intense scrutiny from the experienced eyes and hands of Detective Art Bransome. Jason grinned when Bransome went on all fours, his face inches from the filthy shower stall floor.

"Holy crap." His tweezers pulled a matted wisp of gray hair from the shower drain.

"DNA?"

Bransome turned his head and smiled. "Hope so. We didn't get a decent sample from the envelope flap of Agnes's letter." He paused with the tweezers held inches above the drain and nodded for another photo. "Saw a brush in the medicine cabinet. I'll get some from there, too."

The roar of the SUV engine approached and cut as Bransome dropped the hairbrush into a bag.

"Perfect timing. They can trample the place all they want now. Bet you the bottle of ketchup ends up in one of their refrigerators."

Jason snickered. "The apple juice probably won't make it that far." A cringe snuffed the chuckle.

Bransome smiled.

Jason ran out of small talk within the first ten miles of the return trip, so they settled into the mutual silence of reflection. At least Jason was reflecting—on how he had misjudged Bransome as a bungling back country yokel. Thorough police work appeared to come naturally to him, to the point that it was effortless, without emotion. Yet, he was emotional about his cases. Their interactions from two years ago bore that out, as did their early dealings on this case. But why was he being so accommodating now? Were they really working together, or was this Bransome's way of keeping an eye on him? The quote about friends and enemies came back to him.

Bransome lunged, startling Jason. The detective's burly arm thrust backward and grabbed a bag from the backseat. The cruiser swerved, then corrected.

Bransome brought a clear bag to his face, anchored

it between his teeth, and pulled it open with his free hand. He held the opening out to Jason.

"Pork rinds?"

Jason peered into the bag. A familiar pile of curled, fried pork skins stared back.

"I love those things. But I usually eat so many of them I get a stomachache." Jason reached his hand in the bag and pulled out a modest handful.

"Shouldn't eat them alone. The next step is heroin." Bransome chuckled.

Jason crunched into one and watched Bransome jab his huge hand into the bag and come out with a fist's worth of the contents. Three of the rinds went into Bransome's mouth, two fell to his lap, one fell to the floor of the cruiser, and five still remained in his paw.

Jason watched the detective clear his hand in two mouthfuls and pick off the escapees on his lap before the second swallow.

Bransome reached for the floor with his right hand and the cruiser banked hard to the right. He straightened and brought the car back from the road shoulder. He kicked with his left foot, kicked again, and then reached to the floor, this time with his left hand. He brought up the pork rind, now dusted an even brown on one side—it probably carried a little of Mendocino and Marin Counties on its surface. Bransome blew hard on the rind and wiped it on the breast of his shirt three times before popping it in his mouth. He turned to Jason and spoke, pork rind dust showing his breath. "The five-second rule is waived with pork rinds. It's international law. A real man doesn't let a single one go to waste. The ultimate conundrum is if one falls in dog shit."

Jason reached into the bag again and pulled out another modest handful. "What's the solution?"

Bransome laughed. "It depends on whether anyone is watching and if there's a hose nearby."

Jason added to the air pollution with a hard, dusty laugh.

The next mile passed with the alternate sounds of crunching and crinkling of the bag. The contents were already half-gone.

Bransome looked over at Jason. "I guess I was wrong about you. I didn't have you pegged for a pork rind man."

"My dad used to sneak a bag into the grocery cart when my mom wasn't looking. He wouldn't get away with it very often. When he did, we'd grab my brother and sneak off to our tree fort. We'd knock the bag down straight and chase it with a shared quart of Pepsi. Then we'd all practice burp talking."

Bransome nodded, apparently in approval. "It's the first test, you know." He had a serious look on his face.

"First test for what?"

"To see if a man is a real man, or a girly man. Any man who doesn't like pork rinds raises one of my eyebrows."

Jason snickered. Bransome didn't.

"What's the second test? What gets to your second eyebrow?"

"Fingernails."

Jason looked down at his hands. "Fingernails? Like if they're polished?"

"No. Look at your fingernails."

Jason held his hand up, palm toward his face, curled his fingers down, and inspected his nails.

Bransome smiled. "See? You passed the second test."

"What do you mean?"

"If you ask a man to look at his fingernails, he'll do it just like you did. If you ask a woman, she'll do it like this." He pushed his hand out at arm's length, with the palm away and his fingers slightly spread and straight. "Any man who looks at his fingernails like that is definitely a momma's boy."

All those hours in the gym and what really mattered is how I look at my fingernails? And why does he care? "What's the next test?"

"That's all that's needed."

The crunching resumed.

At the next swallow, Jason looked over at Bransome. "Why'd you need to test me? You know I had a thing with that woman who worked at the old folks' home."

"You could have been a switch-hitter. Any man who can't make up his mind is worse than one who goes all the way over to the other side. I can handle someone if they're up front about it. Even respect them for standing up for it. It's the ones who pretend they're something else that bug the hell out of me."

"And you doubted me?"

Bransome smiled and tilted the bag opening in Jason's direction. "There's one more thing."

Oh God. Now what? "Yeah?"

"About two years ago." The car accelerated. "One part of me can understand what you did."

"A small part?"

"Yeah. But it got bigger today."

Is this an apology? "Yeah? How's that?"

Bransome held up a pork rind crumb. "The tests. I wanted to find out if you were one of those tree huggers or something. Did you do it because it was tofu, sushi trendy, or because of an honest commitment to your job."

"Did I pass that test?"

"You passed. But don't get too self-righteous. My other side is still in control. I think I can put it behind me. I can't forgive yet, but I can understand. I can put it to rest."

Jason wrung his hands. He'd love to put it to rest as well. If only it were that easy.

Bransome drove past the turnoff to the police station and continued up Highway 1, toward Fort Bragg.

"There's a nice motel a couple of miles up the road here. It has a great view, with good surrounding visibility. I sometimes put witnesses up there. You can check in, and then I'll take you down to get your car. I'll get you our discount."

"Can I hang around the station for a while? I know you'll start processing some of the fingerprints right away. I'd like to see what comes up. I can help if you show me what to do."

Bransome looked over like he was sizing him up. "I could use the help, but it would break the chain of custody. All evidence has to remain in the hands of law enforcement personnel at all times, and we have to document every time it changes hands."

"So deputize me or something."

"You watch too many movies."

"Hire me. Part-time. I'll work for minimum wage."

"We have procedures. Affirmative action requirements. Things like that. Besides, our budget is stretched as it is. I can't even scrape up a minimum wage, part-time job right now. Even if I had approval."

"How about a paid volunteer. I'll work for one dollar. You cut an official check to me, and I become an official employee. For one dollar."

Bransome stared at the road.

Jason let a few road signs pass. "Are you thinking what I'm thinking? Prints from the cabin should match those from Ella's room, and from Agnes's letter."

The question seemed to strike a flame of enthusiasm. "Keep going, Sherlock."

"And, if two different sets of prints come up, with one showing a similarity to Agnes's, that would indicate Eddie and Lilin are working together. It would also give us—or you—a lead on Lilin."

"Don't forget your little Agnes. Her prints could show up as well."

"I thought I already won that bet. I've already filled out the deposit slip."

Bransome looked over with a serious squint. "Want to double the bet?"

Bransome stopped at the front desk on the way into the station and held his hand up in a stop sign. Jason froze.

"Can you make an ID card for Mr. Powers?" Bransome said to the receptionist. "And have payroll cut a check to him for one dollar."

The receptionist giggled.

"I'm serious. Do it. And run the usual background check. But expedite it."

He turned to Jason. "You stay here and give Doris

your information. When you're done, come on back. I can show you how to scan fingerprints. That'd be a huge help. But I can't let you into the programs. Lunch will be on you. How's that?"

CHAPTER 28

Jason approached Officer Wilson's cruiser in the restaurant parking lot. The officer lowered his window. "I'll buy you lunch if you want to come in. Just give us a little privacy."

Wilson took a counter seat across the room. Jason joined Agnes.

"I'm so sorry about Ella," Jason said. "I wanted to come over, but I didn't think it was safe."

"What do you mean? I needed you."

"I know. I'm sorry. But I had a little problem in Santa Rosa. Lilin found me."

"What? You saw her? You talked to her? What did she say? Does she look like me?"

"Agnes, slow down. Yes, she looks like you. But we didn't talk much. She tried to kill me."

Agnes went pale and buried her face in her hands.

"Obviously, I got away. So did she."

"When was it?"

"The night Ella died."

"So she didn't kill Ella?"

"No. It wasn't Lilin."

"Thank God." She rubbed her face and exhaled through her mouth. She looked in Jason's eyes. "Are you okay?"

"I'm fine. Nervous as hell, but I'm fine."

"Do you know what she wants? Did she say anything?"

"No. She was concerned about my intentions toward you."

Agnes didn't react. "I'm not so sure I want to find her now."

"Why not?"

"She's not like me. Why didn't Gert and Ella take her, too? It could have been different if they'd taken her. I know it could have."

"Maybe they couldn't handle two little girls. Maybe Eddie wouldn't let them."

"Eddie? What would he have to do with it?"

He was past the drop-off now. He had to swim. "Are you sure you don't remember anything before Gert and Ella?"

"No. Nothing."

"Do you remember anything about a man in your life?"

"No."

"Did you have any medical problems when you were

young?"

"No. Why?"

Jason let the waitress take Agnes's order. His appetite had disappeared.

"I have some bad news about Eddie."

"Is he dead, too?" Her query lacked emotion.

"No. He isn't just your grandfather." Swim fast. "He's your father."

Agnes leaned back in the booth and crossed her arms over her chest. "What do you mean?"

"He fathered you and Lilin with your mother."

Agnes frowned like she didn't understand.

"He molested your mother, his daughter."

"How do you know all this?"

He took a deep breath. "Ella told me."

"More lies?" Tears welled in her eyes. "What else did Ella say?"

"Nothing. I didn't get a chance to talk with her again."

"Did Eddie kill her?"

That would be too much for her right now. "I don't know."

Tears released. "Why is this happening to me? I never hurt anyone."

"I know. I'm sorry."

The waitress brought Agnes's food and a milkshake for Jason. She looked at Agnes. "Is everything okay here?"

Agnes nodded and the waitress left.

Jason leaned forward and put his elbows on the table. "Agnes, are you sure you don't remember anything about a man?"

"I really don't. If I lived with Eddie, I don't remember a thing about it."

"Do you hate him, now that you know about him?"

"How can I hate someone I don't know? I hate what he did, if he did what you said. But that's all."

Jason let Agnes finish her meal, but little of it made it to her mouth. She pushed it around her plate and finally shoved the plate away.

"The funeral is tomorrow," she said.

"You know I want to be there for you."

"I didn't think you'd make it." Hurt stained her voice.

"I really want to, but I don't think it's safe, for you or for me."

"Because of Lilin, or because of Eddie?"

"Both. You're smart not to want to see Lilin now. I speak from experience. Will you be all right at the funeral?"

"Yes."

"I'll call you afterward."

"They're listening in on the phone now?"

"Yes, but don't worry. We can talk."

"Where are you staying? I called the motel, but they said you checked out."

"I'm staying at another motel in the area."

"Which one?"

Bransome's words came back—want to double the bet? "I'm sorry, but I'm not giving that out to anyone. You understand, I hope."

"I don't understand anything anymore."

Jason turned out of the restaurant parking lot and headed directly to the police station, and not just to disguise his current residence. He'd been holed up in the motel for two-and-a-half days. That was enough time for the DNA results to come back from Eddie's cabin. At least the time wasn't wasted. His new abode was wired for the Internet, so he caught up with his backlog of stories, including all of the news releases from the latest on the case.

A dense fog had lifted from the ground during his meeting with Agnes, but it still hung overhead, giving everything a dull gray tone. Days without shadows were usually the most productive for him, although he didn't know why.

Detective Bransome's car occupied the same spot it had three days ago. Did he park there out of habit, or did he stay at the station the whole time? None of the parking spaces were reserved.

Jason found Bransome at his desk, absorbed in a tall stack of computer printouts.

"You must have the most understanding wife in the world."

Bransome peered over the top of his glasses. "At least I have a wife. She's an amazing woman. When I get time with her I make it count."

His answer seemed as unemotional as his crime scene data collection. Jason's mind wandered. If he had a woman like that, he wouldn't be so lukewarm. If he had a woman . . . He turned away. Had he been too demonstrative with Eugenia? Had he driven her away? He had to change the subject. He spun around to face the desk again. "Do the fingerprints from Eddie's cabin match the ones in Ella's room, and from the letter?"

"You get right to it, don't you?" Bransome kept reading the printouts. "Perfect match."

"Anyone else's prints there?"

"No. He was there alone. The only decent prints came from the paper and cardboard pieces. The others were too old. Looks like he left about the time of Gert's death. About the time the car was stolen."

"How did you get that? From the fingerprints?"

"I found a receipt stuck to the bottom of the kitchen trash can. You photographed it."

Jason paused. He'd snapped so many shots that day, they all blended together. "How about the DNA? Anything there?"

"We got some tissue from under Ella's fingernails.

Evidently she put up a fight. The hair from the cabin gave a perfect match. Eddie killed Ella."

"And the fingerprints showed that Eddie sent the letter to Agnes?"

"Yes. Quite a family."

Jason slumped in the chair at Detective Saroyan's desk. Bransome stood. He seemed excited.

"Now for the good part. For an old fart like me, this e-mail thing is a miracle. I sent scans of Agnes's and Eddie's DNA to one of the genetics profs in Berkeley. He confirmed they're related." He paused.

Jason thought about telling him what Ella had said, but Bransome interrupted his deliberation.

Bransome's grin spread his cheeks wide. "But the relationship is more like a father, not a grandfather. They can tell that from the DNA." He paused again. "You don't find that strange?"

"I know about it. Ella told me the same thing."

Bransome took a step forward. His voice filled the room. "And you didn't tell me this because, what, you didn't think it was important?"

"She said it once. I wanted to verify it on the next visit, but she wouldn't talk to me. Then she was murdered. I wanted to find out more about Eddie."

"Is there anything else she said that I should know about?"

"The only other thing she said was, 'family secrets.'

Those secrets probably got her killed."

Bransome plopped on his chair. "Okay. Let's see if we're together on this. Eddie Hahn, or whatever he's going by now, molested his own daughter, Denise, and it resulted in the birth of identical twins, Lilin and Agnes. Denise died right after the birth. All of that is public record, except about who the father is. But we know that now. It appears Eddie had early custody of the twins until Gert and Ella stepped in and took Agnes when she was around three or four years old. Now Lilin is butchering a bunch of men, moving closer and closer to Mendocino, and Eddie has reappeared and killed Ella because she started to talk." He rubbed his chin with his right hand. "Eddie has reappeared . . ." His eyes gazed at the ceiling.

Jason leaned forward in his chair. Was he expected to contribute something at this time?

Bransome slammed his hand down on the desk. "Gert dies, Eddie's car is stolen, and he moves out of his cabin. All about the same time. Eddie is scared someone might find out about what he did to his daughters. But there's something else. Lilin stole the car. I doubt they're working together. He wouldn't have to move out. You following so far? You agree?"

"So far, I'm with you."

"Good. So, Eddie had to move out and go into hiding. Someone must be after him. But what if that someone didn't know where he was?"

"If you're talking about Lilin, she had to know. How else could she have stolen his car?"

"True." Bransome stood and paced in front of his desk. "But what if he disappeared right after the car was stolen? Or even before?" He stopped and whirled to face Jason. "Did Ella say anything about the twins being molested by Eddie?"

"I asked about that, but she wouldn't answer. She faded back out. That's what I wanted to press her about on the next visit."

"How about Agnes? Did she say anything about Eddie?"

"She has no memories from that time. She doesn't even remember a man in her life."

"How about Lilin? You spoke to her. Did she say anything about Eddie?"

"No. I didn't ask."

"Why not? You must have suspected him."

"I was too busy trying to keep from getting my pecker sliced off." The sound of the razor, inches from his ear, came back, amplified. Jason leaned back in the chair and slid his hands into his pockets.

"Did you check hospital records from when the girls were small?"

"I looked. Nothing I can find."

Bransome resumed pacing. "What if Eddie's the target?"

"I thought about that. Either *the* target or *a* target."

"No, what if he's THE target, and all of the killings were done to flush him out? What if the girls were molested, and this is all about revenge? Agnes wouldn't be the one to do it, but Lilin would."

Jason leaned forward again. It did make sense. "And the intent was to put the blame on Agnes?"

"DNA doesn't lie." Bransome snickered.

"But why would all this start after Gert died? If this was eating at Lilin, you'd think she'd have gone after Eddie before that."

"Not if she didn't know where the rest of the family members were until Gert's death. Or—"

"Or, what?"

"Or maybe Lilin and Agnes are both in on it. Working together. You didn't answer before. Do you want to double the bet?"

"That doesn't make sense to me. Agnes isn't the type. And she's really scared now. At first, she wanted to meet with Lilin. Now she doesn't."

"Oh, how good actors can devour the gullible."

"You're wrong on that one."

"Then why don't you double the bet?"

The phone rang on Bransome's desk.

Jason sighed with relief.

"Yes, it's very important . . . Why not . . .? You and every other county. I think you should reconsider . . .

Okay, but if something happens, the papers will know . . . And just as far up yours." He slammed the phone down.

"Problems at home?"

Bransome glared. "The people in Marin County are going to call off the stakeout of Eddie's cabin in two more days. Nothing is happening and they say they can't afford the man-hours. Probably interfering with their donut breaks. They said they'd check for signs of habitation every day or so. Big of them."

"If Eddie really is on the run, I doubt he'd go back. There's nothing there he'd need now that the ketchup is gone."

"Home is home, and living invisible is expensive. They're going to rely on a call from the moron at the post office if Eddie shows up to collect his mail. He gets Social Security checks there, for God's sake."

Jason stood up and stretched. "One other thing is still bothering me about Eddie."

"Only one?"

Jason grimaced. "How did Eddie know Ella was talking? And Agnes?"

Bransome nodded, then looked up at the ceiling. "Good question. My guess is he kept tabs on Gert and Ella. He must have known about Gert's death, and Ella's move to the home. And Agnes's involvement in the murders has been plastered all over the papers and TV news."

"But how would he put all that together? How

would he know I was talking to Ella?"

"The theft of his car," Bransome said with an exaggerated nod. "Why would he go into hiding? Because he has something to hide. Something bad enough for him to murder his own sister. He's probably been watching. Ella. Agnes. Us."

"And Lilin?"

"Probably not. He must not know where she is."

"Huh?" Jason frowned. "Why do you say that?"

"If he knew where Lilin was, he probably would have gone after her instead of Ella."

"I agree with the first part, but he'd still have to silence Ella."

Bransome shuddered. "Poor lady. Most of us have family secrets, but not the kind that lead to murder."

It was Jason's turn to shudder. "Any possibility of beefing up the security around Agnes's house? She's really scared about the letters."

"Not this again. Don't you think what we're doing is sufficient? We have someone watching twenty-four hours a day. That's stretching our personnel, and our budget, like down in Marin County. But I'm doing it anyway."

"She's just really scared."

"I'll alert everyone to go into protection mode in addition to the watching mode. How's that?"

"Is that double-talk?"

"Yes, but Agnes doesn't know that. And you won't tell her, right?"

"It'll probably make her feel better. Thanks."

Bransome clapped his hands together. "Eddie seems to be a key here. How can we lure him out of hiding?" He started for the door but whirled around. "By the way, your Francine Thomas was killed by our serial murderer. But there was something strange about it."

Jason felt a chill. Too many connections were pulling a tightening web around him. He flopped back down in the chair and fingered his collar. "Strange?"

"Yeah. The murderer wasn't menstruating this time. And she didn't use the man's member."

"Then why do you say it was the same murderer if the MO is that different?"

"Other pieces of evidence are consistent. More significant things."

Investigative secrets, withheld from the public. Jason shook his head. "But this is the first woman killed."

"That's why I think this one was a crime of opportunity. There seems to be a grand plan with the others. Not with this one."

"Opportunity? Opportunity for what?"

"Revenge. That's all I can figure. She stole from Ella."

"And what's the motivation for the others? What's the grand plan?"

Bransome's face reddened. "I don't know." He balled his hands into fists at his sides. "Yet."

Jason looked at the floor. And what about Agnes? He thought about the red dress. He'd take the bet.

CHAPTER 29

JASON LET THE TELEPHONE RECEIVER FALL ON THE cradle and looked at the clock. It was eight thirty in the morning. He ignored personal hygiene, except for quick swabs of deodorant and a fast brush run across his teeth. He also ignored the speed limits as he hurried down Highway 1, around the large bend in Reese Drive and up to Agnes's house. The antilock brakes of his Volvo chattered to a stop. Bransome and Officer Wilson huddled on the front porch. Jason threw the car in park, jumped from the seat, and sprinted to the front porch to join them. The front door was ajar, black print powder everywhere.

"What's going on?"

Officer Didier arrived within a few seconds. She looked tired, disheveled.

"The porch light didn't go out this morning, so I checked it out," Wilson said. "No one answered the door. I called her cell phone, but I kept getting her voice mail. I looked in all of the windows, and no one seemed to be home, so I called Detective Bransome and we did a preliminary sweep. She's gone."

Bransome took a spiral notebook and pen from his satchel. He had two cameras over his shoulder. "Powers and I'll do the inside and the back door." He handed a camera to Jason and turned to face Wilson. "You and Didier do the outside and the garage. Her car is still in there. Do all of the house windows. Look for signs of forced entry. Take a photo of each regardless. You may want to phone the station to get a ladder out here. I want all the windows done, even the second floor. And look at all parking areas and the driveway. Look for tire marks and oil spots." He turned back to Jason. "Come on."

Jason followed. "What do you think happened?"

"There's no sign of a struggle anywhere inside, and on a quick look there's no evidence of forced entry. She could have left on her own, or it could be Lilin or Eddie who got her. We'll have to do the whole house, although we'll be more thorough in the kitchen, her bedroom, and the bathrooms. I thought you'd want to be in on it. You have anything going today? It'll probably eat it all up."

"Thanks for calling. She wouldn't go off by herself." Would she? She had said she needed my help. Lilin must have her. Unless . . .

"What makes you so certain?"

"Gut feeling." Unless she is involved.

"Let's see if your gut's right."

They had to step over a few scattered envelopes and a magazine in the entry. Jason photographed the items and collected them into a neat stack. They included what looked like bills, junk mail, and a *People* magazine. He placed the stack on a sideboard, and slipped the three bills into his back pocket so they could check them out at the station later.

It was nearly suppertime when they joined Wilson and Didier on the front lawn for a quick summary. Bransome took charge.

"Forced entry?"

"No. Nothing," Wilson said.

"Any vehicle marks?"

"Nope."

"Not even in the garage?"

"No."

Bransome scratched his head. "Anything unusual about her car?"

"No."

"Odometer?"

Wilson thumbed a page in his notepad. "Just a few miles since the last check."

"Okay. Give me what you have and I'll start process-ing it. Didier, go home. You look like how you probably feel. Wilson, back in the car. We need to watch the place closely for the next few days. I've turned on a light in the extra bedroom upstairs, and a lamp in the front window. Let's leave the porch light off. If any of that changes, call me immediately."

Jason cleared his throat. "Mind if I come along to the station? I'm really charged up about this. I can help scan in the fingerprints again. Dinner's on me."

"The help would be appreciated, as would the meal."

Bransome stopped a few steps from the group. "Wilson, could you go a few extra hours this evening? Didier should get a little sleep. How about switching around nine?"

Wilson nodded.

Bransome worked at Jason's side in the computer room, running the prints as fast as Jason could scan them. He used a direct comparison with Agnes's stored prints since that was faster than going into the AFIS database. He explained that anything that came up negative for a match could be run the more thorough way.

The only prints that did come up different turned out to be Jason's, and they were restricted to the dining room. He was in the database through his work. People in his business covered so many crime scenes, they volunteered their prints so no confusion would result if they touched something inadvertently.

Eleven o'clock came and went, and Jason was tiring. "What do you think? Looks like Agnes was the only one in there."

Bransome rolled his chair back. "I think we can eliminate one of the three."

"Three?"

"Yeah. Lilin, Eddie, and Agnes herself."

"Which one are you throwing out?"

"Eddie."

"Eddie? Why?"

"We can't throw Agnes out based on anything we get from her house. And Lilin killed all those men and only gave us a single, crappy print. She obviously uses gloves. On the other hand, Eddie didn't wear gloves. He'd have left at least one print somewhere."

"He could have worn gloves here."

"Anyone who'd kill his own sister without gloves isn't likely to slip some on to abduct his daughter. People usually don't change their tendencies."

"Experience?"

"Every bit of it."

Jason sighed. "You mind if I knock off? I'm fading fast. I can come back tomorrow and help you finish it up. I've got a lot of free time lately. I decided to take some vacation time."

Decided. What a laugh. It was a tactical move. The gossip had Mulvaney putting Torres on the story and yanking Jason's leash. Mulvaney couldn't argue about the leave. And it was a good compromise. Mulvaney got continued coverage of the story for free. Jason was relieved of the steady stream of piddly assignments that kept him wet to his ankles. Yolanda Torres had backup, which was also good. Despite everything Mulvaney had said, he liked working with Yolanda.

Bransome jolted Jason back to the workroom. "Does that mean you'll be hanging around here all the time?"

"I'm in on it now. You expect me to just give it all up? I can give you more time. You already paid me, and I cashed the check." Jason pulled out his wallet and withdrew a crisp dollar bill.

"You've been a lot of help. I like the way you work and the way you think. It'll free up Saroyan. He has a full plate with other cases. You can roll in when you roll in. I know how to get you if I need to."

"Aw, gee, Detective." He tilted his head and forced a sappy smile.

"I didn't say we were on joking terms. I still don't like some of the things you did in the past or some of the things you stand for. Being on this end of a case may turn your mind around."

Jason smiled. Or help me forget, or at least feel

better about it.

Jason threw his keys on the table in his room, kicked off his shoes, and collapsed onto the bed. He didn't expect to make it into the covers tonight. His mind spiraled outward, but the ring of the phone pulled him back.

"Hello?" The nicotine smell of the receiver nearly made him retch.

Silence.

"Hello . . .?" He grunted to a sitting position. "Who is this?"

Silence.

"Agnes? Is this you?"

Silence.

He swung his feet over the side of the bed. "Lilin?"

Silence.

He listened for breathing or background noises. Nothing.

"Tell me what you want, damn it. Do you have Agnes?"

Silence.

He slammed the phone down, paused, and picked up the receiver. He punched the number for the front desk.

"Did anyone call and ask for my room?"

The clerk seemed annoyed. "We don't screen a

guest's calls."

"Anyone can call a room without going through your switchboard?"

"You got it, dude. Can I help you with anything else?"

Jason slammed the receiver down, walked over to the window, and parted the drapes a crack. Even the sodium vapor lights hurt his eyes. Nothing suspicious in the parking lot. The window lock included a chained pin that inserted into a hole in the frame. No slack in this one. He checked the dead bolt and chain on the door. Secure. Fatigue took hold once again, so he fell back on the bed. There was no way he would get in the covers now.

CHAPTER 30

THE DAY WITHOUT A WORD ABOUT AGNES PASSED LIKE chilled syrup, further congealed by the shift from unique discovery to tedious processing of the humdrum pieces of crime scene evidence. But playing the tourist, or the hibernator, produced more anxiety than relaxation for Jason. Waiting was time wasted, and all he could do was wait, so any small contribution to the forward movement of the case represented added value.

He collapsed on the motel bed. Before he closed his eyes, the blinking red message light on the phone caught his attention.

He pushed the message button and let the short message run through. "A letter? Here?"

He jumped from the bed and hurried out of the room.

The stamp stood alone across the top of the envelope, with no return address, and it didn't have a cancellation imprint or postmark. The letter must have been slipped into the motel mail, either at the motel or through the mail carrier.

He rushed back into his room and threw all of the locks. The envelope had the same cursive loops and circular dots as on Agnes's first letter—the letter from Lilin.

Hair raised on his arms. Lilin knew where he was staying.

He turned the envelope over. Should he open it here, or at the police station? Bransome was at home, and it wasn't a good night to bother him. He'd give up his plans in the time it'd take him to hang up the phone, but he needed the time away with his wife.

Jason sat on the bed. Should he open the letter or leave it until tomorrow morning? Would Bransome be mad if he brought it in opened and contaminated? But how could he wait? It was addressed to him, Jason Powers. It was a message to him, maybe time sensitive. Maybe Agnes's safety was at stake.

He tapped the short end of the envelope on the tabletop a few times and grasped the other end to tear it open, but stopped. Gloves. He had a pair of gloves in his jacket pocket. He pulled them on and tore the edge off the envelope. A single, folded sheet was inside.

He wiped a spot on the top of the thigh-high chest of drawers and carefully opened the paper, pulling it flat on the wood. The hand that addressed the envelope also wrote the message—Lilin's hand.

I HAVE AGNES. SHE'S ALL RIGHT FOR NOW. I'M NEARLY DONE. DON'T INTERFERE. LET ME FINISH MY WORK.

Nearly done? he thought. Kill off Eddie and it's all over? Is that what she meant? Is that the finish of her work? If so, maybe it would be best to let her do it. Eddie's death wouldn't be a loss to the world. If that stopped the killing, it would be a reasonable compromise.

But what about Agnes? The letter said she was all right. For now. What if she was a target? It could be jealousy that was driving Lilin. Jealousy over the life Agnes had, and she didn't.

A strange twinge tugged at Jason's stomach. The sensation felt like fear. The kind of fear one has when someone close was in danger. He had an overwhelming urge to find Agnes. Make sure she was safe. This wasn't a reporter's desire for a story; it went beyond that.

Jason slumped on the bed. Why was Agnes so important to him? Why was she occupying his thoughts, motivating his actions? Eugenia. Was that it? It was strange. When he thought of Agnes, Eugenia didn't pop into his mind. Not like she did with other women. Something in other women always reminded him of his ex, always made him feel like she was there with him, encouraging him, setting him up again. But not with Agnes. Why?

Jason went into the bathroom and splashed water on his face. Was he developing feelings for Agnes, as Lilin thought? Was he being selfish to suggest her life was more valuable than Eddie's? But Agnes hadn't killed anyone. That was his gut feeling, even though it went against Bransome's instincts. Who was right? Who would win the battle of waistline intuition?

Jason walked back out of the bathroom and froze. Maybe Lilin's goal was to kill them both, to clean out the whole family. To pull out all of the family secrets, like weeds. Roots and all.

It didn't matter. Agnes was in trouble no matter how it was figured.

He wished he could induce a temporary lobotomy so he could live in the present without having to plan for the future or to worry about it. So he could go to sleep. So the morning would appear in an instant of conscious time.

There was a way, but it clouded the following day with a hangover. It would also dull his defenses. If Lilin knew his whereabouts, he needed to stay sharp. The swish he had heard go past his ear when he jumped over his patio wall was probably from the razor she used to emasculate her prey. It was close then and it was still close now.

Jason startled awake. His hands groped for his crotch. He last remembered watching the clock flick past three. That was a bad dream ago. He rolled on his side and looked at the clock. It glowed a red 6:05. Bransome would be in by seven, even if he and his wife partied hard last night.

Jason turned the faucet in the shower stall. One of his favorite cinematic sequences was the shower scene from Alfred Hitchcock's *Psycho*, but he always viewed it through Anthony Perkins's point of view, going with the eye of the camera. Now he stood in Janet Leigh's bare feet, the water beating on his shoulders, the steam flowing across his visual field.

He had lined the floor with all of the extra towels he could find and pulled the curtain halfway, so he had a clear view of the bathroom doorway. Through the mirror he could see the edge of the front door. He twisted the water valve toward cold. It would have to be a luke-warm shower today, so the mirror wouldn't fog.

Bransome spread the letter on a clean piece of paper on the laboratory bench. "No sense doing the envelope. If she wore gloves for the letter, she'd wear them for the envelope as well. Besides, there'd be several other sets of prints all over the envelope."

Jason stepped closer. "I disagree. The letter wasn't run through the post office. It doesn't have cancellation imprints. She could have delivered it directly to the motel."

Bransome shrugged. He grabbed the can of ninhydrin, sprayed the letter and envelope, and hung them in the modified film drying cabinet. "We'll have to process all the prints. We'll compare them to yours first. Then we'll see if the motel clerk is in the system. We'll have to do a side-by-side with Agnes's prints to see if there are general similarities. You want to continue with them, or are you getting bored with the grunt work?" He closed the cabinet and flipped the fan switch. "I really appreciate it."

"I better not. I have a funny feeling about handling anything that involves my own prints. Besides, I have to send some information to one of my colleagues in Santa Rosa to keep the paper up on the case. It won't take long." He studied Bransome's face. "How'd it go with the missus last night?"

"We cranked up the fireplace and curled up on the couch in front of the television. It was wonderful. I didn't think about this place for a minute."

"You're a lucky man. I'm stuck in a room that smells like cigarettes and sex, and they aren't even my smells." Jason kicked at the floor. Would marital happiness ever come his way, or was he destined to live with those smells for the rest of his life?

"When are you planning to go back to your apartment?" Bransome said.

"I don't know. Not until something shakes loose with this case. If you're going to take my picture, I'd prefer it be with a smile on my face and my danglies intact."

"A couple of weeks ago I'd have preferred the file shot."

"You're a pal, Detective."

Bransome laughed. "Go to hell. I'll be your pal when we put this murderer behind bars." He slapped his hand down on Jason's shoulder. "How's that for an incentive?"

"Better than a paycheck." Jason gave a single chuckle. "Speaking of that, I think I will double the bet. Agnes is a victim, not a murderer."

"I want to agree with you, but I can't. I still have to go with my intuition. I'm coming in your direction, but I believe I'll drag my feet a while longer."

Jason sat down on the corner of a desk. "I can't stand this waiting. I'm worried Lilin will kill both Eddie and Agnes. Is there anything we can do to find them?"

"I've been agonizing about that. We have APBs on all of them and on the GTO. The people in Marin County are supposed to be checking the cabin at least twice a day. Other than that, we have no leads. On a sitting-or-doing scale, we're way to the left."

Jason stood and clapped his hands together. "There might be something we can do. I was getting hang up calls at the old motel, and now I'm getting them at the new place as well. I didn't tell anyone where I was staying. It's our only means of contact going in that direction. Is there anything I could say that would help flush them out?"

Bransome paced around the desk. "I could put a trace on the phone."

"The caller's too smart. Besides, my guess is they're from a cell phone. All the caller has to do is move around and triangulation will only tell us where he or she was, not where he or she is."

"Yeah. You're probably right. Then we have two choices. You could say something to inflame the situation, hoping it would accelerate it, or say something to defuse the situation. Since we have no clue where they are, the first won't do anything useful and probably will give a bad result. The second's our only choice."

Jason plopped back on the desk. "What if I said the DNA tests proved Eddie didn't father Lilin and Agnes? That could get him off the hook."

"Not if he abused the girls. The family tie may be the only thing that's making her be deliberate with Eddie. If he was a nonrelated abuser, she probably would've whacked him long before now."

"So you suggest I do nothing if I get another call?"

"I don't see any other option at this time. Either way, it'd probably come out bad."

"Just like doing nothing."

"I know."

The phone on Bransome's desk rang. He answered and turned his back on Jason to help mute the conversation. It didn't take him long to get agitated, peppering his side of the discussion with obscenities, which danced in the room like they were shouted in a cavern. He slammed the receiver down and turned to face Jason.

"That idiot postal worker in Inverness called the sheriff's office yesterday afternoon, around four thirty. He told them a man matching Eddie's description came in earlier and got his mail. The man was driving a light-colored foreign car. Compact model. Seems the clerk didn't give a better description because he was admiring a beautiful, black GTO that was parked across the street. When the man left, the GTO left right behind him. That happened around two."

"He didn't call them for over two hours?"

"Right. The officers got on it right away. They drove around all evening looking for the GTO, but they didn't see it. They also stopped by Eddie's cabin last night, and again this morning. It was untouched." Bransome shook his head. "They're keeping an eye out, but they're at the mercy of an idiot witness."

"Didn't they tell him to look for the GTO?"

"Yes, but he said he didn't make the connection."

"Didn't make the connection? Look for a familiar man coming in to get mail. Look for a black GTO. Does the mailman have a problem with a certain white powder?"

"What's done is done. The important thing is that she was on his tail yesterday afternoon."

"She's probably done him in already. His body's probably floating in Tomales Bay."

Bransome tugged his belt upward.

Jason imagined a younger Bransome, without the gut, but with the same thick arms and barrel chest. Almost his height, Bransome was probably more than formidable. Probably scary.

"I don't think so." Bransome said. "She's been very public about the other killings. If this is her finale, I wouldn't expect her to hide it. She'd want everyone to see him with his wiener sliced off. She may even do something symbolic with this one."

Jason shook his head to reset Bransome's image. "Like what?"

"Like kill him in a symbolic place."

"The deputies said the cabin was clean."

"I'll have Wilson go check Agnes's house." Bransome hurried to the door.

"Jesus. Do you think she would? What a perfect way to frame Agnes."

He spun around. "Or for Agnes to make it look like Lilin was framing her," Bransome said as he left the room.

Jason frowned. The closer they seemed to get, the farther they were away. Theories were easy to formulate, but nothing allowed them to rule any out. All they could do was wait and hope. They were doomed to be reactive, as Bransome had said, and Jason hated it.

The day dragged on, worse than the previous one. Bransome had filled him in on the frustrating details. Agnes's house was untouched, inside and out, and the Marin County boys checked Eddie's cabin two more times before they set Bransome off by suggesting they stop making any more drives out to Inverness unless there was other business there. They had said something about crying wolf.

There were no prints on the letter. Two types of prints from the envelope included Jason's and someone whose pattern wasn't even close to Agnes's. Probably the motel clerk's. Bransome delivered the envelope to the lab person to start processing the glue for DNA.

Jason relished the fading afternoon. Back in the motel, he curled up in the bed, inside the covers this time, and looked forward to vegetating in front of the television. He needed to empty his mind, and there were any number of prime time shows that required low double digit IQ points worth of audience involvement.

He chose a reality show with six contestants, three of whom were young ladies in scanty outfits. Poster girls for breast implant surgeons throughout the country. Jason chuckled. One of the girls seriously discussed the importance of mental preparation and strategy before fishing pig uteri out of a vat of mealworm larvae with her teeth. Andy Warhol was right on the money about the fifteen minutes of fame.

The host had admired the complex weaving of tattoos on one of the male contestants when the phone rang, jolting the 99 percent of Jason's brain that was on standby.

He felt the tingling of nervous energy course through his body and his thudding heart jumped into overdrive. It was his cell phone this time. Bransome? Agnes? He reached to the nightstand and pushed the speaker button.

"Hello?"

Silence.

"Hi, Lilin." His heart thumped so hard it seemed to vibrate the bed. "Can I talk to Agnes?"

Silence.

Bransome had said it wouldn't do any good to bluff about Eddie, but what other move was there? It wasn't the first time he disagreed with Bransome. And it beat sitting around, twiddling thumbs.

"Did you hear the news? The DNA evidence says that Eddie isn't your father."

Quiet giggles built into loud laughter.

The laughter was female, but low-pitched, throaty. Creepy to the extreme. "Lilin. Talk to me. Where's Eddie?"

She laughed. "Eddie's at home," she whispered.

The voice reminded him of his apartment. The smell of the eucalyptus. The sound of the razor slicing the air, close to his ear. "At home, where? In Inverness?" Hopefully far away.

Silence.

"Where's Agnes?"

"She won't interfere anymore."

Panic swept his mind, but the reporter took over. He stood. "How about Eddie?"

"He's a bastard."

Her venomous voice surprised him.

"He's trying to protect himself."

Jason walked to the window and pulled back the drapes. "Why does he need protection?"

"No-good fucking bastard."

He rechecked the door locks. "Did he hurt you?"

"Fucking no-good bastard."

"Did he hurt you and Agnes?"

Silence.

Jason backed away from the door and flopped on the bed. "Is that why Gert and Ella took Agnes?"

Silence.

"Why didn't they take you, too?"

"Too late."

"What do you mean, 'too late'?"

Dial tone.

The cell phone startled Jason. Bransome again? He'd just called fifteen minutes ago.

Jason rechecked the clock—2:00 a.m. Had the Marin County boys found something at Eddie's cabin after all? Bransome had said they were pissed about being called on a wild goose chase so late. That they threatened to back-burner the case.

The phone rang again and he fumbled for the *talk* button. "Is there news?"

Silence.

"Lilin?"

Silence.

"What do you want?"

A whisper: "Eddie's at home."

Dial tone.

CHAPTER 31

JASON READIED THE BATHROOM FLOOR FOR HIS HALF-curtained shower. He couldn't get the two phone calls from Lilin out of his mind. The warm water reset his thoughts, then turned his mind loose into freewheel mode. At home, some of his best thinking came at the expense of his water bill.

She could have made the first call from Inverness, knowing he would phone Bransome, and that Bransome would forward the information to the Marin County deputies. She could have been watching as the officers checked the cabin, angry at Bransome for a late night false alarm. That would give her the time, and freedom from discovery, to carry out her plan. But why the second call? To publicize her act? To taunt?

He turned the water off and toweled his shoulders. His reflection in the mirror caught his attention. Maybe she wanted him to find the body. Body or bodies?

He hurried out of the bathroom, wrapping the towel around his waist, and dug in the nightstand drawer for the phone book. He dialed and made a reservation.

Jason paused in the doorway. The police station workroom was empty. He turned to see Bransome stomping up the hallway.

"What's up for today?" Bransome said. "More grunt work? I have a pile."

"I'm heading out on a road trip. A rental car is going to be delivered in half an hour. I have to pay for this one myself so I got a little POS."

"POS?"

Jason smiled. "Piece of Shit. Don't worry. I told the delivery guy to use the back door. Is that okay?"

"Yeah. Where you heading?"

Jason thought about telling him, but decided against it. Bransome seemed edgy on the second call, after the Marin County boys found Eddie's cabin empty. "I'll let you know when I get there." He cringed, expecting an objection.

"I know the feeling. Sometimes I have to get out there and just drive. No destination. It clears the head."

"Something like that." What, really? Reporter's intuition? Lilin sounded different on the last call. There was a finality in her voice, almost like resignation. But that wasn't all. Lilin had Agnes. Would there be two bodies in Inverness? He had to find out for himself.

A white Toyota Corolla pulled up at the rear entrance of the police station right on time. Jason dropped the delivery person off at the rental office and headed south, toward Inverness.

He had a little over three hours to anticipate what he might find, but instead he followed Bransome's lead and emptied his head. Every time Agnes popped in, he forced his thoughts to one of his other assignments. He needed the short break, a brief clearing of anxiety-tainted speculation. A punch of a mental reset button. The relaxation exceeded anything he'd experienced in the last couple of weeks.

As he cruised through Inverness, he backed off the gas pedal. What would he find in Eddie's cabin? Lilin had said Eddie was at home. Alone?

He yanked his foot from the pedal. What if Lilin was there, waiting for him? What if this was a trap? What if he was one of her targets? She had tried to kill him once before.

Was it a mistake to come down here without Bransome? Without alerting the Marin County boys? A good scoop would be worth angering them all, but like before there was something else. And it centered on Agnes. He was worried about her. More. He wanted to find her.

His foot pressed the gas pedal again. Anger replaced apprehension. Three hours wasted, thinking about nothing when he could have been developing a plan for his visit to the cabin. Now he would have to wing it. Make it up as he went. Errors plagued the unprepared, and an error here could be fatal.

Jason turned onto the road to the cabin and pressed on the gas pedal. His anxiety level increased tenfold. The yellow crime scene tape that spanned the front door dangled from the left side of the door frame. Someone, other than law enforcement officers, had been in there. He pushed hard on the pedal and sped by.

He drove on for what seemed like minutes but only registered a mile on the odometer. Off to the left, a turnout led to a narrow driveway and, presumably, to a well-disguised cabin. The driveway was overgrown. Not frequently used. He turned in and slowed the car to a crawl. Twenty yards into the brush, the roadside foliage opened up enough to allow him to turn off the double-rutted driveway and park, invisible from the main road.

He turned off the ignition and sat, trying to catch his breath. A long walk was ahead of him, but it was still shy of noon. No reason to hurry.

The high cloud cover had fragmented, so the sun cast moving shafts of light between trees, across the underbrush. Better to walk through the cover than on the road, to come in to Eddie's cabin from the side. Just in case.

Several thickets of dense, tangled bushes forced detours. After each diversion, he angled back until the road was in sight before turning toward the cabin again.

The clouds thinned even more, and the air turned as crisp and clear as the waters of an alpine lake. The light breeze tickled his body and bathed it in a faint ocean scent. It reminded him of waggish summer days from long ago—before the obligations of adulthood swooped down and swiped their mischief. But there was an edge to the clarity. The horizon held a fog-thick veil of apprehension, like all the clouds were assembling to gang up on him. He wanted to turn and skip in the opposite direction.

Ahead, a large rock, ringed by a horseshoe of short shrubs, looked like an idol to male pattern baldness. His chuckle caught in his throat. The cabin jutted from the tranquil landscape twenty yards beyond the rock. It was quiet, eerily so. Like the twittering birds were all holding their breath.

Circling around behind the structure, he came to the opposite side. He looked to the left, and the right, away from the cabin, searching for evidence of a stakeout.

He crossed the road and made another arc, again looking for evidence of hidden observers. There were none. If Lilin was watching, she was far enough away to give him a chance at detection, particularly with the sparse brush cover in the immediate vicinity of the cabin.

With his circumnavigation complete, he inched to the

side of the front porch. It creaked his trespass and he froze. A window invited his gaze, and he nearly fell backward at the sight. He saw spurts of blood inside, on the walls of the main room. He tapped his pocket and mouthed a curse. He'd left his cell phone in the car. What should he do? Did he need to go in? Did he want to go in?

Agnes popped into his mind. Was this the Eddie show, or was it a double feature? He took a step toward the door, but again hesitated. He wanted to know if Agnes was in there, but then again, he didn't. Could he handle seeing her mutilated body right beside Eddie's? What did Lilin have planned for him?

He heard a car on the road, coming in his direction, so he sprinted around the side of the house, back to the bush-lined rock. An old, beat-up pickup sauntered by, the sole occupant a long-bearded man with his hair pulled into a ponytail. Jason's next exhalation lasted forever.

Back on the porch, he chided himself for his reluctance. He was a reporter. He had a job to do. Any personal connection should be suppressed in a situation like this. Should be. He gripped the doorknob and hesitated. Should be.

He released the knob—forgot to glove up. The latex gloves snapped tight on his wrists. He turned the doorknob with a loud click and stopped. No further sounds. No movement inside. The door pushed open without resistance. He leaned close to the hinge side of the door.

Through the crack, he verified that nothing, or no one, waited behind the door. He stepped through the doorway, slowly closing the door behind him.

Blood was everywhere. The smell nearly turned him around. The scent was metallic, sharp. Was this the smell of a violent death? Whose death? Eddie's? Agnes's? Both? He wanted to run, to get to his phone and call Bransome. But first, he needed to know. Was Agnes here?

Blood had splattered and sprayed the walls and pooled on the floor, mostly in the kitchen area. It looked like the victim put up a struggle, and like he bled out right in this room. He? Hopefully so.

Jason stepped around the stains, taking care to avoid any potential evidence. Red stains ran down from the rim of the sink like it had boiled over with blood. He peered in. A bloody lump of tissue rose from the drain like a leaning tower. It took him a few moments to realize it was a penis, business end down.

He stepped back. He'd seen the photos of the other crime scenes. They were grizzly, but nothing compared to this. This one was more random, more disorganized than the others. More violent? Then, he noticed another difference. Next to the sink was a bloody set of fingerprints. He looked around and saw more prints. And footprints. The killer wasn't wearing gloves this time. And she wasn't careful. She'd slipped up. Or had she? Was this Lilin's grand finale? Artists always signed their work.

But where was the body? It wasn't in the living room. He tiptoed around the bloodstains and through the door of the bedroom. It looked untouched since his last visit. There were no bloodstains, no signs of a struggle. No body.

He went into the bathroom. There were diluted bloodstains in the sink, like the killer used it to wash her hands, but no other signs of mayhem and, again, no body.

Or bodies. There seemed to be enough blood for two murders. Either one body totally bled out, or two were partially bled. And there didn't have to be any blood at all for a life to be taken. He wanted to find a body. One body, not two.

It wasn't in the house. And he hadn't seen anything on his observational circuit of the building, although his attention had been on the surroundings.

He returned to the main room and looked down at the main pool of blood. It ended abruptly on the side nearest the door. He got down on his hands and knees. The dust spoke to him. Slide marks. Going out the back door. She must have rolled the body in something and pulled it outside. Not a rug. There wasn't one in the place on their previous visit. He got up and walked to the bedroom.

The bed was made, as it was on their earlier visit. He lifted the bedspread. Fitted sheet, but no top sheet.

He burst through the back door and walked the

back wall of the cabin. No bodies littered the landscape. He froze. Just off the far corner of the back wall, a shovel leaned against a tree, as if resting from a recent, difficult job. He walked to the tree and paced in an arc, parallel to the back and sides of the cabin. Then another arc, farther out. Then another. He scanned the ground, looking for signs of recent disturbance.

Fifteen yards out from the building, behind a low stand of shrubs, he found it. Freshly dug dirt was mounded in a four-foot by seven-foot patch. He kicked at the dirt midway on the long side, and it scattered easily. A few more kicks and he felt resistance. He used a gloved hand to move away more of the dirt, and a finger appeared.

He stood back and a weak feeling nearly buckled his knees. The plot wasn't big enough for two bodies, unless they were stacked on top of each other. He looked at the dirty fingertip protruding from the soil.

Was it the hand of an elderly man? He couldn't tell. He pulled in a full breath and held it, then pinched the fingertip with this thumb and first two fingers, and pulled. The hand lifted from the dirt, just beyond the wrist. He released the finger, and the hand fell back, stiff.

The air hissed from his lungs. The hand was fairly large, with broad fingers and closely trimmed fingernails. He brushed off some of the dirt, and turned the appendage as much as it would give. Hair on the back of the hand was long, and the skin looked wrinkled. It was a man's hand. Maybe an old man's hand.

He pulled upward a little more, and a white fabric appeared, wrapping the forearm. A bedsheet, no doubt.

He dared do no more to the site for fear of destroying the evidentiary value, but even with a cursory look at the whole picture, he felt relief. Probably Eddie, and definitely not Agnes. He didn't need a complete investigation to sense that Agnes had survived this carnage.

He tapped his pants pocket again and remembered his cell phone was back in the car. Nothing more could be done here, so he headed back for the car, this time walking along the road. His gait pushed the efficiency-driven switch point for a trot.

Back at the car, Jason struggled to punch the buttons on his cell phone. His hands, steady through the grisly discovery, shook so hard he could barely read the phone screen. Was it relief that Agnes wasn't the victim? Or was it nervousness over her unsettled fate? He'd seen many murder scenes, and he'd never reacted this way.

He punched 911 and reported the scene and location to the local emergency people. His next call went to Bransome, who was in his car before the conversation ended.

A third call went to his colleague at the *Santa Rosa Press Democrat*, Yolanda Torres, who had taken over the release of short updates on the mass murder case. He told her to get out to Inverness right away, to get a scoop on all of the competitors. He'd be waiting.

He drove back to the cabin, backed in so he could watch the road, and waited. Would Bransome be mad? He seemed businesslike on the phone.

Two Marin County deputies showed up twenty minutes after the 911 call. Jason followed them through the front door and kept a close eye on them so they wouldn't contaminate the scene. He showed them the grave site, and one put in a call to the county coroner. Jason retired to his car when they began securing the site.

Bransome drove up two hours after his call, beating Jason's drive time by a full hour. To Jason's relief, Bransome was calm, professional.

"How'd you get here so fast?" Jason said. "It's a hundred and forty miles."

"I used the lights and pushed the speed. Don't have to worry about traffic when I do that."

He looked over at one of the deputies, a peach-fuzzed officer who retied yellow crime scene tape on a porch pillar with the care of a Christmas present wrapping.

"I'm Detective Bransome. The lead investigator on the Hahn case from up in Mendocino. Can anyone give me permission to start processing the scene?"

The deputy walked over and held out a hand. "Officer Grossmont. The coroner takes over murder scenes when he arrives. His name's Finnegan. He's a nice old man."

"Mind if I take a look inside? I won't touch anything until he gets here."

"Be my guest. It's pretty gruesome." Grossmont looked at Jason.

"He's with me," Bransome said.

Grossmont stood back and pointed at the front door. Bransome shoved a camera into Jason's chest and walked toward the cabin.

The coroner arrived twenty minutes later and it took him another two to get out of his van. He wheezed in time with the steps of his portly waddle, each shaking generous jowls that obscured his jawline. A kindly look of calm never left his face.

Bransome approached him. "I'm Detective Bransome from Mendocino. I'm the lead investigator for the Hahn case up in Mendocino." He flashed his badge. "I've helped process all but one of the murders. I'd like your permission to do the same here."

"I don't think you need my permission." Finnegan stroked his grizzled chin. "So you think this is tied to the Menstrual Murders?"

Bransome glared at Jason.

Jason raised his palms. "Not from me."

Bransome turned back to Coroner Finnegan. "Yes. The man who owns this cabin is the suspected murderer's father. The body is probably his."

Finnegan held up a hand. "A yes is all I need. I'll trust you. I'm glad to have the help. I've been way too busy lately. You'll share all data right away?"

"Of course."

"I have a form for you to sign back in the van, but we can get to that later. Help yourself to the cabin. I'll start with the body. I understand it's in a shallow grave out back."

Jason and Bransome were partway through processing the cabin when a commotion outside drew their attention. A young woman was pleading with one of the officers.

"Can you do without me for a few minutes?" Jason said.

A head nod answered his question.

Jason stepped around the blood spatters and onto the porch. Thank God. She had come in an unmarked vehicle. Yolanda Torres looked like a college student in her tight jeans and short cropped button-up blouse. An inch of flesh separated the garments, revealing a silver ring in the tight skin of her navel. She was new to the paper but already had passed several of her colleagues in terms of quality assignments. Using a baseball euphemism, she was a three-skill player. She had looks, personality, and smarts. Gobs of smarts.

Jason cleared his throat, hoping the officer would reel in his tongue. "She's a reporter—newspaper, not television. Doing a story on the murders. She's here to observe."

Yolanda's scowl jolted Jason. He knew she could

speak for herself, and her patience was thin for situations like this—where two men talked around her like she wasn't here.

The officer scanned Jason from head to foot and back with a testosterone glare. "I'm not going to let this turn into a circus." He turned his head to Yolanda and his look softened. "I can't let you past the tape."

She glanced at Jason, who shrugged.

"That's fine," she said. "I'll wait out here, if you don't mind. Can I ask you a few questions?"

The officer's cheeks pulled into a smile.

Jason stepped aside, but he couldn't yank the officer's attention from Yolanda. "I'll get back inside. The sooner we get done, the sooner we can get home."

The sequential logic seemed to register with the officer, perhaps because of the "get home" proviso. He nodded at Yolanda. "I can't tell you much."

Yolanda walked over a few steps and motioned to Jason. She leaned close, her voice a whisper. "Thanks. He's a piece of work."

"He's doing his job." Jason smiled. With his ID badge firmly clipped to his shirt pocket, defense of a fellow law enforcement employee came out, as if by default. "You got all of the background information I sent?"

"Yes, but I have a few questions."

"You'd better save them for later. I've got to get back in there. Detective Bransome is all business. I'm just now getting on his good side."

Yolanda's eyes swept up, her angle in line with the open door and what was inside. She gasped. "I'll be here." She walked back over to the officer.

Jason rushed back inside and stopped short. Bransome looked like he hadn't moved. The detective lifted another print and shook his head.

"I don't understand. Why did she leave all the evidence this time?"

Jason picked up the camera. "Question of the year."

"This one is real sloppy. It's not like the others."

"Maybe she doesn't care anymore. If this is her last one, maybe she didn't bother to be neat. Maybe she thought Eddie didn't deserve care and precision."

Bransome stood up straight and stretched his back. "Perps don't change their ways this much."

"Maybe Lilin's planning on disappearing. Maybe this is her final taunt."

"Or maybe someone else did this one."

"Not the bet thing again," Jason said. "Why would Agnes want to kill Eddie? Up until a couple of weeks ago, she'd never heard of him."

"Let's see what the prints say."

Jason surveyed the scene and grimaced. The uniqueness of the view didn't jump out. It exploded. Still, it couldn't be Agnes. She wouldn't do something like this. She couldn't. Could she? "Okay, but if she's involved, she was probably forced into it. Maybe Lilin framed Agnes so she could make her escape."

CHAPTER 32

THE SUN WAS ABOUT TO DIVE INTO THE PACIFIC, producing a narrow band of glare above the pink and orange cloud cover that stood away at the horizon. The drive to Mendocino was boring if one took the inland route and slow with the coastal highway. But speed wasn't a necessity since Bransome had said he wouldn't be able to process anything tonight. He had plans with the missus.

Jason pulled into the parking lot of a poorly marked restaurant in Bodega Bay and let the engine idle. A sudden hankering for calamari and shrimp, and any number of other invertebrates, moved his hand to turn the key in the ignition. He wanted anything that didn't bleed red.

What was his next move? He still wanted to find Agnes, but what would happen if he went out on his own again? Bransome hadn't said a word about the initial trip to Inverness, although Jason sensed an undercurrent of tension, a slight reversal in their treaty.

The memory of Yolanda's pale-faced reaction to the murder scene brought his mind back to Eddie. Yolanda had stayed behind to watch over the body. The coroner was still processing the grave site, with the body in place, when Jason and Bransome had left. The corpse would probably sit there for several more hours before being lifted out and placed in a body bag. Then more processing of the grave would be necessary.

Based on the demeanor of the coroner, Jason guessed that once the body was removed, the site would be sealed for the night. Tomorrow's light would be needed to complete evidence collection.

Jason mouthed a thank-you to Yolanda. Because of her help, he'd have an early night, so he could be at the Mendocino Police Station first thing in the morning.

In his haste to shower and get moving, the bathroom floor didn't receive proper towel cover, and the slippery tile nearly claimed a victim. He dressed in a hurry and swept his coat off the chest of drawers, where he'd thrown it in a heap the previous evening. Three envelopes fell to the floor.

"Shit. Forgot to take them in."

He picked up the mail he had stuffed in his pocket on his last trip to Agnes's house and shuffled through the pieces. All bills: Pacific Gas and Electric, State Farm Insurance, U-Store self-storage center. The last one was addressed to Gertrude Hahn, not to Agnes.

Two envelopes fell back to the floor as the third yielded to Jason's tear. Due: rental for space E-24. He scanned the due date and the last payment information. It was a monthly bill. Agnes had been paying it since Gert died.

The U-Store sat behind Agnes's house, separated by Agnes's five-and-a-half-foot wooden fence, and only inches behind it, a tall chain-link fence topped with razor wire. He'd walked the wooden fence earlier, from Agnes's backyard. It appeared intact, but he hadn't squeezed behind all of the tall junipers. Maybe a detour on the way to the police station was in order.

An urge pulled at him. More of an instinct, from his experience as a reporter. If something smelled fishy, chances were there were scales on the floor. Lilin had been watching Agnes. She had put a package on Agnes's back porch. Only the two fences separated the U-Store from Agnes's backyard.

Jason paused in the motel room doorway. How would Bransome react if he went off on his own again? Bransome didn't have to say anything. Jason had seen the look many times on Christian Mulvaney's face, felt the icy change in demeanor. Neither Mulvaney nor Bransome were subtle.

He looked down at the envelope in his hand. What

if space E-24 held a clue about Lilin? More importantly, a clue about Agnes? He slammed the door and jogged to his Volvo.

A rolling gate guarded the entrance to the U-Store. Evidently, the renters slid a card key into a drive-up receptacle to gain entrance. Jason waited for fifteen minutes, hoping someone would open the gate so he could slip in behind the car before the gate closed. Today didn't bring that kind of luck. Maybe the bright sunshine and the long shadows got in the way.

He swung the Volvo around and parked it on the street ten yards down from the entrance. Slinking to the back of the car, he scanned both ways along the street. Deserted. The trunk hatch creaked like a casket lid in a horror film. A quick shuffle through a mound of meaningful debris produced a rolled and tied canvas tool kit—a Boy Scout's be-prepared dream, with standard and jeweler's screwdrivers, assorted lightweight pliers and clamping devices, cutting and boring instruments, a dental mirror, a magnetic retriever, and, most important, lock picks. In the final pocket, he found an M-80 firecracker and a screw-cap tube of waterproof matches.

M-80s were a kid's fantasy. About an inch-and-a-half long, and as big around as a man's thumb, they packed a punch that could lift a heavy rock. The equivalent of several cherry bombs. A two-inch waterproof fuse jutted from the middle of the barrel instead of the end like other firecrackers. He tried to remember why he put it in the kit. Maybe for a fishing trip.

He shoved the roll into his jacket pocket and lowered the trunk to contact, then pushed hard until it clicked.

The portion of the fence into which the gate rolled wasn't capped with razor wire, just two straight strands of standard barbed wire. He scanned for traffic and waited for a pickup to idle by before he scaled the fence. At the top, he braced himself on one of the vertical spires that held the barbed wire, and placed his hand on the top wire, between barbs. Pushing down, he swung his leg over and found a foothold on the far side of the fence top. His weight shifted without a snag, but then the trailing pant leg caught a spur and compromised his balance. He had a choice to make, to move to an even more unstable position to try to free the captured pant leg, or let it rip with a quick pull. The latter won out. The pants could be converted to cutoffs after this was all over.

The rows of storage units strung away from the gate in parallel lines, building A to the left, building whatever to the right, and building E right in front of him. He walked down the edge of the asphalt driveway, counting as he went. Two-thirds of the way to the end of the long building he came to a stop. Unit E-24 was the size of a single garage, closed by an upward sliding garage-type door. The handle in the middle of the door held a standard-key, recessed lock.

Jason looked up and down the alley-like driveway. Building E was in direct line with the front gate, giving an unobstructed view of the street, or rather, giving those on the street an unobstructed view of what he was doing.

He pulled the tool kit from his jacket pocket and withdrew the lock picks. He worked them in the lock like knitting needles laying down garter rib stitches. His shadow, projected on the garage door by the morning sun, mimicked his actions.

"Bad feeling about this."

The lock didn't yield. It was recessed enough to limit the angular movements of the picks.

"Come on, damn it." He hit the door with his open palm and the rattling sound echoed in the barren alley. He tried again. The tumblers moved, but not quite enough.

His thighs cramped from the crouch, so he knelt on the cold asphalt and leaned back. He moved the tumblers to the catch point again, and gave them a hard jerk. One of the picks fell to the ground, but the lock clicked over. He tried the handle, and it turned.

A final look to the street, then another in the opposite direction verified the grounds were deserted. Jason stood and dusted off the knees of his Levi's. He put the lock picks back into the tool kit and slipped it into his pocket. Inside the garage, he expected to see old trunks, a few pieces of near-antique furniture, and stacks of old, framed family photographs. Boxes of who knows what probably included at least one family treasure worthy of appraisal on the *Antiques Roadshow*.

He turned the handle again and moved the door. It was well balanced and not heavy at all. With little effort, the door slid upward, disappearing into the garage.

He spotted the grill inside the garage at the same moment the engine howled to life. A flash of black. He dodged to his left. Tires screeched. All he saw was black and chrome. He dove, but the bumper caught his right foot, spinning him to the ground. His head thumped the pavement and a rear tire screamed past. Less than six inches from his forehead.

The GTO gained traction through the turn and accelerated toward the gate. Hard braking started a four-wheel skid that brought the car to a stop next to the gate, which whirred into its slow slide open, obviously activated by an electric eye.

The car lurched forward. It didn't wait for the gate to open all the way and the right fender clipped the gate, nearly throwing the car into a spin. It corrected and screeched into a left turn on the road. The low growl of the engine warned Jason not to follow.

He scrambled to his feet and nearly collapsed. A stinging sensation radiated upward from his ankle. He tried to put his weight on the leg but drew it back to toe contact when the pain objected.

He couldn't see the intersection with Reese Drive, but he could hear the unique rumble of the GTO's engine. It roared away to the north.

Jason pulled the cell phone from his pocket and took a chance. Bransome answered on the second ring.

"It's Jason. I found the GTO. It was in the U-Store behind Agnes's house. It just took off. North on Reese Drive. Hurry."

"Get in here. To the station. Now." Bransome's phrases came through the phone like a series of pants, like he was running.

"Can I do anything?"

Bransome hung up without saying another word.

Jason limped into the garage. His foot hurt, but not enough to prevent him from putting some of his weight on it. The trunks, furniture, and boxes were all there, pushed to the back and side walls of the space.

The experience in crime scene data collection told him to leave the garage contents alone. A flick of the lock and the garage door slid down and sealed. He tested the handle. It was locked. He'd get Bransome out to work the site later. Right now he wanted to get to the police station as fast as he could. But he hesitated. Fifteen yards to his right, the chain-link fence loomed, separating the U-Store lot from Agnes's fence. It was every bit of six feet in height, and the coiled razor wire on its top made it look like a prison fence from this side. He walked to the barrier.

In both directions it looked sound. He meshed his fingers and gave it a strong shake. Solid. Was there any way Agnes could get through? The question warranted an inspection.

At the far right of Agnes's yard, her wooden fence came within three inches of the chain link. Another shake confirmed the integrity of the fence. He looked closely for breaks, cut links, or other evidence of trespass. There were none. He walked along the fence, from pole to pole, checking each section. No more than six inches separated the fences, and both were completely intact.

At the other end of Agnes's yard, the wooden fence posted even closer to the chain link—only an inch or two of separation. The U-Store fence was solid, uncompromised.

He couldn't see a way Agnes could get through the fence to the garage. No human could climb over through the razor wire, and the asphalt had been spread after the fence was erected. It embedded the chain link at least a couple of inches at the bottom. He had kicked at the bottom of each section. None gave a hint of a gap.

A flood of questions swamped his mind. Was Lilin that close all along? Was that how she kept an eye on Agnes? And why did Agnes keep paying the bill? Had she ever visited the U-Store? He limped to the front gate.

Who was behind the wheel of the GTO? Obviously, Agnes wasn't around to answer the questions. Was she still alive? It didn't look like there had been two people in the car.

Sirens wailed in the distance. It sounded like they headed north, presumably in search of the GTO. It would be easy to spot, but too many side roads split from the highway to Fort Bragg. They'd have to be lucky.

Jason reached the front gate, and this time his luck was running. A car pulled from the street to the entrance of the U-Store and the driver carded the receptacle. Jason gave a wave as the car passed and ambled through the gate before it closed. His right foot hurt now—the driving foot. It might take a while to get to the station.

Jason pulled into the police station parking lot and grimaced when he pumped the brake pedal. Pushing on the gas didn't hurt, but braking was another story. He'd driven slowly all the way, under twenty-five, taking advantage of the lower gears of the automatic transmission to slow the car when approaching traffic lights or stop signs. He tried to let his mind work between twinges of pain.

If that was Lilin, what was she doing in the garage? Did she sleep there, in the car? It couldn't have been Agnes. Even if she had a way to get through the fence, why would she stay in the garage? She could have snuck back into her house without anyone knowing, and as long as she didn't disturb the lighting trap Bransome had set, she could have gone about her activities, undetected.

A terrible thought stopped him from getting out of his car. He pictured Agnes, lying in her own house, blood oozing from Lilin's razor slices. Only one person in the GTO. The other taking her last breaths while the police, and everyone else, pursued the driver.

A call to Officer Wilson wouldn't do any good. He had undoubtedly joined in the chase. Jason thought about driving to Agnes's house and breaking in, but Bransome's tone was unmistakable. Besides, his foot hurt, and he didn't want to miss any news about the GTO.

He pulled himself from the car and hobbled into the station directly into the detective's workroom. He clipped on his ID badge. Recognized and accepted, he had free run of most of the building. Too bad he didn't know where they kept the fingerprint data from Inverness. He could start processing it.

A computer printout lay on the blotter of Bransome's desk. Jason plopped in Bransome's chair and lifted the single sheet.

"Mother of God."

CHAPTER 33

THE COT IN THE HOLDING CELL WAS A WELCOME SIGHT. Jason's head swirled and his foot hurt. He had to think this through. It didn't make sense.

The scene in the cabin had seemed strange, different from all of the other murders. There was more blood, more of a mess. Compared to the other sites, it reeked of inefficiency and carelessness.

And the prints—none had been left at any of the other murder scenes. Why now? Why so messy? Why so different? He'd rationalized that earlier, but was he just kidding himself? The prints in Inverness were Agnes's. Bransome had come in early and processed some of them. The printout confirmed it, without a doubt.

Jason had trouble catching his breath. Agnes had killed Eddie. But why? Was she working with Lilin all along? Her performance was Oscar worthy if so. But what if Lilin had forced Agnes to kill Eddie? That easily fit in

319

his conceptualized view of Lilin and her desire to get even. And what if all of the prints were planted, and the change in technique was just a frame job? With the U-Store connection, Agnes could be blamed for all the murders. Lilin could go back into the woodwork and vanish.

But then, where was Agnes? Surely, Lilin hadn't planned to be surprised at the U-Store. And now that she was on the run, what would become of her twin sister, unless her fate had already been sealed?

Jason gasped. What if Agnes hadn't even been in Inverness? Lilin could have planted Agnes's fingerprints. A severed finger? No. Some of the prints were of all five digits, complete with a palm print. Jason's next gasp echoed in the holding cell.

Would Lilin know that identical twins have different fingerprints? She'd have to if she'd intended the planted fingerprints to point at Agnes. Maybe Agnes's hands were safe, intact. But the information about the fingerprints of twins was hardly a secret. It could be found on a number of Web sites. Lilin seemed to be thorough, prepared. And smart. Very smart. She knew Agnes had been released following the initial arrest. There had to be a reason for that. Just how much did Lilin know about the details of the case?

A picture of Agnes, her throat slit from ear to ear, one hand severed, came to Jason—all too real. He turned on the cot and groaned. He'd give Bransome the rest of the day. If there wasn't any news by late afternoon, he'd break into Agnes's house again.

Jason startled awake. A commotion in the station stirred the air with sound and energy. He'd dozed off, but for how long? A pull on the shirtsleeve exposed his watch. It was one thirty.

Bransome stomped in and rattled the bars before Jason could get up.

"We got her. We got Lilin Hahn."

Jason swiveled to a sitting position and rubbed his eyes. "You caught up to her?"

"She started out heading to Fort Bragg, but I had a hunch she might have turned on Highway 20 to get to 101. That would be the best way to disappear quickly. I was right. I caught up to her just outside of Willits. Another ten minutes, and who knows where she'd be."

"Is it Lilin?"

"It sure doesn't look like Agnes. I mean, it does, but Agnes wouldn't dress like that or act like that."

"Act like what?"

"She fought us the whole way, and you wouldn't believe her mouth. I've never heard language like that from a woman. And then, once she calmed down in the backseat, she started offering me all kinds of sexual treats if I'd let her go. If my wife heard what she offered me, well . . ." He wiped his brow. "I bet Agnes has never even dreamed about some of the things this woman wanted to do with me. At my age, I don't even know if some of them are possible."

"Tempting, huh?"

Bransome laughed. "The next time with the wife isn't going to be the same. I won't be able to get some of the visuals out of my mind for a while."

Jason stood up and immediately favored his left leg.

"You all right? You want a doctor?"

"Bumper caught me when she peeled out of the garage. It's bruised, but I'll be okay." He limped forward. "What are you going to do with Lilin?"

"After I Mirandized her, I started asking questions. She clammed up. Now she won't talk. At all. I'll try again in a little while, but I'm not optimistic. She turned on a dime. We've got a call in to the shrink who talked to Agnes earlier. Maybe she can help. Wilson suggested we put her on a suicide watch. We don't want to blow this case."

"Has she been booked?"

"Going on right now."

"Did she say anything about where Agnes is?"

"Not a word. That was my first question, and that's when she went silent. Sorry, but we don't have a clue about where she might be."

"I have a hunch. Could you send someone out to

check Agnes's house again? I have a bad feeling about it."

"Good idea. I'll have Wilson stop by on his way to the U-Store. I want him to secure the garage. What space was it?"

"E-24. I didn't touch anything, but I did look inside. I don't think you'll find much."

Bransome shook his head. "This is weird."

"What's weird?"

"I've never been on a case like this. Where I've been so schizophrenic about the suspect. It's Agnes. It's Lilin. It's Agnes. It's Lilin. I've always had a clear suspect in mind. On a few occasions I was surprised, but even then, there was the surprise and then it was done. None of this back and forth crap. And I'm still as confused as I was weeks ago." He took a deep breath. "You know about the prints from Inverness?"

"Sorry. I saw the printout on your desk."

"I left it there for you to see. Even with Agnes's prints, I'm having trouble running with my initial gut feeling about her. Even if she was involved in Inverness, I'm not so sure she did the other murders."

"Sounds like a flip-flop to me."

"Yeah, but ten minutes from now, I'll probably be back on the other side of the fence."

"When do you plan to talk to Lilin again?"

"After the shrink gets here and has a go at her."

Jason fingered his chin. "If nothing else works, you

mind if I have a try?"

"I'll go with anything that'll get some answers. But first, we want to make sure of who we have. The computers are down right now. They probably won't be fixed until tomorrow morning some time. Can you be here first thing?"

"Is everything around a pig's ass pork?"

CHAPTER 34

JASON PEERED THROUGH THE ONE-WAY WINDOW OF THE interrogation room. He felt like a Peeping Tom.

Lilin looked disheveled. Her hair was pulled straight back, but wayward strands fell from the tie like frayed fibers in a worn rope. Her jail jumpsuit hung on her, buttoned to the very top, just under her chin. Her eyes looked unfocused, vacant, peering at a focal point somewhere beyond the interrogation room table.

Bransome appeared angry, or frustrated. Jason knew the look—balled fists at his sides; intense, squinty eyes; reddened face. He'd been on the receiving end of Bransome's look several times. And he had to admit it was intimidating.

Lilin didn't react. No matter where Bransome paced—in front of the table, behind it—she just stared through the table. He leaned toward her and barked a question. Turned away for another. He came right up behind her and whispered in her ear. She just stared.

Bransome threw his hands upward and stomped out of the room, into the hallway. He saw Jason at the two-way mirror and shook his head.

Jason stepped in Bransome's direction. "Has she said anything about where Agnes is?"

Bransome's voice boomed. "That is Agnes."

"What?"

"The prints. From her booking. It's Agnes."

Jason slumped against the wall. His knees nearly buckled. Flashes of information danced in his mind, but a knot of surprise choked off any hope of consolidation. He couldn't speak. His mouth moved, but nothing came out.

Bransome shoved his hands into his pockets. "The answer is no."

Jason squeaked a single word: "What?"

"No. She hasn't said anything. Not a word. It's like no one's home. We don't know where Lilin is. Being nice doesn't work. Threatening her doesn't work. I'm about to pop."

Jason turned back to the two-way mirror. His eyes flicked to one of Agnes's hands, then to the other. He rubbed his eyes into a blaze of fireworks. "Can I talk to her?"

"Not yet. The shrink's coming back in. She thinks she made some kind of a connection last night. She didn't get any information, but she thinks Lilin, I mean

Agnes, was about to talk."

"I can't believe Agnes nearly ran me over."

"If she could carve up Eddie Hahn like that, she could put a couple of tire treads across you without blinking."

"I'm still having a problem with Inverness. It's all too convenient."

"Maybe so, but at least we have one of the sisters. That's more than we had this time yesterday."

Jason and Bransome pressed close to the window side of the two-way mirror. Agnes hadn't moved. The cheap audio system hissed at them through the small, overhead speaker.

CHAPTER 35

AGNES SLUMPED. HER SHOULDERS BARELY MOVED WITH her breathing. The rest of her body was frozen in mannequin stiffness.

"Agnes, do you remember me? I'm Dr. April Leahy. I spoke with you last night, and once before, some time ago. Are you feeling all right?"

Agnes didn't look up. Her eyes burned, but she refused to even blink.

"I know you've been through a lot in the last few weeks. I'm here to help you. But first, you have to help yourself."

Psychiatric double-talk.

"You're in serious trouble now. What you need more than anything is to let someone help you. I can do that."

She felt invisible.

"We know you were in Inverness, in Eddie's cabin. And we know he killed Ella. Is that why you were there?"

Agnes glanced up in time to see Dr. Leahy look up into the mirror on the wall and nod. Agnes tilted her head back down and finally blinked to keep the tears that filled her eyes from falling.

Dr. Leahy reached across the table and put her hand on Agnes's hands, which were folded together, flat on the table.

"I'm so sorry about Ella. She didn't deserve that. And neither did you."

The tears let go and ran to Agnes's jaw.

"I understand how upsetting that must have been. You must've been very angry. And sometimes when we're angry, we do things we ordinarily wouldn't do. I can understand that."

Agnes dropped her head and her shoulders heaved forward. She gripped Dr. Leahy's hand.

"You've got to talk about it, Agnes. It's the only way to get through it."

Agnes lifted her head and returned her gaze to the middle of the table.

"Can you talk about it?"

You can do it.

She bobbed her head.

"You were in Eddie Hahn's cabin in Inverness the night before last, right?"

Agnes sighed and bobbed her head.

"Did you do something to Eddie?"

Another bob.

"Did anyone help you?"

Agnes shook her head side to side.

"Lilin wasn't there?"

You can do it.

Agnes lifted her head and made eye contact with Dr. Leahy, then dropped her head and shook it. She peered upward, under her brow, and watched Dr. Leahy glance at the mirror again.

"Agnes, do you know where Lilin is right now?"

Agnes froze.

"You don't have to tell me where. I want to know if you know where she is."

She shook her head.

"Thank you, Agnes, you're being very helpful. I have a few more questions, then I'll let you get some rest." Dr. Leahy thumbed backward through the pages of her steno tablet. "Are you all right to go on?"

She bobbed her head.

"The other murders. Did you have anything to do with them?"

Agnes bobbed her head.

Dr. Leahy leaned forward. "Was Lilin at any of the other murders with you?"

Agnes cringed then looked up at Dr. Leahy. She shook her head and lowered it.

Good girl.

"Are you telling me that you committed all of the murders?"

Agnes didn't respond.

"It's okay. We can help you. But we have to know all the details. It's the only way." Dr. Leahy stared. "Did you hurt all of those men?"

Agnes slowly bobbed her head.

"All of them?"

A single bob.

"And that woman in Benicia?"

Agnes looked up, her brow furrowed to deep creases. She dropped her eyes and shrugged her shoulders.

"You killed a woman, too?"

Yes.

"Yes."

Dr. Leahy drew out the next exhalation. "And Lilin didn't have anything to do with them?"

She shook her head.

Dr. Leahy gripped Agnes's hands again. She shifted in her chair. "Now, I have to ask a few difficult questions. Please try to answer them. They're really important."

Agnes felt muscles throughout her body tense and hold.

"Was Eddie going to be the last?"

The tension didn't let go.

"Is Eddie the one you were after all along?" She squeezed Agnes's hands. "This is important."

Bastard got what he deserved.

Agnes pulled her hands away.

"Please, Agnes. This information will help you."

No response.

"Okay. I'm sorry. I'll stick to the specifics of the murders. What did you use? A razor?"

Agnes bobbed her head.

"On all of them?"

She raised her head and squinted at Dr. Leahy. "Yes." Her voice was soft, quiet.

"The men were all pretty big. How did you get them to relax?"

She kept her stare on Dr. Leahy, her reply emotionless. "Sex."

"You seduced them?"

"Yes."

"And the man and woman in Benicia?"

Agnes paused. "Sex."

"And you didn't do anything else before you cut them?"

"No." Agnes dropped her eyes back to the table and picked at the wood grain. "I just waited until they relaxed or fell asleep."

"And then you cut them?"

"Yes."

"Didn't any of them struggle?"

She looked into Dr. Leahy's eyes and squinted. Her hands balled into fists. "Eddie."

"None of the others?"

Her hands relaxed. "No."

"So you didn't subdue them in any way?"

"No."

Dr. Leahy took a deep breath. "You're being very helpful. Thank you."

Yes, thank you.

"You're welcome."

"Can I ask a couple more questions?"

Agnes shrugged, but maintained eye contact.

"Why did you kill all those people?"

Agnes held her expression. She shrugged her shoulders.

"You don't know?"

She shrugged again.

"Why did you kill Eddie?"

She felt her eyes well again. Tears released. She looked down at the table.

"Can you tell me?"

Agnes's shoulders bounced with her sobs.

"I'm sorry to upset you, but I have to ask once more. Do you know where Lilin is?"

"No."

"Would you like some time?"

Her sobs continued.

"Thank you, Agnes. I'll give you some time now."

Good girl.

CHAPTER 36

JASON LUNGED FROM THE TWO-WAY MIRROR TO THE interrogation room door before Dr. Leahy turned the knob. He couldn't believe what he had heard. Agnes killing all those people? Using sex? No way.

Dr. Leahy walked into the hallway and let the gas piston close the heavy interrogation room door. She turned and faced Jason.

Bransome hurried to their sides. "Great job. You remember Jason Powers?"

Dr. Leahy smiled and lowered her eyelids partway. She held out her hand, knuckles up, like he was supposed to kiss it instead of shake it.

Bransome shoved his hands into his pockets. "She didn't do them?"

Dr. Leahy shook her head. "No. I don't think she did. Except for Eddie. She could have done that one. Did you see the way she reacted to the questions? No emotion with all of the others. She broke down when we talked about Eddie."

Jason feathered his hair with his fingers. "You don't think Agnes was involved in any of the murders except Eddie's?"

Dr. Leahy and Bransome answered, "No," in unison.

"What do we do now?" Dr. Leahy inquired.

Bransome pulled his hands from his pockets. "I'll get with the DA and see what he suggests. We have a confession. Let's see what he wants to do with the case."

"Does Agnes have to stay in that room?" she said. "It's intimidating to her."

"Do you think a cell's any better?"

"Yes. It's probably a safe place to her. Besides, she can lie down. She's very emotional."

Bransome shoved his hands back into his pockets. "Please don't sedate her like you did last night. We'll have to talk with her again later today. I'd like the DA to hear her confession."

"Wait." Jason edged back into the conversation. "I don't get it. Why would Agnes cop to several murders she didn't do? Even if she did kill Eddie, why would she claim the others?"

Bransome huffed. "Good question."

"I have a theory," Dr. Leahy said. Her eyes met Jason's and she smiled.

Both men stared.

"Okay." She tugged on her jacket lapel. "Look what Gert did for Ella. Gert was driving the car the night they had the accident that took Ella's leg. Agnes said Gert rejected suitors because there wouldn't be anyone to look after Ella. Gert gave her life to her sister, Ella."

"And you think Agnes is doing the same thing for Lilin?" Bransome said.

"Holy shit," Jason said. "That sounds like the Agnes I know."

"Guilt is a powerful emotion," Dr. Leahy said.

"Why should Agnes feel guilty?" Jason said.

"She had a good life," Dr. Leahy said. "Maybe Lilin didn't. Maybe Agnes felt partially responsible."

Bransome smiled. "But do you think she killed Eddie?"

"Yes," Dr. Leahy said. "I think she did that one."

"She could have been manipulated by Lilin." Jason's voice elevated an octave. "Or Lilin could have planted the fingerprints. I talked to her. That sounds like Lilin to me."

Bransome smiled.

CHAPTER 37

District Attorney Scott Grayson joined Bransome, Dr. Leahy, and Jason in a conference room. They all remained standing.

Jason scanned the little man—midforties, with dark, intense eyes that moved slowly, as if he were decelerating everything into slow motion.

"Who's this?" he said, pointing at Jason.

Bransome waved his hand in Jason's direction. "This is Jason Powers. He works for the *Santa Rosa Press Democrat*. Jason, this is District Attorney Scott Grayson."

Grayson looked down at Jason's hand but didn't shake it. "Are you crazy? A reporter? Come on, Art. You know these discussions are privileged."

"He's okay. We hired him for part-time work. He's been helping process the data. A good part of the information we have in this case came from his research. He helped break it."

Jason fingered his ID badge and smiled.

Grayson eyed Jason for what seemed like minutes. "Conflict of interest, wouldn't you say?"

Jason broadened his smile.

Grayson didn't blink. "Everything said in here is off the record. Got it?"

"Agreed," Jason said. He wanted to salute, but thought better of it.

"If you leak one word, I'll have your ass." He looked at Dr. Leahy. "Sorry."

She looked at Jason and giggled.

Jason glanced at Dr. Leahy and smiled. "You have my word."

Dr. Leahy's eyes went to the floor, then back up to Jason's.

Grayson shot ferret like glares at Dr. Leahy and Jason, then fixed his stare on Jason. "You two want to get a room somewhere?"

Bransome's voice boomed. "So what do we do with Agnes?"

"This is a tough one, but I think I have a solution." Grayson kept his eyes on Jason. "You have the evidence to convict on the Edward Hahn murder, right?"

Bransome puffed his chest. "Yes."

"Solid?"

"As granite."

"Good. With that, you could tie in the other murders, too. Right?"

Bransome nodded, bending at the waist. "It would be circumstantial, but with the Eddie Hahn tie, we may be able to pull it off."

Grayson turned his gaze to Bransome. "Doesn't sound so solid."

"No. A sharp jury would probably throw out the others."

"That's what I think, too," Grayson said. "And what about Lilin Hahn? You said you don't think she'll kill again, that this was all about getting Edward Hahn. Right?"

Bransome looked at Dr. Leahy and then at Jason. "That's the consensus."

"Normally, I'm not one to risk that, but we do have to think about the public. Other than the Edward Hahn murder, which ones have the most complete forensic evidence?"

"From our point of view, that'd be the Anchor Bay, Point Arena, and Fort Bragg murders." Bransome tapped his lips with his right forefinger. "Only because we worked those scenes from the start."

"Perfect. We let Agnes confess to Anchor Bay, Point Arena, and Fort Bragg as well, and keep the other ones open, in the inactive file. If Lilin decides to kill again, or if we catch her, we can work the other murders on her, and then bring those three back from Agnes to Lilin."

Jason slapped his thigh. "That's not fair to Agnes. You let her confess to murders you don't think she committed, and then say you'll pull them back later if you get Lilin? That sucks. It's not ethical."

Jason felt Grayson's stare burn through him.

"There's a clear benefit to Agnes in this plan," Grayson said. "If we do it this way, I won't seek the death penalty. She'll get life without parole. She could get death from the Edward Hahn murder. The public is that worked up about it."

What a weasel. "It doesn't sound so fair to me."

Grayson frowned and exhaled through his nose. "I have to answer to the people of this state. The public is on edge. They need to have some closure on this case. They'll take the confessions and not want blood, as long as they know the murderer will be behind bars for the rest of her life."

"But the murderer won't be behind bars," Jason said. "Are you willing to gamble that Lilin won't kill again?"

"I'll stand tall and admit my mistake once we catch Lilin and put her away. We may even consider making Agnes parole-eligible in that case."

Jason looked at Bransome and shook his head. He felt his face heat up. "And if Lilin murders again, what are you going to say to the families of the victims? They're people of this state."

Bransome looked at the ground.

Grayson slid in front of Jason, facing Bransome, the back of his head just under Jason's face. "Are we agreed?"

Jason shuffled back a step.

Dr. Leahy raised her hand. "I have a question."

Grayson nodded.

"Agnes needs help. Have you considered the possibility that she's not mentally competent? I could make a good case for it."

Grayson's face turned maroon and his lips tightened into thin, straight lines. "I can parade a line of prominent psychiatrists by you who agrees she is. God damn it, she slit Eddie Hahn's throat. Do you think the public's going to stand by and let her go to a mental hospital with a chance of getting out if one of you people think she's suddenly cured?"

"She sliced off his penis and threw it in the sink, too," Dr. Leahy said. "Doesn't sound normal to me."

"She knew exactly what she was doing. He abused her. She got revenge."

"You have good evidence for abuse?" Dr. Leahy asked.

Grayson's mouth opened, but nothing came out for a full three seconds. "I don't want to face the public on this one without the minimum of a life sentence."

Dr. Leahy took a step forward. She was a full inch taller than Grayson. "You don't want to face the public without it, or you don't want to face reappointment?"

Bransome forced his way between them. "All right. All right. Let's see if we can work this out. Let's agree we still have some issues and see if we can find some common ground."

"Wait." Jason stepped around next to Bransome and stabbed a finger at Grayson's chest. "I get it. Eddie Hahn's murder occurred in Marin County. And the early ones in Sonoma County. But if she confesses to Eddie's, along with the three that happened here in Mendocino County, you can run the show up here instead of letting the Marin County people handle it. You can get the credit for putting away the dreaded serial killer, and the men in the Bay Area can go back to picking up women in bars. As long as she confesses to the ones that occurred here. Very clever. But she isn't the serial killer."

Grayson slapped Jason's hand away. His eyes narrowed. "She confessed to all of them. I can take that and run all the way to the needle."

"And I can go back on the off-the-record thing." He inched forward and poked at Grayson's chest again. "How do you think the officials from the other counties will react?"

Bransome thrust his forearm into Jason's chest and moved him back a step. "That's enough. Let's see how Agnes's lawyer reacts."

Jason held Grayson's stare. Silence fell on the air, broken by the ring of Jason's cell phone.

CHAPTER 38

JASON PUT HIS PALMS ON THE GLASS OF THE ONE-WAY window. Agnes looked like she was fading—like she had lost twenty-five pounds in the last couple of hours. Twenty-five pounds she didn't have to lose. Her skin was the color of milk.

She slinked across the interrogation room and sat at the table next to her lawyer, who'd entered the room a few minutes earlier.

Bransome walked to the door of the interrogation room and looked at Jason, Grayson, and Dr. Leahy.

"Here goes nothing."

Agnes didn't flinch when the door opened and closed. Her focus remained on the table. Her lawyer nodded without altering his frown.

Bransome pulled out the chair across from them and flopped down. "Hello, Agnes. Are you feeling okay?"

Agnes didn't respond.

"Thank you for talking with Dr. Leahy earlier. It was very helpful."

"Why wasn't I called?" the lawyer said. "Are you trying to pull something here?"

"I told the desk clerk to call you. She said she left a message on your pager."

"I didn't get a message."

"Well, we sent one. Besides, Agnes agreed to talk."

"To a psychiatrist?"

"Dr. Leahy talked with her before, remember? She's on Agnes's side."

The lawyer shook his head. "This is classic Grayson. That little prick is going to go down." He pulled a legal pad and pen from his briefcase. "Get on with what you want. And don't try to pull any more end runs."

Behind the glass, Jason looked at Grayson and smiled. The speaker made their voices sound high-pitched, almost cartoonish.

Bransome straightened in his chair and turned to face the lawyer. "You know she's confessed to all of the killings?"

"I want to hear her say it to you now." The lawyer turned to Agnes. "Did the detective, or any other people force you to say anything you didn't want to say?"

Agnes shook her head.

"You have to answer out loud. Did they force you to say anything?"

"No."

"Did you tell them you committed all the murders?"

She nodded. "Yes."

"Remember what we talked about? Do you still want to say that you did them all?"

Another head nod. "Yes."

The lawyer looked at Bransome. "What kind of deal does that weasel, Grayson, have cooked up? Where is he anyway? Why isn't he in here?"

Bransome looked at the mirror out of the corners of his eyes. "He has a case."

Jason chuckled and looked at Grayson. Quite a play going on here.

Grayson's face twitched red, like a lobster dropped in boiling water.

"I'm sure he does," the lawyer said.

Bransome cleared his throat. "She pleads to Inverness, Anchor Bay, Point Arena, and Fort Bragg, she'll get life in prison, no chance of parole. If it goes to trial, Grayson will go for the death penalty."

"Grayson is amazing. He doesn't want to share this one, does he? Power-hungry turd." The lawyer leaned over to Agnes. "Do you understand what all this means?"

She nodded.

"And you agree to it?"

Her eyes didn't leave the table. "Yes."

He turned to Bransome. "How long do we have?"

Bransome glanced at the mirror.

Jason thought he looked worried.

"Uh. I don't know. We didn't discuss a time limit."

"Okay. I'll let you know tomorrow. I want to sleep on it, and I want Agnes to sleep on it, too."

Behind the glass, Grayson spun around and whispered a curse.

Bransome stood and shook the lawyer's hand. They both walked to the door.

Jason looked around as Grayson scooted down the hall and disappeared around a corner.

The lawyer exited the interrogation room first and hurried out toward the front doors.

Bransome approached Jason and Dr. Leahy. Grayson peeked, then stormed around the corner in their direction.

"What was that all about?" Grayson said.

Jason's cell phone rang. "Excuse me." He walked down the hall, in the opposite direction of Bransome, Dr. Leahy, and Grayson.

Jason moved to the door of the interrogation room and looked up the hall. Bransome and Grayson still argued. Dr. Leahy pressed her face close to the one-way glass, as far from the other two as she could get.

Jason took a deep breath and entered the room.

Agnes straightened in her chair when he rounded the table. A faint smile dimpled her cheeks.

"Hi, Agnes. Are you doing okay?"

Agnes stood and pushed her chair back with her legs. "I'm fine. I know what I'm doing."

Jason walked around and took Agnes's hands in his. "Do you know where Lilin is?"

"No. I don't."

"Can you call her? Do you know her number?"

"Yes."

Jason pulled her a little closer. "You should call her and let her know you're okay. Does she know what you're doing?"

Agnes looked down at the floor. "She knows."

Jason reached into his pocket. "Here. Use my cell phone. You won't have to worry about being traced." He flipped the cover open.

Agnes punched in a series of numbers and put the phone to her ear.

Jason shuffled back two steps and stopped.

"Hello, Lilin? . . . It's Agnes . . . Yes, I'm all right . . ."

Jason walked to the door and stopped, his hand on the knob.

". . . I've done it . . ." Agnes turned and gave Jason a smile. "You're free . . ."

Jason opened the door and Bransome grabbed his shirt and pulled him through. The door eased shut.

Bransome slammed Jason against the opposite wall as Grayson ran up to them. Jason's head spun. Bransome pulled him away and slammed him against the wall again.

"Why the hell did you do that? We had a phone wired up for her, you asshole. You blew any chance we had to get to Lilin."

Agnes's words rang out from the speaker. "I love you, too . . . You're welcome."

Jason managed to spin loose from one of Bransome's hands and avoid a third wall slam. "Wait." He held out his hand.

Bransome looked down. "What's that?"

"The battery," Jason said between breaths. "For the phone."

Dr. Leahy put her hand to her mouth. "Oh my God!" She ran to the window.

Agnes folded the phone and put it on the table.

Dr. Leahy brought her other hand to her mouth as well. "Oh my God."

It took several seconds for it to register with Bransome. He let go of Jason's shirt and took a step back. "How'd you know?"

Grayson lunged at Jason. "What's going on here? Why'd you let him go?"

Bransome stopped Grayson with a stiff arm. "Shut up and listen for once."

Jason leaned against the wall and tried to catch his breath. "The phone call I just got. It was from Yolanda Torres. Out at Inverness. They were working up Eddie's grave site this morning. They found something else."

"What the hell's he talking about?"

Bransome turned to face Grayson. "Just shut the fuck up, okay?"

"Underneath Eddie's body. Something was wrapped tight in sheets." He took several short, deep breaths. "It was another body. Wrapped so tightly it was partially mummified."

Dr. Leahy joined them.

"It was the body of a little girl. Maybe three or four years old. The coroner thinks it's more than twenty years old."

Dr. Leahy gasped. "Oh." She ran back to the window and pressed both palms to the glass. "It's Lilin. My God. Poor Agnes."

"Is somebody going to tell me what the hell is going on?" Grayson said.

Bransome stared at the DA. "Scott, put your hands on your ears."

"What? I'm not in the mood for playing games."

Bransome took a step closer. "I mean it. Put your hands on your ears." His voice boomed in the hall.

Grayson put his hands up near his ears.

"Now, pull your head out of your ass." He turned to

Jason. "Does the coroner think it could be Lilin?"

"He thinks they can get DNA from the bones. We'll have to wait, but in the meantime, I'll lay a handsome bet on it."

Grayson walked over to Dr. Leahy. "Can you tell me what's going on?"

She pointed at Agnes through the glass. "It's Lilin."

"I thought the fingerprints proved it was Agnes."

"It is. She's both of them. She must have seen the whole thing. When she was only three or four. She must have seen her father kill Lilin and bury her body in the backyard. No wonder she shut everything out. No wonder Gert and Ella took her away."

Grayson stomped his foot and balled his hands into fists. "You mean she's schizophrenic? She's both Agnes and Lilin?"

Bransome came up behind Grayson. "Welcome to the obvious, champ."

Dr. Leahy seemed excited. "It's not schizophrenia. It used to be called multiple personality disorder, but now it's DID—dissociative identity disorder. And ever since Charcot and Babinski, most psychologists think it's therapy induced. Not in this case. There hasn't been any therapy. This is the real thing."

"How do you know she isn't cooking all this up?" Grayson kicked at the floor. "To let Lilin get away?"

Bransome started to say something, but Jason interrupted. "We'll let the DNA answer that question. Until then, you may want to contact Agnes's lawyer. And you better meet him face to face instead of having Detective Bransome fake a phone call. I don't think you're going to get your life sentence on this one, so you better start preparing your opinion brief. You agree, Dr. Leahy?"

"She's going to need to be institutionalized, but not in prison. If the DNA comes back as a twin sister, your team of psychiatrists won't disagree with me on this one."

Grayson stomped down the hall and disappeared.

Bransome looked at Jason and smiled. "Sorry about slamming you. Are you all right?"

"I could use a couple of aspirin. But first, we have one more detail to cover. Can you give Wilson a call? There has to be a way to get from Agnes's backyard into the U-Store lot. I checked the fence from one end of Agnes's backyard to the other, but there might be a breach somewhere else. There has to be an opening, or we've got a loose end to explain."

"Done," Bransome said as he walked to the workroom.

Jason opened the door to the interrogation room and hesitated. Agnes turned in the chair and smiled. He walked to the table and slipped the phone back into his pocket.

Agnes stood and reached for him. She put her hands on his shoulders and pulled close, leaving a small gap between them. "Thank you. You are one of the good ones."

He kissed her cheek and took her hands off of his shoulders. "You're welcome. Everything's going to be all right now. They'll take good care of you."

Jason walked to the door and grabbed the knob.

"You'll wait for me?" Her voice sounded different.

He turned around. The smile on her face looked like a blend of Agnes's dimpled grin and Lilin's vicious sneer. The hair on his arms stood straight up as he pushed through the door.

CHAPTER 39

Jason stood in the middle of his living room and
stretched his arms straight out at shoulder height. It was
nice to be back in his own apartment again, listening to
the curses of the golfers on the sixth hole, smelling the
cat pee odor of the wet eucalyptus trees, trying to force
himself to go out on the patio after dark.

It wasn't nice to remember what happened the last
time he was here. He couldn't believe it was Agnes's
hand that held the razor that sliced the air inches from
his neck. Even if it wasn't her mind, it was her hand.
Yet, through it all, Lilin had just used Agnes. Used her
to get to Eddie. Used her for all of the murders. The
only good thing—now Agnes would get the help she deserved. Maybe she could get back what Lilin had taken
from her. Maybe she could be Agnes without Lilin. If
so, Jason wanted to be there.

The Rolling Stones broke into "Beast of Burden"

on the stereo, probably a little loud for the day-sleeping neighbor above. And even though his future at the *Press Democrat* was more unsettled than before, normalcy seemed within reach.

The alternation between guilt and justification had settled at dead center for now. After all, it was his reappearance in Mulvaney's office that had sent the editor into the tizzy that ripped the bulging cerebral artery, depriving the better part of the right side of his brain of oxygen. It had taken Jason a full ten seconds to pick up the phone and dial 911, mostly due to the shock of watching Mulvaney crumple to the floor. If anyone would die standing up, it was Christian Mulvaney.

The latest news helped settle the sliding scale. Mulvaney's family was about to take him off of life support. The doctors found so many nodules in his lungs they'd have an easier time cutting out the good tissue. And the ventilator was about to blow a gasket trying to adequately work lungs that were well below 50 percent functional.

Jason walked to the sliding patio door and unlocked it. He could get two, maybe three hours of work done on the laptop before dusk chased him back inside. The assignments from the interim editor were all simple ones. Easily banged out in fits of effort. He'd fill in the gaps working on his book.

Collecting his computer and stack of notes under his arm, he paused. His favorite part of the song was coming up.

The doorbell interrupted the moment. Jason strode to the door, setting his burden on the credenza. He was mellow enough to be polite to a salesperson. He peered through the peephole and froze. His hands thrust against the door propelling his body backward. He stepped up and looked again.

Light brown hair in a slightly ratted shell. She stood sideways, her face turned away. She turned her head and dipped it forward. Her hair slid across her cheek.

Jason pushed his face into the door.

Her hand fished down into the scoop neck of her deep maroon blouse and adjusted her breasts upward.

He shoved away and ran to the patio door. It was hard to throw the small lock lever with his hands in a violent Parkinsonian shake. He scanned the apartment. Too late to turn down the stereo.

The doorbell rang again.

Thoughts sprinted past. Agnes. Deception. Lilin. Razor. He ran to the front bedroom and pressed his face against the wall next to the window. He could see the edge of the front porch, but no one was there.

His little toe caught the bed frame as he ran to the window in the back bedroom, and the pain swamped his desire for silence. Two hops and he fell backward on the bed, his initial scream subdued into rhythmic grunts. It was the same foot the GTO had mashed.

A loud curse came through the back bedroom window. Probably a golfer. Please be a golfer. He rolled off the bed.

The only window on the side wall facing the parking lot was a small, sliding bathroom window, more than five feet above the tub/shower. He stepped up on the edges of the tub and growled. Too early to put weight on the toe. His balance was awkward, making time inch. The parking lot was deserted except for two cars—his and his upstairs neighbor's.

Jason stayed on the tub until a cramp in the arch of the already traumatized foot redoubled his limp. What should he do now? No answer came. Lie low? Wait? He slinked back into the rear bedroom and slid onto the bed. His mind swirled on alert, further slowing the clock.

The sun burned directly through the bedroom window, low in the sky, sliced into parallel beams by the nearly closed mini-blinds. Jason rolled away on the bed, but then bolted upright. Can't stay here. Especially after dark.

He grunted as he slipped his shoe over his sore toe and gathered his keys, jacket, and laptop before he realized he didn't have a destination. Where was safe? At work? Not a good idea. Mendocino? At the police station? That might be expected.

He closed the door behind him and keyed the dead bolt. An explosion of adrenaline accompanied the clunk of the lock. Just drive. Away from here.

The sprint to the car was tempered by tightness from the shoe on his injured little toe. His pedal foot. The pain had settled into a dull, pulsing ache. Driving would ratchet it up. "Least of my problems," he said to himself as he jumped into the driver's seat and slammed the door. The electric door locks calmed him like a pacifier plugged into a teething toddler.

He selected a random path through the city, complete with U-turns and serpentine veers, all the while conducting a rearview scan for a trailing vehicle. It wouldn't be the GTO. It was in the police impound lot in Mendocino. The more aggressive itinerary, compared to the night of his initial meeting with Lilin, required repeated, painful shifts between the gas and brake pedals, but the pain was less than expected. A raised glass to natural endorphins.

Fifteen minutes of random turns and twists left Jason only a mile and a half from his apartment. A yellow light gave him time to think. Where to now? Only one thing was certain. He didn't want to be alone. Even a loner like Mulvaney went out in company.

The police. Go to the police. But could he positively identify the person as Lilin Hahn? No. So, what could they do? Take a report and send him on his way, no better protected than now. Bransome came into his thoughts again, but like before, the drive was rejected. Too dangerous if it was Lilin. Who else could help? The light turned green.

He pulled his wallet from his pocket and fumbled in the bill compartment. An embossed card provided a business address and phone number but not a home address. He knew who to call to get the information, but he'd have to leave the safety of his car. In his haste, he forgot his cell phone in his apartment. Were there pay phones near the police station?

The metal phone cord stretched tight across his neck, but he needed to keep his eyes on the street. The pay phone was a block down from the station, within sight, but barely. Every car that crawled by presented a challenge in the dimming light. He ignored the ones with more than one occupant. But most were drivers-only.

He needed a miracle. And he got it. "Hey, big brother. I need a home address." The information on the card should be enough.

Two more single-occupant cars came by and decelerated. The phone was too close to the corner. A voice in the phone broke the tension.

Jason realized he had a pen but no paper. He rested

the pen on the back of his hand and circled it on his skin until it left ink. "Go ahead."

The condominiums were on the far side of the city, with cultured lawns and shrubs pruned to a millimeter tolerance. Dr. April Leahy lived three buildings in, near a swimming pool, hot tub, and exercise complex. Climbing to the second-floor condo, Jason suppressed a grunt. His toe throbbed with raw pain, topped by a dull ache in his ankle. He hoped the trip was worth it. Then again, maybe Dr. Leahy could lend some sense to his confusion. At the very least, she would be company.

Jason paused at the door. What would he say? Hello. Lilin really exists, and she's on my trail? Care to put up a condemned man? Should he leave her in the dark and pretend it was a social visit? Pretty lame all around.

He took a deep breath and rapped on the door with the knuckles of his right hand. His left hand was embedded in his jeans pocket. He thought he heard shuffling inside, then the light in the peephole blinked. The doorknob turned.

He forced a smile.

The door flew open and a returned smile nearly filled the doorway. "Jason. What a surprise."

He stood motionless. Voice cracking like a teenager's,

he stammered, "You cut your hair." His eyes drifted to the scoop neckline of the maroon blouse.

April fingered the cut ends of her hair, now at jaw level. "Yes. I needed a change. I'm glad you stopped by. I was at your apartment earlier. No one answered."

Jason's shoulders slumped. He thought his eye blink would last forever. "It was you."

"You were there? Why didn't you answer?"

"I'm embarrassed to say. Not to be forward, but maybe a beer would loosen my tongue."

April's smile widened as she stepped aside.

Jason flopped on the leather couch like he was in triple gravity just as April rounded the kitchen wall with a pair of long, narrow beer glasses. A slice of lime floated in each.

"Mexican okay?"

"Top choice."

She sat on the couch and turned to Jason, pulling her leg up so the knee touched the back cushion.

His first drink drained the glass halfway. "So, what brought you to my place?"

She raised her eyebrows. "You first."

He drank until the lime hit his nose, leaving an inch of beer. His face burned. "You ready for this?" He raised the glass but stopped short of his mouth. "I looked out the peephole and I thought you were Lilin."

April's face matched the hue of her blouse. Between them, the temperature in the room went up ten degrees. She adjusted her neckline upward and fingered the permanent crease on the leg of her slacks. "I don't know how to take that."

Jason's tongue preceded his mind. "Lilin was one of the most alluring women I've seen in a while. Even if she did try to kill me." He leaned back slightly and looked down. "Sorry."

"You're empty." She stood. "Want another?"

He held out his glass, glad for the interruption.

April offered the full glass, with a fresh lime slice, and sat. Closer this time. Her knee nearly touched his thigh.

He grinned. "Your turn now."

"Business."

He studied her expression, but came up blank. "What kind of business?"

"Agnes Hahn business. She wants to give you power of attorney over her assets and her property." April shifted on the couch and pointed across the room toward a large, rolltop desk.

"She made the request through me, so I offered to deliver the paperwork."

"I thought there were couriers for that."

April's face reddened again. "There are." She took a deep breath. "I wanted to see you again." She turned back and her knee brushed his thigh. "I'm glad you came here."

He was torn. He wanted the flirting to continue, but he also wanted to take her off the hot seat. "Why me?"

She laughed. "Why me, like in why did I want to see you again, or like in why did Agnes pick you?"

He let a large mouthful of beer slide down his throat. He'd felt the initial tingle of the alcohol a few minutes ago. Now he had head-to-toe prickles. "The second one first."

"I'm not sure. She said you're one of the good ones. Does that mean anything to you?"

"Yes. I'm hoping it's the answer to both parts of your question."

She settled into an awkward silence.

Jason took a long drink. "What does Agnes have besides the house and what's in it?"

"I have a list in the folder." She started to move.

He put a hand on her knee. "Don't get up. Just a summary."

"She has a heck of a lot of money in the bank. She wants to give some to the animal shelter. She also has some stocks. I think most of it came to her from Gert and Ella. And she wants to rent the house. She doesn't want to sell it. She was very adamant about that."

"She expects to get out?" Jason removed his hand from her knee, and she looked down and frowned.

"She could, you know. I don't think she was in her body when she killed Eddie. I think it was Lilin, just like all of the others."

"But you can't let Agnes out without letting Lilin out, too."

"With proper therapy, it could happen. I've volunteered to head up her treatment. Pro bono. I got her into Napa State Hospital."

"Imola?"

April giggled. "What?"

"Imola. Napa State Hospital."

"Why do you call it that?"

"The address. Napa-Vallejo Highway and Imola Avenue. When I was young, everyone called it Imola. It meant the 'nut house.'"

"Agnes will be in their new annex just outside of Napa, in American Canyon."

"Still Imola to me."

"It fits. Anyway, I'll work with her once a week. It's a bit of a drive, but I can deduct it."

"I feel better now that I know you're helping her." Jason put his hand back on her knee. "Thank you."

"You're welcome. But it's not totally altruistic. It's an incredible case."

"She, not it."

April wrinkled her brow. "Sorry. She could give us tremendous insight into dissociative identity disorder. Like I said in Mendocino, some cases are actually therapy induced. Therapists get the patients to overcome their horrible memories of abuse by having them playact through a fictitious person. The patients are so impressionable the fictitious personalities become real to them. This isn't the case with Agnes. Her alternate personality was spontaneous. It came directly from her abuse." She looked into his eyes. "Sorry. I'm talking too much."

"So you think Agnes was abused?"

"It had to be something really bad. Most cases of DID come from childhood sexual abuse."

"You think she'll open up?"

"It'll be a tough one. I wish we knew more about the abuser." April stood. "You're empty again. Another?"

"Not unless you want me to sleep on this couch tonight."

She hurried into the kitchen. Two more bottle caps whooshed.

CHAPTER 40

JASON'S HEAD SWIRLED. THE SPIN, AUGMENTED BY THE buzz of alcohol, blurred the artwork on the wall of April's condo. His own apartment was safe after all, but it was the last place he wanted to be right now.

His interaction with April had accelerated exponentially through the evening. Talking. Flirting. And kissing. But why was he holding back? With one foot on the boat and one foot on the dock, he'd have to make a decision soon. If he was right about her expectations, the boat was about to sail—the next step was down the hall.

He stood, to a mild protest. "I'll be right back."

"It's down there, on the left." She pointed.

"No. Not that. I need to get something from my car."

April sat upright. "You're coming back, aren't you?"

"Yes."

He limped down the steps and paused at the back of the Volvo. The alcohol spun his thoughts into loops instead of straight lines. He had noticed April's raised eyebrow of interest as far back as the dinner after their first meeting. Their recent interactions at the Mendocino Police Station, and her visit to his apartment door cemented her intent in his mind. But could he really give her what she wanted, and could he get that someone else out of his mind long enough to see if she could give him what he needed? She provided the allure—intelligent, kind, pretty. But why did he see it as a temptation instead of a simple attraction?

The trunk of the Volvo complained at being violated at such a late hour, but yielded. Jason rummaged in its depths and came out with a small, sealed package. He tore at it and a string of three wrapped condoms fell back into the trunk. He retrieved it, paused, and pocketed all three. The stairway to April's door seemed like three flights instead of just one.

He let himself in to find an empty couch in a dark room. The only light came from down the hall so he followed the glow.

He braced himself in the doorway of the bedroom. April was in bed, the blanket pulled up under her bare breasts. Was she one of the good ones? He had to find out.

He kicked off his shoes on the way in the room. His shirt hit the floor before he reached the bed and his pants followed within seconds. He bent, pulled the pant legs from his feet, and fished in the right pocket for the condoms. One tear separated one from the other two, another tear opened the sleeve. He rolled it on.

April pushed up on an elbow. "You don't need one of those."

He yanked the covers to the foot of the bed and she met him halfway to the mattress.

Her touch was urgent but tender. Not like the buckle-your-seatbelts,   you-must-be-this-tall-to-go-on-this-ride experiences he'd had with Uh huh. Pure lust was fun, but unfulfilling.

That was something a guy would never acknowledge out loud, at least not to other males. But since he'd experienced the depth of a loving physical relationship and lost it, there was a void that lust alone couldn't fill.

He relaxed into the bed then reached out to feel. His quest was both simple and complex at the same time. It was rooted in the physical, but it went well beyond that. Even with the alcoholic haze, he craved the intimacy, the tenderness of an emotional touch.

He slid his right hand down April's side to her hip. Across her flat stomach. He wanted to take his time. Build the mutual tension. The nervous energy. The desire to please. He envisioned cooing exhalations wavering in his ear, a lip-nibble on his neck.

A hand gripped his wrist, pulling it upward. April moved it off her tummy and wriggled her hips against his, pushing herself under him. Her other hand slipped past his navel and grabbed him.

She guided him to her and, with a muffled grunt, inside.

He listened to her exhalations. Waited for her nibbles. Hoped for this union to go beyond the physical.

The afterglow was certified by a close, gentle snuggle. April turned away, pulling on his arm. He pressed into the spoon and exhaled. "That was nice, Ag—" He felt her tense.

"Name's April. Remember?" She sounded distant, like she was conversing with a passerby on the street.

"I'm so sorry."

"Did you and Agnes—"

"No. But I've been living and breathing her for the last several months."

"And you're still thinking about her."

"She makes an impression."

"Seems that way."

He pulled away and moved to the edge of the bed.

She spun around and caught his arm. "Don't go. My ego's wounded, but you'll make it up to me. After we get Agnes out of your mind." She fluffed her pillow against the headboard and sat semi-upright, covers pulled to her neck. "You mentioned a book about her. How's it coming?"

He kissed her cheek and leaned against the headboard next to her. "I'm up to the analysis of the Inverness grave site."

"Anything that I don't know about?"

"I'm sure you know the DNA evidence from the small corpse came back identical to Agnes's."

April nodded.

"The coroner referred the case to a forensic anthropologist. Did you hear about that?"

She shook her head.

"There were significant signs of physical abuse. Broken bones that were healed without setting, a fractured skull, nearly healed. There was no way to tell how she died, or if she had been sexually abused. Even though some of the soft tissue was mummified, it wasn't possible to tell."

"Is there any doubt in your mind?" The voice from the pillow came back professional.

"Not really. I e-mailed the anthropologist to see if I could get some photos, but he hasn't responded."

"I wouldn't hold my breath if I were you."

"Reporters can breathe underwater. Didn't you know that?"

"And under the covers, too."

He chuckled. "I didn't notice. I was busy."

She didn't laugh. "I want to talk about Agnes now. Since I'm treating her, I want to know everything you know about her."

"Here? Now? Don't you know a man is supposed to fall asleep right after? It's a law."

"Break this one and maybe we can break some others later on." A comical wink punctuated her giggle.

"There isn't much else. Officer Wilson found a way through the U-Store fence. There were a few cut rungs in the chain link at the extreme southern corner of the lot. He couldn't fit through, but he said someone smaller could. He went around to the other side and found a couple of loose boards in Agnes's wooden fence on the side up close to the house. The house was in just the right position to block the view from the stakeout site." He snuggled close.

She relaxed into him, then stiffened. "Next time, if you call me Lilin, I'll play the part and do some slicing."

"Warning noted and filed."

April shifted upward against the headboard. Her breast peeked from under the blanket. She pulled the fabric upward. "You have anything at all on Eddie?"

"He's a real mystery man. Nothing comes up besides useless details of his existence."

"Any hints about what he may have done, and why? Anything here would go a long way for Agnes's treatment. I need some hints to get her to open up about her time with Lilin. And with Eddie."

"Sorry. I can't give you anything. I'll keep checking, but the dead ends could fill a graveyard. My source is banging his head against a wall as well." He slid to the edge of the bed.

She collared him and yanked him back, pressing his head against her chest. "I thought you were supposed to fall asleep. I want you to get some rest." She pointed at the two attached condom packets on the adjacent nightstand. "If you came in expecting three, you'll get at least one more before you go. Maybe you'll get my name right."

CHAPTER 41

AGNES'S EYES STRAYED TO THE GLASS PANEL IN THE DOOR of the dayroom. One of a restricted number of doors in her new world—unit T-6 of the medium security section of the state hospital annex. She shifted her glance to Dr. April Leahy, who sat across the table, then back to the door. She rubbed her eyes. It was him.

The door opened and Jason entered, his hands behind his back.

Agnes stood, nearly tipping her chair. "Jason. Thank you for coming." She rushed into his arms for a full body hug.

He accepted the hug, but kept one arm behind him.

Agnes released and Jason turned to Dr. Leahy and smiled.

"Sit here." Agnes pulled out a chair next to hers.

"I'm sorry. I can't stay today. I'm on my way to Vallejo. They've got a strange hostage story going."

Agnes's eyes lowered. She reached out and touched his right arm. "What are you hiding?"

He turned square to her. "I have a present for you. I know how much you miss the animal shelter, so I brought you a stray." He held out a stuffed dog—a golden retriever, about a quarter life-size. "I wanted to bring the real thing, but there was no way they'd allow it." He moved in her direction. "He needs a good home."

She gathered it in her arms and hugged it tight to her cheek. Tears filled her eyes. "It's perfect." She lunged into a one-armed hug, squeezing the puppy between them. "Thank you."

Dr. Leahy stood and walked toward them. "How thoughtful. We were talking about Agnes's work at the animal shelter."

Agnes thought she detected an edge in Dr. Leahy's voice.

Jason lifted Agnes's arm from his neck and pecked her cheek. "I have to get going. Duty calls."

"Is this work for the *Press Democrat* or the *Chronicle*?" Dr. Leahy said.

"Both."

"Good for you." She hooked her arm in his. "I'll walk you to your car."

Stop her.

Agnes moved next to them. "No. I want to talk to Jason."

"He can't stay, Agnes. I'm sure he'll come back for a longer visit soon." April squeezed his arm.

"Yes. I'll be back next week. I'll want to see how the puppy is adjusting to his new home."

She's fucking him.

Agnes grabbed Jason's arm, unhooking Dr. Leahy's. "If he has to go, why are you going to talk to him?"

"I'm going to walk him out. I'll be back in ten minutes."

"I want to come."

"Agnes. You know you can't." Dr. Leahy pointed at the TV corner. "Please sit down. I'll be right back."

Agnes remained standing. She looked at Jason. "You'll come next week?"

Jason gave her another hug. It was tight from Agnes's grip. He whispered in her ear, "I'll come back next weekend. We can have a whole day."

Rub into him. You've got to fight for him.

Agnes pushed into him. "Will she be here?"

"Not on a weekend."

Agnes let go. "Next weekend."

She watched the dayroom door close behind them, and hugged the puppy tight to her chest.

He is one of the good ones.

Two hallways away from the dayroom, April hooked her arm into Jason's again. She turned him and pressed her lips to his. "Thanks for coming. I've missed you. When can we get together again?"

Seeing April with Agnes created mixed feelings for him. April was desirable on a physical level, but when he was with her, other thoughts interfered. And that was the strange part. The thoughts weren't of Eugenia, like in his other relationships. They were of Agnes.

"Jason? Can't you answer me?"

"Soon. I'll give you a call."

"Promise me."

"I promise."

She pulled on his arm again.

Jason frowned. The look on her face was a little too serious.

"What do we have?" she said.

"We have what we have."

"And the future?"

"Let's relax and see where it goes."

She squeezed his arm. "I know I wasn't the reason you came today."

"I knew you'd be here." Jealous, or possessive? Either way, not good.

"The stuffed animal was a nice touch."

"And nothing for you, right?"

Her face reddened. "How's the book coming?"

"It's not."

"Why not? I thought you were almost done."

He shook his head and looked at the buffed tile floor. "I can't do it."

"Why not?"

"I can't do it to Agnes. Her story has been told in the newspapers. I need to drop it for now. For her."

"It'd be a best seller."

"I don't care. I can't do it to her. She's been through too much." It might keep the wounds open, delay her return to innocence.

April swung around in front of him. "Hey. You got something going with Agnes Hahn? I hear she's a real cutup." She kissed him again.

"Real funny." He felt his face heat up. "She deserves the best. Thanks again for getting her into Imola."

They pushed through double doors and walked outside into the crisp fall air. It smelled productive, and not just because the famous wine country started a few miles up the road. It was pruning time, the first step in regrowth. Renewal.

April steered him to a bench under a large oak tree. The grounds were deserted; only piles of yellow and red leaves surrounded them.

"I can't believe you gave up on the book. You're walking away from some serious money."

"Maybe. But it finally hit me. Everyone wanted to

jump into the Agnes Hahn case, but for all the wrong reasons. I should know."

"It's an interesting case. From all corners."

Jason glared. "You sound like the damn district attorney. He never once mentioned Agnes. It was always the case, or her, or she. The only reason he paid any attention to her was to be the big shot. To further his career. I guess justice was served, though."

"What do you mean?"

"You didn't hear? The little prick was mugged outside his office. In the parking lot. He was hurt pretty bad. I'd hate to put together a suspect list for that one. Probably in the hundreds. Bransome took the case. My guess is he's put it in the cold case file already." He mimed the toss of a file into an imaginary wastebasket. "Bransome. That reminds me. Do you have a stamp?"

"Sorry. Are you pen pals?"

"I have to send him two dollars."

"Two dollars? What for? Some kind of joke?"

"I went for the double-or-nothing."

"A guy thing?"

Jason leaned away. "Tell me again why you're driving all the way over here once a week. Pro bono."

"An unequivocal case of dissociative identity disorder doesn't fall in the lap of the psychiatric world every day. One that's definitely not therapy induced."

Jason shook his head. "What about Agnes?"

"What do you mean? This is about Agnes."

"It's an interesting case. From all corners."

"I don't think I like the insinuation. It's possible that a professional can do what's best for the patient and become energized by the intellectual merits of the case. I'm here for Agnes. To make her better."

Jason slumped against the bench back. "Good answer." He rested his hand on her knee. "How's it going with her? Is she happy?"

"She seems to be. She seems to be at peace."

"Have the honchos looked at your treatment regime proposal?"

"I hear they're going over it right now."

"Has Lilin surfaced?"

"Not that I know of. The danger is if Agnes is struggling with Lilin and not telling me."

"I don't understand how Agnes held her in for all those years. Until Gert died and Ella went into the home."

"That's what my proposal is about. I think Lilin is a relatively weak personality, easily controlled by a strong one. Gert was a forceful person to Agnes, and she raised Agnes to be good. Because she was strict, she held Lilin in check for Agnes. Once she died, Lilin was released."

"But you got my e-mail. Agnes went to UC Davis. Why didn't Lilin surface there?"

"My guess is that Gert was still in control. I doubt if she let out too much leash, even when Agnes lived in

Davis. I bet she called every night, came home every weekend."

"So what do you propose? You want to make Agnes strong so she can hold Lilin back?"

"In a way."

"You have some magic wand or something?"

"Something like that. It's called training. I'm pretty good at what I do."

"I'll say." He Grouchoed his eyebrows. Something about her glowed with highlights from the autumn sun. Right now he could use a dose of her therapy.

She hit him on the arm. "Not that. I mean professionally."

"You're a professional? What street corner do you work?"

"You're an asshole. For a moment there, I thought you were interested in my work."

"I am. How do you intend to get Agnes to control Lilin?"

She turned to face him. "First, I have to get her to acknowledge Lilin's existence."

"The real Lilin, or the one in her mind?"

"Both."

"What will you wear when you do it?"

She raised her fist. "God damn it. I'm being serious. Do you want to hear this or not?"

Jason stood and kicked at the yellow and brown leaves. "Okay, but you're kind of distracting me."

She smiled. "All you have to do is call."

"I know. Tell me about how you're going to get Agnes to acknowledge Lilin."

"That's the tricky part. I'll have to make her aware of what Lilin is like. What she's done. All of that. Agnes needs full disclosure. I think Lilin's acts highlight her weakness. I need to convince Agnes that Lilin acted out of cowardice and selfishness. Agnes has so much good in her she'll react strongly against those negative traits."

He put a foot on the bench and leaned on his bent knee. "I don't know anything about psychiatry, but it sounds kind of risky to me. What if Lilin proves to be stronger than you think? If she puts up a fight?"

"I don't think she will."

"But what if you're wrong?"

"Then we risk getting Lilin, not Agnes, and she stays here for the rest of her life."

He pulled from the bench and shuffled through the fallen leaves again. After a half lap around the bench, he turned to face the building in the distance. The low angle of the sun threw crooked-armed shadows of the bare trees across the walls. They looked like cracks, threatening to crumble the structure. "Do you have alternatives? You know, a contingency plan?"

"You don't have confidence in me?"

"I didn't say that. I'd hate to lose Agnes."

"You do have feelings for her."

He turned to face her. "She's important to me."

April turned her head slightly and squinted into his eyes. "Is there anything I should know?"

"About what?"

"About you and Agnes."

"You'll find it under *P*."

"What?"

"Paranoia. It's under *P*. Surely you've heard about it."

"Screw you. Maybe you'd like her better as Lilin. I hear she's a sexual force."

Despite the warmth of the direct autumn sun, the hair on Jason's arms stood, accompanied by a chill. Would he ever see Agnes without the threat of Lilin? He covered his crotch with one hand.

April shook her head. "You really have a one-track mind today."

Jason didn't laugh. A quote came to mind, but not the source. He spoke it aloud. "Never befriend the oppressed unless you're prepared to take on the oppressor."

"Where did that come from?"

He regripped his crotch and gave it a shake. "Right here. It was more for me than for you."

CHAPTER 42

AGNES LOOKED AT THE CLOCK—JUST A FEW MINUTES left. In the last four weeks, the sessions had dashed her initial antagonism. She only felt on edge when Jason was there. Otherwise, she felt relaxed, calm whenever she and Dr. Leahy talked. Chatted. That's what Dr. Leahy called it. It created a new freedom. Agnes could say anything during their chats.

Dr. Leahy cleared her throat. "Have you heard the voice since our last meeting?"

"No. Nothing."

"Nothing at all since you've been in here?"

Agnes dropped her eyes and smiled. "Not a word."

Dr. Leahy tugged at the hem of her skirt. "Think back. When you did hear the voice. Was it ever in the first person? You know, *I . . .?*"

Agnes gazed at the ceiling. "In the letters."

"No. I mean the voice. Did you ever hear her use *I*?"

Agnes's eyes scanned the ceiling tiles. "No."

"How about *we*?"

"Not that I recall. Is that good?"

"Everything seems to be falling into place. Let's use the last few minutes to review. You understand that your sister died when she was around three, right?"

"Lilin."

"Right. She's dead now, so she can't bother you anymore. Do you understand that?"

"Her name is Lilin. Why won't you say her name?"

"Because she doesn't exist anymore. I'm sorry. I know that's harsh, but it's the kind of hard truth you have to embrace." She pressed her fingers to her chest and flicked both hands away, like she was shooing something away. "She's gone. She can't bother you anymore. You're strong enough to stand alone now. Right?"

"Yes."

"That's all? Just yes?"

"I know Lilin's dead. That she only existed in my head. But she was weak. Recognizing that makes me strong. Stronger than she could ever be."

"Good girl. What's the next step?"

"I have to stop talking like she's real. Do I have to stop using her name?"

"Can you do it?"

"I don't know. I'll try."

"Good girl. What encourages me most is that she

hasn't said a word since we've been chatting." She surveyed the dayroom. "Do you ever get mad in here?"

"I get frustrated."

"And you don't get that uneasy feeling you mentioned you felt before the voice came to you?"

"No."

Dr. Leahy bobbed her head three times. "That's because of you. You know that, don't you?" She smiled.

"Yes."

Dr. Leahy stood. "You are a very strong woman, Agnes Hahn. And you're getting better already. I can see it."

Agnes stood and leaned into Dr. Leahy's outstretched arms. She accepted the hug.

Agnes leaned back.

"Will I ever see Jason again? I mean, outside of here?"

"I can't . . . make any promises, Agnes."

"Will you make me better so I can?"

"You know I'm trying to make you better."

Agnes leaned back into the hug and her hand brushed Dr. Leahy's neck. She felt the jaw pump the invisible wad of gum.

Right there. We pull the razor right there. I can show you how to do it. We can do it together. She's not one of the good ones.

CHAPTER 1

Boyston, Tri-Counties, 1982

GABE LEANED FORWARD in the confessional and eased the door open a crack. Light from the church flowed into the dark chamber in a narrow slash. He squinted the altar into view. In two years of early morning visits to the All Saints Catholic Church, Father Costello had never been late.

That wasn't the only thing wrong with today. The air carried an abnormal chill for this far into the spring. Gabe had overheard his father talk about it—this growing season had more than its fair share of unexpected thunderstorms and strong, dust-laden winds. And then there were the fogs. They rarely extended more than a mile from the swamp up north, and hardly ever as far as Boyston. But this year, they were enveloping the town two or three times a week. Today's was a doozy.

Gabe squirmed in the confessional, which he jokingly called the inhouse. It was the same size as the outhouse his grandfather had built at their farm. And even though the farmhouse had indoor plumbing, his father had maintained the structure for sentimental reasons—to teach a lesson on appreciation for what one has, his father had often said.

Gabe pushed the door open a little farther, enough to open a crack on the hinge side. Enough to get a view of the massive double front doors of the church. Nothing there either. He let the door slide shut. The hard wooden seat, and the near blackness, would help him think of another sin or two.

He wasn't Catholic but he liked the idea of confessing his sins. The recurring comfort of the lifted burden and the cleansing feeling of official acknowledgement and forgiveness gave him a sense of reverent calm. As he had done so many times, he had left home early to ride his bike to town to confess his week's worth of moral hiccups to Father Costello before heading up the street to join his family at the Lutheran church service.

Their interactions didn't have the formality of the official sacrament. Father Costello was just a good friend. In the confines of the dark confessional, with a screen between him and the good father, twelve year-old Gabe could talk about anything, especially things he was uncomfortable discussing with his real father.

A door slammed and an unrecognized, high-pitched voice brought Gabe out of his search. It came from the back room, behind the altar. He pushed on the door and squinted at the business end of the church. For an unsettlingly long time, no one appeared, but he could hear the voice, muffled, at a distance.

I could run for it, he thought. But the inhouse was closer to the altar than the front doors, and the huge latch that bolted the doors was hard to throw open in a rush. His mind was made when the door of the back room opened and Father Costello walked out, in full white robe, followed by a small man, only three-quarters of the Father's height. The small man leaned forward as he walked, apparently to counterbalance a half-full gunnysack that was slung over his right shoulder. A red stain wimpled the bottom of the sagging sack.

Gabe slid his butt back on the inhouse seat and closed the door to the narrowest crack that would allow a view of the two men. His breathing echoed in the small, dark space, so he switched to mouth breathing to avoid the occasional nose whistle that sounded an exhalation.

The small man dropped the sack on the first step of the altar and walked to the side of the church, out of Gabe's sight. He reappeared in only a few seconds, carrying a bare metal chair that he unfolded and placed at the front, center of the altar. He motioned to Father Costello, who walked to it, robot-like, and sat, feet together, hands on his thighs.

Gabe leaned closer to the gap. Father Costello's eyes seemed to follow the small man, but they were wide, unblinking, like the eyes of hypnotized people in the old black-and-white television movies.

The small man reached into the sack and pulled out a limp animal. It looked like a dog. He placed it on the top step, to Father's right, and fished his arm into the sack again. Over the next minute, he pulled two more animals from the bag. One was definitely a cat. Then, he brought the sack to the center of the altar, right in front of Father Costello, and reached in. The bottom of the sack went limp when the object was lifted.

Gabe's forehead pressed into the door as he strained to see, but his visual angle, and the railing of the first row of pews, prevented a clear view. Whatever kind of animal it was, it didn't have fur. He was sure of that. The brief glimpse he got was of an animal about the size of a small dog, but with grayish-pink, wrinkly skin. Once it was set down, all he could see through the wrought iron railing was the tip of one of its appendages. He stopped down his eyes with an exaggerated squint, but the image still blurred.

An idea struck—a trick from school that allowed a better focus at a distance. He pinched the tips of his two thumbs and two forefingers together into a square and peered through the pinhole created by the space between the tips of the four digits. The view of the altar sharpened, but it didn't help. The obstructions still prevented a full view. He pushed the door open a little more with his forehead and looked through his fingertips again. A little more came into focus. He pushed farther. When the image cleared, an involuntary breath sucked his lungs full. His back hit the rear wall of the inhouse just as the slit of light narrowed and extinguished. Knees to his chest, he strained for his next breath. He thought he saw toes.

Gabe's mind swirled, accompanied by a dizziness that nearly turned the feeble light that seeped around the edges of the inhouse door to pitch black. When the sensation passed, he leaned forward for another peek.

This time, his vision was tuned to an acuity that was almost painful, as if vision were his only fully functional external sense. It was silent in the church, and there were no smells.

In the close quarters of the inhouse, Gabe's internal world was anything but quiet. The lub-dup of each heartbeat reverberated as if branches of his heart extended to every part of his body. And the tensile stretch of his lungs, on each inhalation, felt like the rasp of wood dragged across cement, until it gave way to a twang of elastic recoil and an exhalation. In the darkness, he was keenly aware of the position of his own body parts—every joint spoke to him of its position—and he knew if he moved one, it would scream its swing.

He inched the door outward to enlarge the crack and gasped again.

Father Costello sat perfectly still on the bare metal folding chair. All around him were animal parts and blood. The pieces were so small, and so carefully carved, it was impossible to tell what they had been in life. Gabe saw they half surrounded the priest in an arc that ran from one end of the altar to the other, and that they were being purposely arranged, as if to highlight the altar, or to degrade it.

Gabe's eyes flicked to the artist, who was engrossed

in his work on the carpeted canvas. The strange looking little man didn't change his evil grin as he went about his task. Precise and efficient at his craft, no blood seemed to spill beyond where he wanted it to go. The knife he wielded appeared sharp enough to cut through bone without perceptible resistance, and it cut so swiftly blood flowed from its cuts without the slightest splatter, forming enlarging, smooth-edged pools. Everything was rounded—the pieces of flesh, the pools of blood, the semicircular arrangement of parts around the altar. Just like the features of the little man, there were no sharp edges.

Gabe was mesmerized by the developing masterpiece. And by the way the little man carefully placed each new severance and then paused to scan the altar, as if he were gaining a wide perspective on his artwork.

Gabe pinched himself. The pain was real. Blood flowed from each of the little man's cuts—it was real. This wasn't a dream.

When Gabe regained his focus, the little man was at the far side of the altar. With a stiff-necked spin, the man shuffled up to Father Costello, his evil grin unchanging, like a painted on clown face. A small voice echoed, the only sound in the cavernous church.

"You don't want to miss this part." The man's lips barely moved when he spoke. "I've saved the best for last."

Father Costello didn't react. Not even an eye blink.

"That's right, Father. You look right here. You think you've defeated me? I can assure you that I always take the game in the end."

The man lifted a gold communion chalice toward Father Costello.

"This is HER blood, shed for me because of your sins."

He extended both of his arms, so his small body formed a cross, with the chalice still gripped in his right hand. A loud "Ha" sound reverberated in Gabe's ears, and the chalice flew from the man's still hand. It impacted the Father's chest with a dull thud, spilling its crimson contents down the front of his white robe and up onto his neck and face.

Gabe's eyes widened and the scene blurred, then came back into sharp focus. Droplets of blood fell to the carpet in slow motion. One drop suspended from the priest's chin for an agonizing instant, gaining volume, before releasing, then splattering onto the lap of his satin robe.

The little man stepped forward and picked up the chalice and turned it in his grip, inspecting it from every angle. "Now, for the final touch to my masterpiece."

Gabe wanted to look away. To curl up in the corner of the inhouse and turn his mind to another time and place. But it wouldn't turn. He felt the same sense of perverse curiosity that captured him a year ago when he had witnessed a head-on collision on State Route 27. A passenger in one of the cars went through the windshield, all the way to his ankles, and his leaking, lifeless body colored the white hood with streaks of maroon, like painted-on flames of a hot rod, but going in the wrong direction. He had felt sickened then, but he couldn't look away.

Gabe's eyes flicked to the animal pieces and their surrounding pools. The blood that spilled on the royal blue carpet drew the red and blue hues to a neutral, dull gray. But the blood that adorned the white, satin robe of the priest emitted a metallic sheen that resonated to an intensity that was hard to look at straight on. His eyes returned to the primary actor in this gruesome play.

The little man reached down and pulled Father Costello's left hand from its resting place on the father's thigh, and turned it palm up. He placed the stem of the chalice across the palm and pushed the father's fingers closed around it, then gently lowered the hand back to the thigh. When the little man stepped back, Father Costello's grip on the chalice had a slight tremor, like he was straining, strangling it.

"You're ready, now," the man said. He pivoted and ambled toward the front doors of the church. "I'd like to stay and watch the show, but my services are needed elsewhere. I hope to see you again, later rather than sooner." The church doors unlatched with a dull metallic clunk.

Gabe jumped. Nudging the inhouse door, he peered toward the front doors. Pressing his head a little closer to the hinge-side crack, so his forehead was against the door, he strained to expand his field of view.

Something hard smacked against the door and slammed it shut. Gabe screamed. His head ricocheted off the sidewall, and then the back wall of the confessional, and he slumped to the floor with a loud thud. His head spun and a stinging sensation crept up his back.

The door of the cubicle swung wide open, and the invading light lent more confusion to his sensory world. Both hands extended toward the light—he tried to shade his eyes and fend off the blurred image at the same time. He squinted between his spread fingers. A small, round head hovered above him. It was backlit with the harsh light of the church, but he made out high arching eyebrows and a strange, tight-lipped grin. And the scars. Both corners of the mouth had thick scars that turned upward, forcing the face into the wicked smile. But the rest of the face didn't smile. The eyes were black with anger. Or evil.

Gabe pulled his knees up to his chest and folded his arms over his head and face. And prayed.

A high-pitched voice came from above, with a Yankee accent. "You'll forget what you saw today if you know what's good for you."

The spin of Gabe's world accelerated and then went dark.

ISBN# 9781933836133
Mass Market Paperback / Horror
US $6.99 / CDN $8.99
Available Now

For more information
about other great titles from
Medallion Press, visit

www.medallionpress.com